Praise for Dawn Brown's *Living Lies*

Rating: 5 Angels and a Recommended Read "Wow! What to say? Stop reading and go buy this book!! Living Lies by Dawn Brown is everything a romantic suspense should be...Ms. Brown has penned a novel full of tension and nail biting suspense. The climatic ending had me on the edge of my seat. Her skill at bringing to life her characters is nothing short of brilliant and every one of them is three dimensional and very real. Living Lies is THE best book I've read in months."

~ *Fallen Angels Reviews*

Rating: 5 Hearts "Living Lies by Dawn Brown is, I believe, her debut novel. She masterfully weaves a tale of mystery and suspense and I shall be watching this author very closely for future releases. She clearly has a lot of talent for writing a thoroughly gripping mystery that is oozing with tension. Living Lies is filled with enough twists and turns to keep the reader on their toes and on the edge of their seats as the story unfolds."

~ *The Romance Studio*

Living Lies

Dawn Brown

A SAMHAIN PUBLISHING, LTD. publication.

Samhain Publishing, Ltd.
577 Mulberry Street, Suite 1520
Macon, GA 31201
www.samhainpublishing.com

Living Lies
Copyright © 2009 by Dawn Brown
Print ISBN: 978-1-60504-167-4
Digital ISBN: 978-1-60504-047-9

Editing by Tera Kleinfelter
Cover by Angela Waters

First Samhain Publishing, Ltd. electronic publication: June 2008
First Samhain Publishing, Ltd. print publication: April 2009

Dedication

For Nana. Thank you for your faith.

Prologue

"Hareton sits on the edge of the Snow Belt, that's why the snow is so much heavier out this way."

Sandra rolled her eyes, but said nothing. She couldn't care less about the weather patterns of some middle-of-nowhere town. Her husband, Brian, was much too busy fiddling with the radio to notice.

Sighing, she turned her attention back to the front window. Not that there was much to see. Outside, small flakes of snow danced in the narrow beams of the SUV's headlights. Occasionally, the yellow light of a house broke through the inky blackness and veil of falling snow. A welcome relief from the monotony.

A tall snowbank to her right suddenly loomed closer as the front of the SUV swerved dangerously toward the edge of the highway.

"Brian, the road!"

He jerked his head up and straightened the wheel.

"Can you please stop playing with the radio and drive?" she snapped.

"Sorry. I was trying to find the game. What's with you? You've been miserable all night."

"There's nothing *with* me. I just have no desire to find myself flattened against a snowbank so you can get a hockey score."

"Fine. But your attitude started long before now."

He may have had a point. She'd been on edge since they turned onto this highway. It was probably just a combination of the weather and having gone nearly a half-hour without seeing another car. The isolation made her tense.

"What were Rhonda and Jimmy thinking when they moved out here?"

Brian grinned. "Low mortgage payments."

"I guess. It just seems so far from civilization."

"We're forty-five minutes from home."

"I know." She sighed. "This weather is making me twitchy. I wish we had just stayed home."

"If you don't want to go to their housewarming, then why are we?"

"Because Jimmy and Rhonda are our friends, and it's their first house. They want to show it off."

"They're *your* friends."

"They're your friends too..." Her words trailed off as she spotted a small, lone figure trudging through the snow along the side of the road.

"Who would be out here in weather like this?" Brian asked.

As they drew closer, Sandra saw it was a girl. Wisps of blonde hair whipped out from under her hood.

"Stop the car," she said.

"Are you nuts? She could be anyone."

"There's no one else out here. If we don't pick her up, who will? Besides, she's small. I think between the two of us we could take her if she turns out to be a psycho."

"Famous last words," Brian muttered, but he slowed the car and pulled over anyway.

From the side mirror, Sandra watched the girl trot up to the SUV. She slowed as she grew closer and hesitated before opening the back door. When she finally did, the overhead light illuminated the interior. The girl peered into the dim car and eyed Sandra and Brian suspiciously, but she stepped forward, her shoulders sagging a little when her gaze fell on the empty baby seat.

"Thank you for stopping," the girl said, climbing in. "Are you going to Hareton?"

"Yeah." Brian pulled back onto the road. "Can we drop you

somewhere?"

"Just a ride to town would be great. I'm Michelle, by the way." She looked young, eighteen maybe nineteen.

"I'm Sandra. This is my husband, Brian."

She turned to face the backseat. Michelle was pretty, the cheerleader type. Long, blonde hair fell in soft waves from under her hood. Her face was small with a pert nose, flawless skin and a smile toothpaste ads would pay a fortune for. But something about her eyes, dark and empty like bottomless wells, bothered Sandra.

"It's an awful night to be out walking," Sandra said. "You must be freezing."

"I am."

"Did you break down?" Brian asked. "I didn't see any cars farther back."

"No, I didn't." A rueful smile touched Michelle's lips. "I had a fight with my boyfriend."

"And he just left you out here?" Sandra asked, appalled.

"It's not that bad. Someone always stops."

What an odd thing to say. Sandra turned back around in her seat.

They continued the rest of the way in silence. As they neared Hareton, the lights from the town reflected pink off the falling snow, shimmering like a halo in the night sky.

"This isn't right." Michelle's voice broke the quiet.

"What's wrong?" Sandra turned to look at the girl. What she saw stopped her heart and turned her bowels to water.

Wide, sunken eyes stared out from Michelle's gaunt face, her skin so pale it appeared almost blue. The heavy winter coat, faded and tattered, hung off her bony frame.

Michelle's hand reached out, trembling as if lifting it took great strength. She wrapped her skeletal fingers around Sandra's wrist like an icy vise, sending waves of frigid chills coursing through her body.

Michelle pulled herself forward. Closer. Until her face was mere inches from Sandra's.

"He used to send me flowers," she whispered, cold against

Sandra's ear. Michelle's breath smelled of rot and made Sandra's stomach roll. Fear, like nothing she had experienced before, held her in place until, at last, Michelle released her. Sandra turned away, sinking back into her seat.

With her heart thundering against her chest, her breath came in quick shallow gasps. Out of the corner of her eye she saw Brian frown before glancing up at the rearview mirror.

"Where did you want us to let you off? What in the hell?"

Sandra was afraid to look. Afraid that whatever Brian saw was worse than Michelle's cold hand or rotten breath.

"She's gone."

"What?" Sandra turned sharply. The back seat was empty.

"She's gone," Brian said again. "She just disappeared."

Chapter One

Haley leaned against the doorframe and looked down at the small, withered husk of a woman passed out on the floor.

"Good morning, Mom," she murmured, but her mother remained sprawled across the pale rose carpet. The frayed edge of her nightgown bunched high on her thighs, exposing dark varicose veins spidering down skinny, white legs.

As Haley stepped into the room, her heart rate accelerated and a shiver slid down her spine. She hated this room—Michelle's room—though she hadn't thought of it that way in a long time. For more than a decade it had simply been *The Shrine*. A pretty pink bedroom kept as perfect as a museum exhibit, all in memory of a sister who was gone and never coming back.

She knelt, hooked her hands under her mother's arms, and half dragged her down the hall. The putrid stink of alcohol oozed from her skin. Haley swallowed hard to keep from gagging. God, she hated that smell.

With her hip, she nudged her mother's bedroom door open and rolled her onto the bed. Haley stood there for a moment, her throat tight and her chest sore, while pity battled revulsion. Who was this creature, with sallow skin and hollowed eyes? Surely she couldn't be the same woman who had raised her for her first fifteen years. Her mother had been warm, quick to laugh and full of life. Unlike the creature wheezing before her, this doppelganger who had assumed her mother's life the day Michelle disappeared twelve years ago.

Haley left the room, wiping at the tears pricking the corners of her eyes. She showered and dressed, dry swallowing two

Tylenols in an effort to combat the steady throb behind her eyes and the ache in her shoulders, the results of yet another sleepless night.

In the kitchen, she took the coffee from the pantry and started her morning ritual. As she filled the pot with water, she spotted a note in her brother's handwriting propped against the wall behind the faucet.

Coward. She set the coffeepot down and lifted the torn scrap of paper.

Haley

Had a breakfast meeting this morning and didn't want

to wake you. Finally spoke to Paige, she'll be here

later today. I'll see you tonight.

Garret

Anger surged within her as she crumpled the paper into a tight ball, tossing it into the garbage. What her brother wouldn't do to avoid both her and their mother.

And now Paige was coming, as if things weren't bad enough.

According to the clock on the wall, she still had a little over an hour before she needed to open the store. And spending that time in the silent kitchen, with only her dark thoughts for company held all the appeal of a sharp stick in the eye.

The walls felt like they were closing in on her and the air too hot to breathe. She flicked off the coffee machine and snatched up her coat. She had to get out of there.

Outside, the cold air stung her cheeks and made her eyes water, a relief from the overwhelming stuffiness inside. Deep blues and purples streaked the eastern sky, barely lighter than the star-dotted black in the west. She jammed her bare hands into her coat pockets and started down the sidewalk, bending her head against the icy wind.

As she walked, the pounding in her skull eased some. Whether from the Tylenol or simply being away from her mother's house she couldn't say for certain.

She turned onto Main Street and wondered absently why every small town in North America had a Main Street. Plastic garland, twinkle lights, tinsel and wreaths decorated the storefronts. The kind of tackiness only Christmas could inspire. Even the lampposts were adorned with green and red lights in the shape of candles.

Most of the store windows were dark, except for the Java Joint. Warm light spilled from the small coffee shop's window onto the pavement outside. With time to kill before she opened Hareton Furniture Restoration, Haley decided to stop. Maybe flip through the newspaper and get lost in the functioning world for a while.

A chime overhead announced her arrival as she pushed the door open. The warm air smelled of rich coffee and freshly baked goods. Chairs at the small, wrought iron tables stood empty, and the only other customer sat hunched over his newspaper at the counter that ran the length of the front window. He glanced up at the sound of the bell, then turned back to his paper.

Karen Murphy, the shop's owner, stood behind a counter at the rear of the store, placing cookies neatly on a platter. She smiled as Haley approached. "Coffee?"

Haley nodded, shrugging out of her coat before sliding onto a stool.

"I wondered if you would stay home today." Karen set an oversized cup down before her.

"Why?" Haley asked.

"I heard they identified the body. That it was Michelle."

God, word traveled fast in this town. "We only found out Friday. How did you hear already?"

"There was an article in the paper." Karen pointed to the folded newspaper at the end of the counter. Haley reached for it and spread the out pages.

The words "Body Found" screamed in one-inch bold letters, then in slightly smaller print, "Remains identified as local girl missing twelve years". Haley pushed the paper away.

"I shouldn't be surprised. This is probably the most exciting story the *Gazette's* published since Michelle went missing." She added three heaping spoonfuls of sugar to her coffee before taking a sip.

"Are you okay?"

"I'm fine." Haley waved her hand as if swatting away a fly, ignoring the ache in her throat. "I've believed for a long time Michelle was dead. When they found the skeleton I knew it would be her."

Karen put her hands on her bony hips. "Liar. Who do I look like? That idiot brother of yours? I've known you far too long for you to sit there and tell me that you're fine and dandy."

"I didn't say I was *dandy*." Karen was a good friend, but sometimes all her touchy feely let's-talk-about-our-emotions crap got on Haley's nerves. Still, she knew from experience, if she wanted to drink her coffee in peace, she would have to throw her something. "I admit, going from twelve years with Michelle just being gone to having her body found and identified inside of three weeks has been hard."

"And it has to be kind of freaky that she was buried in your grandmother's basement."

"It was." And terrifying and horrifying.

"That's so weird. Your family kept the house all that time after your grandmother died, and then, almost the minute it sold, Michelle is found."

"Yeah. Strange." Haley took another drink from her cup and wished Karen would shut up. She hated thinking of the years spent waiting and wondering, when all along Michelle had been buried under the dirt floor practically beneath their feet. Stop being morbid, she told herself, trying to push the image from her mind.

"How's your mom?"

"The usual." No need to bore Karen with tales of her mother's drunken tirades or sobbing fits.

"Has Garret been any help?"

"He's dealing with the police and that kind of thing, but other than that, he's avoiding me. He did leave me a note this morning."

"A note?" Karen's eyebrows, nearly as blonde as her straight, cropped hair, drew together in a frown.

"Yeah, nice, huh? I wonder how early he had to sneak in to do that."

Karen chuckled. "What did it say?"

"Just that he finally spoke to Paige, and she'll be gracing us with her illustrious presence sometime today."

"Have you spoken to your sister at all since—"

"No," Haley interrupted. "Not in four years. Anyway, I feel like I've been eating and breathing all of this forever. Let's talk about something else. Anything that's unrelated to Michelle or my lunatic family."

"Change of subject coming up." Karen lowered her voice to a conspiratorial whisper. "Check out tall, dark and brooding over there."

Haley turned toward the man at the counter. His back was to her, but his face reflected on the glass, translucent against the brightening background like the image of a ghost. His head bent, he stared at the newspaper in front of him, and Haley couldn't get a good look at his features. Still, there was something familiar about him.

"I've seen him before," Haley whispered, turning back to Karen.

"Me too, but I'm damned if I can remember where."

He stood suddenly, his chair scraping the tile floor, and left the shop without a backward glance.

Karen's cheeks turned pink and a giggle escaped her lips. "Oops. Do you think he heard us?"

Haley shrugged and drank her coffee.

Well, Lawson, you handled that brilliantly. Dean climbed into his car, heart pounding, body bathed in icy sweat. Way to tackle an issue head on. Run away with your tail between your legs. He didn't have a tail, but his nuts were sucked so far up inside him he might never see them again.

Damn it. All the planning, all the scenarios that had played in his head over the years, all the things he'd intended to say had evaporated the minute Haley Carling walked into that coffee shop. Instead, he nearly fell off his stool when her whiskey-colored gaze touched him. When she thought he looked familiar, panic's fist squeezed his insides, and he knew he had to get out of there. It was only a matter of time before she recognized him.

But wasn't that the point? He'd returned to Hareton prepared for the attack, and this time do a little attacking himself. Then, at the first opportunity, he ran. Just like he had twelve years ago.

He started the car, but hesitated before pulling away from the curb. Where to go? He considered checking into a hotel, but the minute the clerk saw his credit card, the whole town would know he was back. And at this point he wanted to keep a low profile at least until... Until what? What the hell was he doing here?

He could think of only one place to go. He pulled onto the street, made a U-turn at the next set of lights and circled back the way he'd come. As he drove, he thought of Haley.

So, she and Paige weren't speaking. He wasn't surprised. The girls in that family had bickered constantly the entire time he knew them. He supposed that wasn't likely to stop just because they had grown up. Just because Michelle was gone.

Back then he'd been the hired help, watching the antics of his employer's children like the audience at a movie. Until Michelle turned her dark eyes and brilliant smile on him. Of the few things in life Dean regretted, that day stood chief among the others.

Michelle had been blonde and beautiful, fun and a little bit wild. And after dating her for two months he realized she was also flaky, self-absorbed and immature. He felt bad thinking so. After all, one shouldn't speak ill of the dead.

Paige had been Michelle's polar opposite. Dark and angry, with a mouth on her that should have been reserved for locker rooms and cock fights.

Haley fell somewhere in the middle. While she wasn't outgoing like Michelle, she didn't hate the world like Paige either. She was only fifteen when he knew her, awkward and skinny, quiet with a dry sense of humor that seemed a little old for her.

The awkwardness had gone now. Her hair had deepened to a dark caramel color, but her eyes were still like liquid gold. He always thought she had amazing eyes, even back when he was too old for her.

He turned off Main onto Shepherd, and followed the street to the edge of town. A small cluster of rundown houses, set far from the clean, pretty homes on the north end of Hareton, formed the neighborhood where he grew up. He brought the car to a halt in front of a dilapidated, red brick, two-story that probably had been nice in the 1940s.

After grabbing his bag from the back seat and hoisting it over his shoulder, he trudged up the unshoveled path to the front door. Like many of the houses in the area, this one had been converted into a duplex. According to the name written in faded marker on masking tape next to the buzzer, Allister Glit lived in the apartment on the second floor.

Dean pressed the button and waited. After a few moments, the door opened and Allister, dressed only in his boxer shorts, stood before him.

His arms crossed his thin bare chest, and his black eyes went wide. "Dean, what are you doing here?"

"I'm not sure."

"When I told you about Michelle, I didn't think you'd come."

"Yeah, well, *surprise*. And until I figure out what I'm going to do, I need a place to stay."

"You can't stay here. Celia will kill me."

"She's back?"

"Well, no, but if she finds out you were here, she'll never come back."

Dean smiled tightly. "She left eight months ago. I don't think my being here will impact her decision one way or the other."

"Forget it, Dean."

"Come on, be a pal."

"I work for Haley Carling. If she finds out, she'll fire me."

"I just saw Haley at the coffee shop."

Al's eyes rounded. "What did she say?"

"Nothing, she didn't recognize me."

"Thank God for that. I wonder what she was doing there."

"I'm going to go out on a limb and guess having a cup of coffee before work."

"She's going to work today?"

Dean could hardly believe someone as white as Allister could get any whiter. "Yeah, I overheard her say so to Karen."

"Crap, she'll know I was late again." Raw panic filled Allister's voice.

"I could go back, maybe stall her. Maybe tell her what a great guy you are. I would know, after all, since we've stayed in touch all these years."

Allister raked his fingers through his greasy black hair, leaving clumps standing at strange angles when his arm fell back to his side. "Fine," he snapped. "You can stay, but no one can know you're here."

Dean nodded and followed Allister inside. He tried not to let Al's words bother him. He'd been a pariah here for so long he thought he'd be used to it by now. He'd been wrong.

Yellowed walls and sparse furnishings covered in a thick layer of dust made up Allister's apartment. The smells of fried food and body odor hung heavy in the air. Dean forced himself to suppress a shudder as he watched something scurry across the filthy kitchen floor.

"Make yourself comfortable," Al said. "I'm going to take a shower. Haley will kill me if I'm late again."

"So, she runs the store?" Dean asked, pretending idle curiosity, then sneezed. The dust was getting to him.

"She sure does."

He would have to be deaf to miss the sarcasm in Al's voice. "Is she a hard ass?"

"Tries to be." Al shrugged. "Not as bad as her old man, but she was just a kid when we started there. I don't know who the hell she thinks she is telling me what's what."

Al disappeared down the hall, leaving Dean alone in the small living room. He sneezed twice, his eyes turning watery. He couldn't stay here. Never mind his dust allergy, or the way the smell turned his stomach, there was just no way he could be around this kind of mess without going a little buggy.

Through the kitchen, he spotted a door that led outside. He sneezed three more times crossing the small room, trying to ignore the food crusted on the stove and the cloud of fruit flies hovering over the dirty dishes piled in the sink. Fruit flies in December. He shuddered openly this time.

As he opened the door and stepped out onto a square deck, the wood creaked and shifted under his weight, and the snow nearly reached his knees. But he'd rather freeze his legs off than go back inside with the fruit flies and whatever had scurried over that floor. He had to find somewhere else to stay. Maybe Matthew could book a room over the phone with his credit card. They were business partners, after all. Matt knew he was good for it.

As he searched for a solution to his habitation dilemma, he spotted the roofline to the shitty little house he'd grown up in. The morning sun glared off the patches of snow covering the peeling shingles.

He knew his mother had gone. He had tried looking her up before coming back, but there was no forwarding address or phone number. For all he knew she might have lit out of this town right after he did.

The bitterness surprised him. He had a pretty good life now. His own business, a nice house, friends. But being here brought back all those old feelings of inadequacy and powerlessness. He supposed they were never really gone, that they were always there, gnawing at the edges of his soul with rat-like teeth.

So what was he doing here? He had no plan and no place to stay. What could he possibly hope to gain in a town where everyone called him a killer?

Chapter Two

One day. She could survive one day. Paige rested her forehead against the cold glass of the living room window. Outside, the late afternoon sun glittered pinkish-orange off the snow-covered lawn.

Home again after four years and not an ounce of warmth or sentiment within her. Only jittery nerves and a sort of tight strangling sensation that left her desperate for escape.

She'd arrived mid-morning and spent most of the day working from the kitchen table. Her mother hadn't come downstairs at all. Thank God.

Paige had heard her mother stir only once. Heavy footsteps overhead, the flush of the toilet, more footsteps, then nothing. All the while she sat frozen, afraid to breathe, afraid the slightest sound would summon the old witch. After what felt like a lifetime, Paige had exhaled a slow, steady breath, got back to work and tried not to think about her mother.

Working kept her mind from wandering, but now, as the day wound down, there was nothing she could do but think. And remember. She flopped down on the couch, drew her thighs to her chest and rested her chin on her knees, trying to forget the image of her father standing at the big picture window.

After Michelle disappeared, he had stood there almost every night, like a sea captain. His legs spread shoulder-width apart, his hands gripped together behind his back.

By late summer, Michelle had been gone for nearly eight months. Paige remembered sitting on the couch in the darkened living room, just as now.

"You should go to bed, Daddy," she'd said.

Her mother and father had given up playing parents, and Paige had the first real inkling they would never again reprise the roles.

"Whenever any of you were late," he told her, "I would wait by the window until I saw you coming up the driveway. I could never sleep until I saw you. I keep hoping if I wait long enough, she'll come up the driveway, and she'll be fine. We'll all be fine."

Paige didn't know what to say. She stayed curled up on the couch, looking at her father's back. At some point she'd fallen asleep, and when she awoke, her father had gone.

He died four years ago of a heart attack and though she'd been away the last years of his life, she was sure he had stood at the window every night, hoping Michelle would come walking up the driveway.

The shrill ring of her cell phone snapped her back into the present. She left the living room and picked up the phone from the kitchen table cluttered with her laptop and papers.

"Paige Carling."

"It's Lucy," her assistant said. "I got your email."

"Good." Static crackled through the earpiece, and she circled the kitchen, searching for a better signal. Lucy's voice suddenly came in clear, and Paige froze.

"Say that again. I missed most of it because of this piece-of-crap phone."

"Should I fax out the new paperwork to reflect the rates you gave me?" Lucy asked, raising her voice to a yell.

Paige held the phone away from her ear and rolled her eyes. "Yes, then wait a half hour and call to follow up. See if you can't get them back signed by the end of the day. I would like this deal booked by Friday. Is that clear?"

"Crystal," Lucy replied.

Paige suspected Lucy might be doing a little eye rolling of her own. The floor above her creaked followed by a loud thump. *Damn it, she's awake.*

"Lucy, I've got to go. Let me know if you have any problems. You can reach me online or on my cell."

"Sure, I'll call you if I need anything."

"Do that. I'll check in with you before the end of the day," Paige added and snapped her phone closed. She imagined Lucy would be cursing her now. After all, she'd just dashed any hope Lucy had for sneaking home early. Paige smiled to herself. Her boss used to do the same thing to her, until she finagled her way into his position and him out the door.

She tidied the papers on the table and folded away her laptop. The sounds above had stopped. Her mother was probably back in Michelle's room.

Maybe she'll stay there. Unlikely, unless she had a bottle hidden away.

Paige carried her things into Garret's old room off the kitchen. Her childhood bedroom upstairs had been filled with so many boxes and forgotten bits of furniture she could barely open the door. It would seem sweet Haley could hold a grudge.

Yeah, well, let her. This room was as good as any other to spend the night. And besides, by this time tomorrow she would be home in her apartment, with her childhood repressed deep inside her, as it should be.

Hesitant footsteps on the stairs followed by three quick thuds told Paige her mother had fallen. She went out to the hall and found the old woman sitting on the bottom step.

She looked up at Paige with dull brown eyes, her gaunt haggard face expressionless. Did she even recognize her?

"Where's Haley?" Claire asked at last.

Paige did her best to ignore the way her insides twisted into tight knots. "Work, I imagine."

Without a word her mother stood, shuffled past her through the kitchen and into the den.

"And hello to you too, Mother," Paige muttered. She slumped down on the bottom stair, resting her elbow on her knee and her chin in her hand. No need to worry about an emotional welcome home in this house.

A loud crash shattered the quiet. First one, then another. Paige jumped to her feet and ran into the den. Her mother stood at the bar, her face bright red and her hands balled into tight fists on either side of her thighs. Paige half expected her to start stomping her feet like a child in the throes of a good tantrum. The shattered remains of a crystal highball glass and a bottle of what looked like vodka littered the floor opposite her. Clear liquid ran down the wood paneled wall.

"Do you know what your bitch sister did?"

Paige shook her head but didn't speak, afraid the next bottle might be thrown at her.

"She filled the bottles with water." Her mother's voice rose to a piercing screech. "She thinks I'm too stupid to notice."

Claire unscrewed the top of another bottle, sniffed loudly, then, like a baseball pitcher smoking one over home plate, she hurled it against the wall. Paige cringed at the sound of exploding glass, and lifted her forearm to protect her face from any stray shards. When she lifted her head, her mother had moved on to the next bottle.

"I can't handle this," Paige muttered, turning away. Another explosion of tinkling glass made her jump. *One day? I'm never going to last.* She went to her room and closed the door.

For a moment, there was quiet from beyond the closed door, then the sound of metal clattering to the tile floor in the kitchen. Now what?

"Paige," her mother called. "Paige."

Paige opened the door and found her mother standing in a pile of forks, knives, spoons and various cooking utensils. Two empty drawers teetered on the edge of the counter.

"Paige," Claire began. "I need you to take me to the store. I think Haley hid my car keys again."

Paige bit the inside of her mouth to keep from smiling. So, Saint Haley had finally grown a spine.

"I'm not taking you anywhere. How about I make you some coffee and something to eat?"

"You have to take me!"

"I don't *have* to do anything," Paige said. A mirthless smile curved her lips.

"I'll go myself then. I'll take a taxi or walk."

"Do what you have to do." Paige shrugged. "But you might want to get dressed and give that hair a brush before you go."

"You're a horrible daughter." Her mother screeched so loud Paige thought her ears might bleed, then the old woman stormed out of the kitchen.

Paige knelt and gathered the silverware from the floor. One day, she reminded herself, just one day.

"We need Christmas decorations. Something bright and cheerful to really get people into the spirit."

Haley tugged on her bottom lip with her teeth and continued dabbing furniture stain onto the wide headboard, ignoring her teenage part-timer. She didn't see the point in telling Billy that with her sister's body found, and her mother home drunk and passed out, and her other sister—the same one who made out with her now ex-fiancé at their father's funeral—arriving today, other people's Christmas spirit was actually quite low on her list of concerns. "I have other things on my mind," she summed up instead.

"Well, you *need* to think about this."

Haley lifted her gaze from the intricately carved fruit and glared.

"All I'm saying," he went on quickly, "is Christmas spirit sells. Real Christmas spirit, not this peace on earth and good will toward man crap. That's a myth. Christmas spirit is cold hard cash. It's buying the perfect gift and trying to top other people's gifts. It's all about money."

"How is it possible for you to be this cynical at sixteen?"

"Call it cynicism if you want. I call it realism."

"Whatever you call it, if you want to see Christmas spirit on your next check, I suggest you get back up to the counter where you belong."

"Why? The shop's empty."

Thanks for the reminder. "Because I've got a lot to do here, and you're distracting me."

"You can't talk and work?"

"No, I can't. I told Mrs. Beaumont I would have the suite done by Saturday." She swung her arm out at the bedside tables and dresser, all in various states of completion. "Al's on a delivery and I'm on my own here until he gets back. So, either sit at the counter or don't speak."

"Oh, I almost forgot to tell you," Billy said, lowering his

voice to a hush. Why he bothered, she didn't know. They hadn't had a customer in nearly two hours. The skinny wooden paintbrush dug into her flesh as she tightened her grip.

"What?"

"I think Al might be gay."

Haley snorted. "Why would you think that?"

"Some guy came to see him while you were getting coffee, and Al got all nervous and embarrassed. He wouldn't even talk to the guy in the store."

Something fluttered in her stomach, and her skin turned cold. "Who was the guy?"

"I've never seen him before. I don't want to sound mean, or anything, but I think he's a little out of Al's league."

"I doubt Al's gay. He lived with Celia for over a year." And how Celia could stand him Haley didn't know.

"Then, who's the guy?"

"He could be anyone. Some friend or relative of Al's, maybe his bookie or drug dealer. Who knows?" Maybe the guy from the Java Joint. She tried to suppress the shiver running down her spine. So what if he was? Why would that bother her?

"Do you think Al's into drugs?"

Haley sighed and tossed her brush down next to the can of stain on the newspaper. "No, I don't think he's into drugs. I swear, you're worse than an old woman when it comes to gossip."

The telephone on the counter rang and she said a silent prayer of thanks. "Can you get that?"

Billy shrugged and slipped through the door from the workshop into the store. She liked the kid. He worked hard for her three nights a week and every other Saturday. Best of all he worked for minimum wage, but sometimes his non-stop chatter drove her crazy.

She peeled off her blue, latex gloves, tossed them into the trash and washed her hands in the bathroom sink. When she emerged, Billy was waiting for her.

"That was Al. He delivered the table, but he said he won't be back in."

"Oh?" She should fire him, she knew she should. He was

late more often than on time, he called in sick at least three times a month, usually on a Friday or a Monday, and he argued with her every time she made a change. So why didn't she? Because her father hired him? A throw back to a time when her world had been okay?

Billy shifted from one foot to the other. "'Cause it's four now, and by the time he gets back it'll be nearly six."

"Is he planning on walking back? Is that why he'll take two hours?"

Billy shrugged.

"Sorry, I didn't mean to snap at you. It's probably for the best anyway. That's two hours I don't have to pay him for." She sighed. "There's not much going on. If you want to take off early too, you can."

Deep frown lines grooved his usually unmarred forehead, while he wrestled with the decision. Clearly, choosing between money and free time was not easy for him. But finally, after careful consideration, going home won out over getting paid.

He grabbed his coat off the hook and left with a quick good-bye. At last, a quiet moment.

She tidied the project she had been working on, then sat behind the counter to go over the bills.

The sky had turned dark and so had her mood by the time she tucked the folder away in the drawer. Working on payables did that to her every time. And the idea of returning to her mother's house and seeing Paige again wasn't helping.

She stood, stretched her aching back muscles, and walked to the front door. Outside, tiny flakes of snow fluttered gently to the sidewalk. She flipped the sign in the window to "Closed", but didn't bother to lock the door. With not a single customer for the better part of the afternoon, she'd relish one now. Anything to keep her from having to face her family.

She was about to turn out the lights when the bell above the door dinged. *A customer, thank God.*

She poked her head out from the workshop. A tall, skinny man, bald except for blond fringe circling the back of his head like a hair horseshoe, stood with his back to her, his attention focused on a painted kitchen set.

"I saw the 'closed' sign," the man said, "but the lights were on and the door was open. I hope you don't mind."

She knew that voice. "Nate?"

He turned, a wide smile spread across his narrow face, and held his arms open. "How have you been?"

"I'm so glad to see you." She moved in for the hug. His arms wrapped tight around her until she couldn't breathe, then he released her.

"The place looks good," he said, slowly walking the perimeter of the shop. "Hell of a lot better than when your father and I ran it. Must have needed a woman's touch."

"I don't know how true that is." Haley couldn't remember the shop ever going an afternoon without a customer when her father and Nate had been in charge.

"It's true. You always had a feel for the place. Not like Garret or that sister of yours. I knew when I sold you my share that this place was meant for you. Your father would have been so proud."

Haley fought to ignore the hot, suffocating sensation sliding over her. "Thanks. I was so sorry to hear about Joan," she added.

He dropped his gaze and a pang of guilt pierced her conscience. Maybe she shouldn't have mentioned Joan. He'd only lost his wife a little more than a month ago to ALS, Amyotrophic Lateral Sclerosis, or more commonly Lou Gehrig's Disease.

"It's terrible thing watching someone you care for suffer for so long." His voice was soft and far away. "When the end came, it was almost a blessing."

"I wanted to come for the funeral, but with my mother..." She didn't need to explain. Nate knew both she and Garret couldn't be away from their mother at the same time, and Garret was his son-in-law.

"I know you did." He took her hand in his and gave it a squeeze. "How are you holding up since Michelle was found?"

"I'm fine."

He gave her a look that told her he clearly didn't believe a word, but he didn't press and she was glad.

"Claire?"

"It's been hard on her."

"And on you."

She slid her hand from his grip. "This has stirred everything up again. In time, it will settle."

"You're probably right." He smiled and nodded toward the door. "I should be going. I want to get to Garret and Erin's before the grandkids are off to bed. It's been too long since I've seen the girls."

"They're getting big," Haley told him as she walked him to the entrance.

He stopped before leaving. "If you need anything, I'm always here for you."

"Thanks, Nate. You're very kind."

He nodded and slipped outside. As she closed the door behind him, she waved. Nate had always been a good friend to her family. Family. With a sigh, Haley gathered her things, set the alarm, and locked the door behind her. *Her* family waited.

Chapter Three

Dean slouched in his seat and drummed his fingers against the steering wheel. When Nate Johnson emerged from Hareton Furniture Restoration, Dean's hands stilled and he slunk down farther.

"Relax, he can't see us," Al said, shoving a handful of French fries into his mouth. One fell from his fingers and slipped between the seats. Dean rolled his eyes when Al made no effort to retrieve it.

Al was right, though. No one could see them tucked into the shadows with only the front bumper touching the pink circle cast by the streetlight. Still, Dean held his breath as Nate climbed into his car and pulled away from the curb, passing them only a few feet away.

Moments later, Haley stepped out of the store. His stomach jumped, and his skin grew damp as he watched her lock the door, then start walking down Main.

"Should we go in?" Al asked around a mouthful of burger.

Dean shook his head. "Not yet. Wait until she's out of sight. Then we'll slip around back. I don't want to risk being seen."

"If you're so worried about being recognized, here's a tip." A shred of lettuce clung to Al's bottom lip. "Don't show up at the store again."

"I waited for Haley to leave." Dean watched as she crossed the street and disappeared around the corner.

"Billy saw you."

"So? He doesn't know who I am. If you hadn't been so weird, he wouldn't have looked twice at me. Anyway, she's gone.

Let's go."

He climbed out of the car and crossed the road. The cold air nipped at his cheeks and hands.

"Damn," Al muttered, breathing into his cupped hands and rubbing them together. "Feels like thirty below out here."

Dean nodded and followed Al down a tight walkway between Haley's store and the used bookshop next door. The path opened into a narrow alley running behind both buildings. He tucked his hands under his armpits and shivered as Al fumbled the key into the lock. The sound of something plastic rattling inside the huge metal Dumpster set his teeth on edge. He didn't like being there, exposed, despite the alley's obvious emptiness.

"Got it," Al whispered, yanking open the heavy steel door.

Dean relaxed a little as he followed Al inside. A piercing electronic beep filled the store while Al punched numbers into the alarm system on the wall, then, finally, silence.

"You are going to get me so fired," Al said.

"If that happens, you can come work for me. I owe you one after this." He sincerely hoped it wouldn't come to that.

Al flipped on the fluorescents over head. Their faint hum filled the air and an eerie white light fell over the dull gray walls and bits of unfinished furniture.

Dean stood rigid, determined to ignore the goose bumps spreading over his skin. God, it was like stepping back through time. Almost nothing had changed. From the pungent odors of turpentine and wood stain, to the tools scattered over the workbenches.

"So what's next?" Al asked.

His voice snapped Dean out of his reverie. "This will only take a minute."

He opened the gate on the tool cage, an oversized chain link box in the back corner of the room, and worked his way past cans and jugs of chemicals. From the other side of the steel fence, Al watched him move dusty boxes of forgotten accessories and bolts of fabric from rotted wood shelves then, at last, the shelves themselves.

"I didn't know there was something behind there," Al said

as Dean stooped to move into a small crawlspace.

Until the day he was fired, Dean hadn't known either. That day, with Darren Carling's hard gaze forever branded in his mind, and Carling's tight angry words still echoing in his ears, Dean had walked into the back room, shaking and sick, his face hot with shame. He snatched his jacket from the hook next to the bench and started to set his store key down, but the thin metal slipped from his sweat-slicked fingers and bounced into the tool cage, disappearing behind the shelf.

Even now, the ping of metal on the concrete floor reverberated in his head.

Now, the crawlspace was empty. Only a thick layer of dust on the floor and tattered cobwebs clinging to the stout ceiling remained. Gone was the green plastic garbage bag he'd found there twelve years ago with an old quilted blanket and a pair of navy coveralls inside, both dark and stiff with reddish-brown stains.

When he had shown them to Nate, the older man tried to convince him it was just a furniture tint. But Dean had never known furniture stain to smell like that. Sweet and meaty. Still, it was better to believe that than the other. Especially when he thought of those reddish brown stains splattered over the bright white stitching of the name *Carling* on the patch.

"So, what's in there?" Al asked.

Dean moved back into the tool cage and started fixing the shelves in place. "Nothing." Had he really expected otherwise after more than a decade?

Finding them would have made life easier. A smoking gun. Everything he'd gathered on his own may be compelling, but it was all still circumstantial. It might be enough. There was the house, after all. Why had Carling held onto it for so long? Fear of Michelle being found?

"What were you looking for?" Al asked.

"Something I forgot before I left."

Dean wished he had paid more attention when he took the boxes from the shelves. Hopefully, it had been so long since Haley had been in there she wouldn't notice if something had been moved.

"So, I guess that's it, huh? Now you'll just go home."

"Not yet." He had other avenues still to explore.

There were two cars in the driveway when Haley got to her mother's, both blocking her old rust bucket in the garage. She recognized Garret's green SUV. The convertible Mustang could only be Paige's.

With a deep breath, she squared her shoulders and went inside.

"I can't believe you didn't make dinner," Garret was saying as Haley entered the house.

Paige leaned over the sink with a cigarette in her hand and blew smoke out the window. "I'm not her maid and cook."

"If she's drinking like that she needs to eat something." Garret crossed the room and flung the fridge door open. It banged hard off the cupboard next to it.

Haley leaned against the doorframe between the kitchen and the hall. Both Garret and Paige were far too absorbed in their argument to notice her. There was something disconcerting about watching them fall back into the older brother and bratty sister roles after so many years. She half expected Michelle to bounce into the room.

"I asked her if she wanted something to eat, she said no." Paige turned on the faucet and ran cold water over the cigarette's glowing tip. It went out with a sharp hiss.

Garret cracked an egg into the glass bowl on the counter. "Well, of course she'll say no. You have to fix something and then make sure she eats it. Haley knows this."

"Good for Haley." Paige closed the window. "When the hell does she get home anyway?"

"Right now," Haley said. They both whirled to face her.

"I just saw your father-in-law at the store," she told Garret. "He's on his way to your house."

"Oh, great. Nate's back in town." Paige rolled her eyes.

Haley ignored her. "Anyway, I'm not staying. I just came to get my things. I need you to move your cars so I can get mine out of the garage."

"What do you mean you're not staying?" Paige asked with

something akin to panic in her voice. Dark pleasure welled inside Haley.

"I'm going home tonight."

"Who'll take care of Mom?"

"You're here, you can do it."

"Oh, I see." Paige rested her hands on her hips. "You're mad, and this is how you're going to punish me."

The hair on the back of Haley's neck bristled as she clamped down on the urge to punch her sister in the mouth.

"If taking care of Mom is a punishment," she said through gritted teeth, "I've been serving a life sentence. So, aside from being born last, what the hell did I do to deserve it?"

Haley didn't wait for a reply. She turned on her heel and stormed up the stairs. Her mother was nowhere in sight.

Fury pounded at her temples as she went into her bedroom, slammed the door and fell back against it. Where had the anger come from? Her fingers trembled as she raked them through her hair. She breathed deeply in an effort to pull herself together before she dealt with her sister again.

"I suppose I walked right into that," Paige said, shaking another cigarette from the package. After having quit nearly a year and a half ago, her lungs burned and her mouth tasted like day-old gym socks, but since her mother's little explosion earlier, she needed something.

She slid the window over the sink open again, while Garret searched for something in the cupboard. He stopped long enough to give her a disapproving glare as she lit up.

"Where is the goddamned vanilla?" he muttered, resuming his search.

"Perhaps Mommy Dearest drank it on a dry day," Paige suggested, exhaling through the screen into the cold night.

Garrett didn't reply as he put a frying pan on the stove.

"I can't believe she's still mad. It's been four years," Paige said.

Garret slopped a spoonful of margarine into the pan. "You

kissed her fiancé."

"He kissed me."

"You kissed him back."

"Well, I didn't want to be rude." Paige shrugged. "I actually did her a favor. He didn't love her. She shouldn't marry a man who doesn't love her."

Garret rolled his eyes. "This talent you have for rationalizing everything you do never ceases to amaze me. Even when you know you were wrong, you can still find a way to twist it around." He slapped the egg-soaked bread into the pan.

"You're no better than me. You live two blocks away, but how often do you help look after Mom? Once a week? Once a month? Ever? Yet you smugly lecture me about rationalizations when you go home every night and hide behind your family."

"You don't know what you're talking about."

Paige shivered next to the open window while Garret turned back to the French toast frying in the pan. He always took Haley's side.

After running the tip of her cigarette under water and tossing the butt in the garbage, she closed the window and sat down at the table.

"Where's Mom?" Garret asked, setting the French toast on a plate. Paige looked up and realized he wasn't speaking to her. Haley again stood quietly in the doorway. How long had she been there? How much had she heard? Heat stole into Paige's cheeks.

"She's in the shrine," Haley said. "I need you to move your car."

Garret walked past her toward the stairs. "In a minute."

Haley flopped down in the chair at the opposite end of the table, still wearing her coat, her bag at her feet, and stared in stony silence at the window.

"How's the store?" Paige asked. Sitting without speaking like two angry children was ridiculous.

Haley turned and glared. "Fine."

"Good. This was always a busy time of year."

"Give it a rest, Paige. You've never been interested before, so don't pretend to be now."

Why couldn't the floor just open up and swallow her? Anything to escape this place.

"We have to talk," Garret said when he returned.

"Move your car," Haley repeated. "I'm tired, and I want to go home."

He plopped more egg-soaked bread into the pan. "You can't leave yet. There are things we need to discuss."

"Such as?" Haley ground out.

"Mom wants a funeral." He didn't look at either of them when he spoke. Instead, he kept his gaze fixed on the bread sizzling in the pan.

"So, we give her a funeral. What's the big deal?" Paige shrugged. Her fingers itched for another cigarette.

"What would we bury?" Garret asked as though she were the stupidest person alive.

"When will they be releasing the body?"

"After a trial. And, funny, I don't see that happening anytime soon." Garret set a tub of margarine and plastic syrup bottle in the center of the table.

"Did they tell you how she died?" Haley asked.

"Marks on the bones suggest her throat had been cut, but with only skeletal remains the investigators can't be sure."

"This is morbid." Paige realized she was holding her neck and forced her hand down to the tabletop as Garret set a plate of French toast in front of her. "You've got to be kidding."

He set a second one in front of Haley. She pushed it away.

Garret finally sat down with his own plate, and seemed not to notice that neither of his sisters touched the food in front of them.

"Maybe we could have a memorial or something," Haley suggested.

Garret nodded. "That's what Mom's going to want."

"Or," Paige said, "we could just tell Mom no. Make her deal with reality, whether she likes it or not."

Haley snorted. "That's a great idea. And since you're not here to deal with the aftermath, what do you care?"

"Just because I'm not willing to waste my life playing

nursemaid to her doesn't mean I don't care. She acts the way she does because you and Garret let her."

"Oh my God, Paige, you're so wise. How do we get by without your sage advice in our everyday lives?" The thick sarcasm in Haley's voice scraped against Paige's nerves.

"You are such a martyr."

"Shut up, both of you," Garret exploded. "Could we get through one conversation without the two of you going at it? Let's just get this done. There will be a memorial service."

"Fine," Haley said. "Who's going to make the arrangements?"

Paige turned to her, as did Garret.

"Forget it," she told them. "I did Dad's funeral. You two can work it out on your own."

Garret turned to Paige. "I'll call you tomorrow and we can figure out what to do then." He glanced at his watch.

"Fine." Paige sighed. So much for getting out of here tomorrow.

"If we're done, could you please move your cars?" Haley pushed her chair back.

"All right," Garret agreed.

He stood and Haley followed. Paige went to fetch her coat from the end of her bed. The room was dark except for the light spilling in through the open door from the kitchen. She picked up her coat and swung it over her shoulders. As she slid her arms into the sleeves, she froze in mid-motion. Someone was at the window.

Her heart leapt and her breath caught in her throat. She was certain she'd caught a glimpse of a shadowy figure peering inside. Or, at least, she had been sure. There was no one there now.

Paige pulled her coat around her and went to the window. Leaning forward, she cupped her hands around her eyes to block the light.

Outside, the gnarled, skeletal branches of two crab apple trees in the far corner of the backyard swayed in the blackness. Everything else was still.

Relief turned her taut muscles to jelly. She'd probably just seen her own reflection in the glass. With the light behind her as she threw on her coat, the movement must have caught her eye.

Paige wanted to laugh at herself for jumping at her own shadow, but couldn't quite manage it.

With trembling fingers, she pulled the thin cord, lowering the blind from behind the window ruffle. She turned the plastic wand, closing the slats and shutting out the dark.

"Paige." Garret's voice made her jump. "We're waiting for you."

"I'm coming," she called. Her voice only warbled a little.

Chapter Four

Lara Williams gripped the letter opener in her sweaty fist, sliding the silver tip between the edge of the desk and the top drawer. With her heart pounding, she ran the thin blade slowly along the crack until the lock stopped her. After a quick glance over her shoulder at the closed study door, she jabbed the opener back and forth until the obstruction clicked and gave way. She was in.

Carefully, she returned the opener to its allotted space, centered between the phone and the edge of the desk. She tapped the tip with her finger until it lined up with the top of the matched magnifying glass. Now her husband would never know she had been there. And saw what he hid.

She ignored his date book and expense ledger, interested in only one thing. The same thing she always looked at when the guilt gripped her. Her fingers closed over a small, velvet ring box tucked into the back of the drawer. She lifted it out and opened the lid. The hard, winter sunlight, spilling in through the window, glinted off the solitaire diamond inside. The perfect symbol of her sin. Her heart ached with the thought.

Was the ring a symbol for Jonathan too? Did it represent sins and a guilt all his own? It must. After all this time, why keep a ring meant for a dead woman?

Heavy footsteps on the marble floor in the hall made her jump. She snapped the box closed and listened as the sound grew louder.

Her breath came quickly as she put the box back with trembling fingers. She checked to make sure everything was as she had found it then closed the drawer.

"Wondering where it all went wrong?" The voice was deep and male, but not Jonathan's. Every muscle in her body sagged with relief as she lifted her gaze to meet the cruel mirth dancing in her brother-in-law's pale blue eyes.

"Something like that." Lara rose from the large leather chair and tucked her hair behind her ear. She would wait until she was alone again to lock the desk with an unraveled paper clip. "What are you doing here?"

Richard grinned and slung his suit jacket over his shoulder. "I wonder. You look good in black. You should go to memorials more often."

"This isn't a joke. Michelle was my closest friend." His tie was loosened and the top three buttons of his shirt undone. The familiar tug of need stirred inside her.

"Clearly. Jonathan is an excellent example of just how close the two of you were."

"Shut up, Richard," she snapped.

He chuckled. "Why is it when someone dies they suddenly become a saint? Let's face it, Michelle was certainly not that, as my brother could attest."

Her insides tightened painfully. "What do you want?"

"You know what I want," he said, closing the heavy oak door, shutting them off from the rest of the house. "Where's Jonathan?"

Lara's heart rate quickened. This was such a stupid risk. "He left already."

"Not attending together? He's not even bothering to keep up the pretense of a real marriage. Ever wonder if your days are numbered?"

"Leave me alone," she said, but she didn't mean it.

He stepped toward her, his eyes bright and hungry. "Struck a nerve, have I?" He pulled her against him before letting his hands run up her thighs, under her skirt.

She shivered and tipped her head back so his teeth could graze the column of her throat. His hands gripped her bottom and he edged her toward the desk.

"Not here," she murmured, taking a step away.

"Yes, here." He lifted his head and his dark satisfied gaze

met hers, making her blood cold. "Here is just perfect."

The calm before the storm. Erin stepped into her mother-in-law's kitchen, a tray of sandwiches balanced in each hand. The eerie silence that greeted her left her uneasy. Quiet in this house was just unnatural.

She set the trays on the kitchen table while she cleared a space for them in the fridge. After sliding them both in, she stood back and admired her handiwork. The shelves were full, but only with the food she brought. Erin shook her head. What had Paige and Claire been eating for the past three days?

No one had shopped. Claire never did, and Haley and Paige were at a standoff. Erin gritted her teeth at the thought of her sisters-in-law and their constant feuding. Poor Garret had enough to worry about without the added stress of his sisters' squabbles. She closed the fridge harder then she meant to and the condiments rattled in the door.

Perhaps she wasn't being fair. After all, she had to accept some responsibility for Garret's sleepless nights. The lies and secrets sat heavy on her shoulders. If things didn't settle down soon, her knees would buckle and she would collapse under the crushing weight.

So many times she had wanted to tell Garret the truth. The words had almost fallen from her lips, but fear kept her silent. And love. The same fear and love that put her in this position to begin with. As the years passed, she remained silent. She and Garret built a life together. A happy life. A loving life. And the secrets and lies faded, turning fuzzy, like a dream upon waking. But now, with Michelle found, those lies and secrets snapped back into focus as sharp and clear as ever.

"I didn't hear you come in," Paige said.

Erin jerked at the sound of her voice. Dressed in a stylish black suit that hugged her slender form, Paige looked like she was going to a business meeting rather than her sister's memorial. Her dark hair was swept into a twist, away from the delicate features of her face. She would have been a pretty girl if it weren't for her eyes. Dark and hard, they shone like shards of black glass.

"Just putting some things in the fridge," Erin said. Her muscles tensed and she hoped Paige would just go away. She wasn't up for a confrontation now.

Paige nodded and disappeared into her bedroom. When she returned, she was smoking a cigarette. The acrid smell assaulted Erin's nostrils and stung her eyes. She frowned, but said nothing. After today, Paige would slither back to whatever life she led and everything else would return to normal.

"Garret's at the funeral home already," Erin said in an attempt to make conversation.

"I'm sure he is," Paige muttered, flicking a stray ash from her skirt. "Anything to avoid *Mother*."

Erin sighed. "Why do you have to make everything so much harder than it needs to be?"

"I don't know. Why do you have to whine when you speak?"

Erin's jaw hurt from grinding her teeth. "I'm going over to the funeral home, unless there's anything else you need."

"See you later." Paige blew a cloud of blue gray smoke into Erin's face and watched her leave through the side door. A slow smile spread over her face.

"That wasn't very nice."

Paige turned to find Haley leaning on the doorframe between the kitchen and the front hall. "I wish you'd stop doing that. How long have you been there?"

"Not long." Haley flopped onto one of the kitchen chairs. "Could you have been any ruder?"

Paige grinned. "Much."

"What's your problem with Erin?"

Where to start? "She's a phony," Paige said, opting for the short version.

Haley rolled her eyes. "Well, obviously."

"I'm serious. She pretends to be all nice and sweet, but I'm telling you, she's a calculating bitch."

"Takes one to know one."

Paige detected no real heat in the insult, and relaxed a little when Haley smiled. "Oh, my, such scathing wit. Erin's whole family's the same. I can't stand any of them."

"I don't know how you can say that. Nate was Dad's closest friend."

"He gives me the creeps."

"As far as I'm concerned, the man's a saint. I would have lost the store if he hadn't let me buy him out in installments, and small ones at that."

"You know, I caught him staring at my breasts when I was sixteen."

"You think everyone is staring at your breasts."

Paige glanced down at her chest. Possibly. "I'm not talking a sneak-a-peek here, I'm talking full on ogling. It was gross."

"I imagine you said *something*."

"Of course. I told him if I caught him again I would blind the son-of-a-bitch." After she'd threatened to tell her father, but Nate had only chuckled. "*Tell all the lies you want, Paige,*" he'd said. "*Your father would never believe that I would do something like that.*" Even now, the memory sent a chill through her.

"Charming." Haley shook her head. "Where's Mom?"

"In her room I think."

"How is she?"

"Strangely lucid." And thank God for that. If Paige had to go through another one of Claire's drunken sobbing fits, she'd put her mother through a wall.

"I'll see if she needs any help. We have to go soon."

"Haley." Paige didn't know what exactly she wanted to say. She should apologize or something, but this was the closest either of them had come to an actual conversation in four years, and she was afraid just mentioning Jason would lead to another blow out.

Haley waited for her to continue, but the words stuck in her throat. "I'll go warm up the car."

Haley shifted on the hard, wooden bench and kept her attention focused on the window and the fluttering snowflakes against the steel gray sky. If she looked away, or even thought of the people packed into the small chapel, her skin broke out in a cold sweat and she could actually feel the blood drain from her face. Was this an anxiety attack? Christ, she hoped not.

She fought to push the thought away, while the minister's words droned meaninglessly in her ears. She needed to keep all thoughts of Michelle tucked to the far recesses of her brain. Too late. Memories of her sister flooded her mind as if released by a great dam. Michelle, the sister she barely knew.

Six years had separated them in age, and while it didn't sound like a lot, when she was fifteen and Michelle twenty-one they lived in different worlds.

What did she remember, really remember, about her sister? Her heart pounded and her throat ached as she realized she couldn't remember what Michelle looked like. Fragments danced in her head. Michelle's smile, her hair, the sound of her laughter. But she couldn't get a clear picture of her.

Haley let out a soft sigh and tried to find something else to focus on. She glanced back over her shoulder and her gaze locked with Samuel Williams. He sat on the opposite side of the chapel, flanked by his sons, Richard and Jonathan.

What was he doing here? According to rumor, he rarely left his home since retiring. He hadn't even liked Michelle. When she and Jonathan had dated, he made no secret of his feelings.

Samuel's pale gray eyes held hers until she finally looked away. A shiver crept up her spine.

She shouldn't be surprised. Michelle had been a town legend for more than a decade. Haley doubted anyone even briefly connected with her family would miss this.

So this was how it ended for her sister, whose image she couldn't quite conjure, entertaining the whole town while her killer roamed...somewhere.

Suddenly, she desperately needed to be away. Away from the room packed tightly with people and the hot oppressive air she could barely breathe.

She stood abruptly and the minister's words halted. She glanced his way and shook her head then eased past Garret and Erin toward the far side of the room.

Garret gripped her arm. "Where are you going?" he demanded in a harsh whisper.

After yanking her arm free, Haley ignored him. She could

feel people's stares as she made her way to the nearest exit. Even with her head lowered she couldn't miss the curious looks and raised eyebrows when she passed. Oh, they'd talk about this for a while. So what. She'd certainly given these people more interesting things to talk about over the years.

Haley hurried through the foyer, pushed open the heavy glass door and burst out into the cold. With deep, gulping breaths, she sucked in the icy air as if she'd been suffocating. God, she must have looked like a crazy woman.

Shaking her head to herself, she started down the cement steps to the path and followed the winding concrete, crusted with frozen slush, to the parking lot where she would wait for Paige and her mother. The small heels of her boots wobbled dangerously on the slick ground and she wondered enviously how Paige managed to make much higher heels appear like mere extensions of her feet.

Twice she nearly fell, only barely managing to keep her balance and stop herself from tumbling face first into a snow bank. Concentrating on her shuffling feet, she followed the path until it opened into a large square lot at the rear of the building.

The sound of someone else's footsteps in the hard packed snow made her look up. The man from the Java Joint hurried toward one of the cars.

"You," she said, as her feet slid out in two different directions, pitching her forward. Her arms pinwheeled wildly in a desperate attempt to keep her balance, but it was too late. She landed with a solid thump. Pain shot from her right knee up her leg. Her hands slid forward in the wet, brownish snow until they scraped against the pavement below.

"God damn it," she muttered, pushing herself back on her knees. She wiped the gritty slush from her burning palms on the front of her coat. The side of her knee throbbed, and through a nickel-sized hole in her nylons the skin had turned dark red. She would no doubt have an ugly bruise there later.

"Here," the man said, thrusting his hand at her. Oh God, he was still there. Her cheeks grew hot when she thought about the spectacle he'd just witnessed.

She tilted her head back and looked into his face. Where did she know him from?

His hand closed over hers, warm and rough with thick calluses.

"Thanks," she said, as he helped her to her feet.

He shrugged and started to turn away. Who was he and how did she know him? The answer hovered in the back of her brain the way a song title danced at the tip of her tongue after hearing the first few notes on the radio.

"Did you know Michelle?" she asked quickly.

He stopped and faced her, his expression impassive. "I did."

Her eyes narrowed as she studied the sharp angles of his face, his light green eyes, and the dark hair curling over his jacket collar.

"Were you a friend of hers?" She stepped closer, as if proximity would somehow make him more recognizable.

He took a step back and glanced quickly over his shoulder. She followed his gaze. People from the memorial were trickling into the lot. "I was."

"How did you know her?"

He turned away and walked to the black Maxima parked near the road. "From a long time ago."

"I've seen you before."

"No, you haven't," he said as he climbed into the car.

Oh, but I have and more than once too. Haley watched as he drove off.

"I want to talk to you."

Haley looked up as an angry Paige gripped her elbow and dragged her toward the far end of the parking lot.

"What is your problem?" Haley asked, trying to shake her sister's hold while her feet slipped and skidded beneath her.

Paige hauled on her cigarette. "What were you doing?"

"My God, is that all? I started to feel claustrophobic inside, so I decided to wait for you here."

Haley watched Garret help their mother into his van while Erin stood by the open passenger door staring at her and Paige.

"That's not what I'm talking about," Paige said. She dropped the well-smoked cigarette butt and ground it into the snow with the pointed toe of her boot. "I'm talking about who you were with."

"You know him?"

"Erin saw you, Haley. She told me who you were talking to. I want to know what the hell you were doing with him."

"Who is he?" Haley asked. How did everyone else seem to know who he was except her?

"Dean Lawson," Paige said. Contempt dripped from her voice like icicles in a thaw. "Michelle's killer."

Haley's insides turned cold and her stomach dropped to her shoes. "I thought he looked familiar."

Chapter Five

Haley sat on the sofa, wedged between Mr. Greene, Michelle's high school science teacher, and her mother's neighbor, Nancy Yolken. Only half listening to Mr. Greene's awkward condolences and Mrs. Yolken's probing questions, she hoped she made the appropriate responses in the right places.

Dean Lawson. How had she not recognized him? In all fairness, he had been the last person she expected to see at Michelle's memorial.

"Such a shame," Mrs. Yolken said again. Haley gritted her teeth until her jaw ached. She wished the woman would find someone else to pump for information. When it came to gossip, Yolken was like a circling vulture, barely waiting for her prey to stop twitching before swooping in.

Mr. Greene slowly got to his feet. "I should see about another coffee."

The idea of Mrs. Yolken claiming her undivided attention sent a wave of panic through her. "Let me get that for you."

"Nonsense, Haley." He waved her off and headed for the kitchen, probably as eager to get away from the other woman as she was.

Crap.

"I just can't believe she was in your grandmother's house all that time." Mrs. Yolken shook her head.

Not this again. *That's right, while my grandmother was staying here, caring for her drunk daughter, someone buried my sister in her basement.* She should have drawn up some kind of FAQ to hand people as they came through the door.

"Strange your father never sold the house."

Haley smiled and looked away. How could she lose this woman?

"One might think he knew Michelle was there all along."

Haley turned sharply. "What did you say?"

"Oh, dear, I didn't mean *that*." Mrs. Yolken's tiny, black eyes shone malignantly in her long, horse face. "Just that it seems he almost sensed it."

"Is that how it seems?" Haley's stomach churned.

"I hope you don't think *I'm* implying anything. I've known your family for so long I couldn't bear to hear a bad word said about any of you."

Of course not. Haley bit the inside of her lip. *Unless, you were first to pass the sordid details along.*

"I know your father adored you girls. Even if people are talking, I certainly wouldn't say a word to encourage such stories."

Haley opened her mouth to speak, something sharp and scathing, but snapped it shut. The last thing she needed was to give the woman a reaction and something more to talk about over her next bridge game.

"I'm glad we can count on you," she said instead.

Mrs. Yolken frowned. "Do the police think he killed her there?"

"Who killed her?" Haley asked, her tone sharper than she would have liked.

"Dean Lawson. The police still think he was the one, don't they?" A hint of a smile touched her thin lips.

"There was never enough evidence to connect him to her disappearance."

"Ridiculous, after he had been stalking her like that."

"There was no proof." But he was back and what did that mean? "Michelle never went to the police and accused him of anything."

"Half the town saw her screaming at him right there on Main Street, then she vanishes the same night. I'm as sure as my own name, he killed her." Mrs. Yolken was quiet for a moment. "Will the police search for him now?"

They wouldn't have to search far. "I don't think so, there's still nothing to connect him."

"But now that Michelle's body has been found surely new evidence will be found as well. Is Dean Lawson still the only suspect, or are there others?" Her eyes almost glowed with greedy excitement.

"As far as I know, there are no new suspects. If you'll excuse me, I really should see if Erin or Paige need any help." Haley stood, her head spinning.

Damn it. How did she not see this coming? Back when her grandmother died, people found it strange her father didn't eventually sell her house or even rent it out. Now that Michelle had been found, that was all anyone was talking about. Was her father a suspect? The thought brought an icy sweat to her skin.

She needed answers, and she didn't want to wait until after everyone left.

Slowly, careful not to draw anyone's attention, she made her way to the front hall and gathered her coat before slipping outside. She climbed into her rusted Chevy Nova and turned the key in the ignition. The motor sputtered, then went silent. After a muttered prayer to the-heap-of-junk car gods for the beast to make it through just one more winter, she tried again. This time the engine caught.

While waiting for the car to warm up, she shivered. She rubbed her hands together and peeked over her shoulder like a guilty teenager sneaking out of the house after curfew. Ten minutes later, an eternity, she pulled away from the curb.

What she really wanted to do was go home, soak in a hot tub and pretend this day had never happened. But first, she needed to make a stop.

She drove down Main Street and parked in front of her store, not bothering to put money in the meter. She didn't plan to take long.

Inside, Billy stood behind the counter helping a twenty-something couple. He frowned as she entered, but said nothing. She sailed past him into the workshop, and closed the door behind her.

Al jumped at the sound and tried to hide something behind his back. Smoke streamed steadily from a cigarette burning in an ashtray fashioned from an old soda can on the workbench.

"No smoking back here." The hairs on the back of her neck bristled as she tried to clamp down on her growing anger. This wasn't the first time she'd caught him. With the flammable chemicals they worked with, it was a wonder he hadn't blown them all sky high. She tossed the cigarette and ashtray through the open back door into the alley. As she turned to face him, she caught a glimpse of the magazine rolled behind his back and a big, pink nipple on the cover. She sighed. "Break time?"

"Yeah." Al shrugged. "What are you doing here?"

Probably making a huge mistake. "Where's Dean?"

His eyes went wide. "I—well—um—how would I know?"

"I know he's here, I spoke to him at the memorial, and I know you know where he is."

"Did he tell you that?" His usually pasty skin turned pink.

"No, but you don't need to be a brain surgeon to make the connection. Have you stayed in touch with him since he left?" Why did that bother her?

His eyes narrowed and he wiped his mouth with the back of his hand. She could almost see his mind turning.

"Look," she said, her patience all but gone. "I'm not going to fire you for knowing him, but if you don't tell me where the hell he is, I will."

His shoulders slumped in defeat. "He's staying at the Mountainview under the name Matthew Clarke."

"Thank you," she said, her voice like saccharine. "And if I catch you smoking back here again, I really will fire you."

The Mountainview Motel was neither on a mountain nor did it offer a view of one, as the name implied. Little more than a row of shabby rooms slightly north of town, Haley was surprised the place managed to remain open.

As she drove into the lot, she spotted Dean's car parked in front of one of the rooms and pulled up next to it. What was she doing here, really? Hadn't she had enough drama for one day?

Maybe, but she needed to know why he was back. Why now?

With a sigh she opened the door and stepped out into the cold. The walk running the length of the motel had been shoveled, exposing weathered wood planks. She crossed to his door and knocked loudly before she changed her mind.

After a moment, the door swung back and Dean filled the opening. He didn't look at all surprised to see her. Al had probably called to warn him after she'd left.

She could understand how she hadn't recognized him. The boyishness had left his face, making his features sharper, almost predatory and, if at all possible, more attractive. Even his body seemed harder and leaner than she remembered.

Her heart rate quickened, and something fluttered in her stomach. Could he really have killed Michelle?

Killer or not, she would have to say something soon. She couldn't just stand there staring like a twit all day.

"I didn't recognize you earlier," she said. Better than silence, but only marginally.

Dean leaned casually against the frame. "I figured."

"Erin recognized you." She should have stuck with silence.

"What do you want, Haley?" His voice was deep and quiet.

"Why are you here?"

He sighed and moved aside. "Do you want to come in?"

She hesitated. If she went inside that room, would anyone ever see her again? Allister was the only person who knew where she was and she didn't have a whole lot of faith he'd come to her rescue if she needed him to.

"People know where I am," she said at last.

Dean smirked, but said nothing as she stepped inside, closing the door behind her.

"Nice place you have here, Matthew Clarke," she said, taking in the faded beige wallpaper and gold shag carpet. An ugly oil painting of a gnarly sea captain hung over the sagging double bed.

"I wanted to keep a low profile."

"I thought you would have stayed with Al."

"Have you seen Al's apartment?" A faint smile touched his

lips. "This place is a palace."

He had a point. She had seen Al's apartment once and had gone straight home and showered.

"Sit down," he offered, gesturing to the only chair in the room. As she pulled it away from the desk, she noticed a thick envelope and file folder with bits of paper curling around the edge stacked neatly in the top corner. She would have loved to go through those pages. To see just what Dean studied on alone in a grubby motel room.

"So," she said. "Why are you here?"

"Maybe I just wanted to pay my respects." He sat on the corner of the bed, his eyes bright and his mouth still twisted in that slightly mocking smirk.

"By lurking in the parking lot?"

The grin vanished. "I wasn't in the parking lot the whole time. I watched the service from the door. When I saw you get up and start to leave I decided to go."

"You came back for the memorial?"

"Maybe." He shrugged.

"Or maybe you're worried there's something to link you to Michelle after all."

A tiny muscle twitched in his jaw. "Is that what you think?"

I don't know what to think, and you're not giving anything away. "I don't think you came back here just to watch Michelle's memorial from an open door. So why not tell me what you're really doing here?"

"What do you want me to say, Haley? That I did it? That I killed her?"

"Did you?"

"If I did, it wasn't too smart to come looking for me now, was it?" His voice was quiet, but there was an edge, jagged, like a serrated blade.

A tiny ember ignited within her. A slow fury growing hotter and brighter each time he spoke. "Are you threatening me?"

"No," he said on a sigh, suddenly sounding very tired. "No, I'm not."

"Why are you here?" she asked again.

"I'm not ready to tell anyone yet, but when I am, I'll tell you first."

"That's it? That's the best you can do?"

He nodded.

"Well, sorry, not good enough. Tell me why you're back. I'm not going anywhere until you talk."

"Suit yourself." He shrugged. "I was thinking about ordering dinner. Pizza or Chinese?"

"This isn't a joke, Dean. My sister is dead."

"I know. And I will tell you why I've come back, but not yet. I need to be sure of some things first."

"Fine. You have until tomorrow. If I don't get some answers before the end of the day, there isn't a person in this town who won't know you're here."

Haley stood and strode out the door, suppressing a smile at the sight of his stony stare.

As she marched to the wreck parked next to his car, Dean stood in the open doorway, half shocked, half irritated, shaking his head.

She'd threatened him.

It took her three tries to get her heap started, taking a little something away from her dramatic exit. But not much. As he closed the door, he could hardly believe it. Quiet little Haley, who used to watch him with those amazing eyes so long ago, had threatened him. And he didn't doubt for a second that she meant what she said. To think, he actually felt sorry for her for a second there.

He would have to get things done tonight. That was probably better anyway. The sooner he finished, the sooner he could get the hell out of this town. He snatched his coat from the end of the bed and headed out the door.

Lara watched her husband from across Claire Carling's living room as he spoke to Paige. Dressed in a dark gray suit and crisp, white shirt he looked as immaculate as ever. Perhaps Lara did feel something for him, after all. Wishful thinking. She should have at least had some stirring of jealousy as she watched him devote his attentions to Paige, while he hadn't spoken a single word to her all day.

With a sigh, she turned away. She should be mourning the passing of her best friend and not obsessing over the state of her marriage, but she couldn't help herself. If it was possible, he was more distant than usual. And she was afraid of what that meant.

Could he know about Richard? Dear God, what had she been thinking? She didn't even like Richard and now she might have jeopardized her lifestyle because of him.

"You look good enough to eat." The hot, whispered breath against her ear made her jump. As if simply thinking about him had summoned him, Richard stood behind her grinning. She turned quickly to see if Jonathan noticed. Thankfully, he was still engrossed in his conversation with Paige.

"Are you insane?" Lara demanded, her voice a harsh whisper. "He could have seen."

"Yes," Richard said, trying to keep his expression serious, and failing. Hard, humorless mirth sparkled in his eyes. "I don't think he would care."

"I do." Lara lowered her voice when some of the other guests turned their way. "Enough is enough. This, whatever it is, is over."

"Keep telling yourself that," Richard said as she stalked off. He didn't follow, but she could feel him grinning at her without even looking.

He probably assumed this was just a new game, something to make their affair more illicit and exciting. That she would actually reject him was a concept he couldn't grasp. He was an attractive man and women rarely told him no. She hadn't, after all.

She threw on her long, black fur coat, not politically correct, but there was little chance of being drenched in red paint on the streets of Hareton. As she made her way to the door, Erin stopped her. The fear in her eyes turned Lara cold.

"We need to talk," Erin said softly. "But not here, there are too many people."

"I'm leaving now. Call me later and I'll meet you." She didn't want to, though. She had enough intrigues on her plate, the last thing she needed was for Erin to add to them.

"Fine, but it has to be soon. Something's happened, and it's not good."

Lara nodded and escaped, leaving Erin and her dire predictions behind.

Barely five o'clock and the sky was almost dark. She hated this time of year. The short days and frigid cold. Houses up and down the street glowed with brightly colored Christmas lights. A sad attempt to make winter somewhat less ugly.

Clutching her coat around her, she crossed the street, unlocked her car, and climbed inside. As she slid her key in the ignition and started the engine, the passenger door opened, making her jump. She expected Richard, continuing his stupid game. Inhaling deeply, she prepared for her most dramatic of irritated sighs. But the breath locked in her throat and her eyes went wide as Dean settled into the seat next to her.

"Hello, Lara," he said quietly and slammed the door shut.

Her mouth hung open, but no words came. Christ, things were unraveling fast.

Chapter Six

Jonathan drank deeply from his glass. The whiskey burned like molten fire down his throat to his gut, but did nothing to warm him. He stood facing the window and the impenetrable darkness outside marred by his own faded reflection.

Funerals were depressing and Michelle's had been no exception. Worse maybe. While coming face to face with his own mortality, he had no choice but to acknowledge the unfortunate role he had played in Michelle's demise.

Outside, the wind gusted, lifting a cloud of powdered snow from the ledge. There had been snow the night Michelle vanished. Large, feathery flakes had swept over her tracks, erasing all sign of her.

Again he drank, this time draining the glass. He set it on the edge of the desk and turned away from the window, lowering himself into the chair. Memories of Michelle filled his head, despite his best efforts to push them away.

He needed to work. If he busied himself with contract bids, there would be no room for Michelle. He could tuck her image away to that shadowy corner of his brain. Forgotten until the next time he saw a woman with the same blonde hair or caught the scent of Michelle's perfume.

He lifted his briefcase from the floor and popped open the latches with two simultaneous clicks. From inside, he removed some file folders and a key ring.

He slid a small silver key into the lock on his desk drawer and tried to turn it, but it wouldn't open. With a frown he pulled it away from the drawer to make sure he had the right one. He did.

He tried again, and again the key wouldn't turn. Then, with a burst of sudden inspiration, he rotated the key in the opposite direction. The lock clicked loudly into place.

Open. The drawer had been open. How could that be? He hadn't left it that way last night. He twisted the key again before pulling out the drawer, then turned it so the silver latch popped up.

Someone had broken into his desk—he ran his thumb over the metal, scarred with several deep grooves—and not for the first time.

His expense ledger and the few other items he kept in the drawer appeared untouched. He reached farther inside until his fingers closed around the small velvet ring box. Someone had been in his desk on the day of Michelle's memorial. Coincidence? Not likely.

"Anything out of place?"

At the sound of his father's voice, Jonathan released the box as if burned and quickly closed the drawer. The latch, still in the locked position, kept him from closing it all the way and he struggled to clamp down on the irrational sense of panic rocketing through him. He lifted his gaze to his father's huge frame filling the doorway.

Had his father been the one in his desk? Jonathan's saliva dried up and he had to clear his throat before he spoke. "Should there be?"

"I know you like things just so and I wasn't sure your brother or your wife would remember to put everything back in order after he finished banging her."

Relief washed over him. Thank God his father hadn't seen. The old man was very astute; he would have known instantly what the ring meant.

Lara and Richard. Had they been searching together or had one interrupted the other? And would either of them understand what the ring symbolized?

"I told you when you married her she was trash."

"That you did." Jonathan struggled to keep from rolling his eyes. He'd known about Lara and Richard for months. If his father had only just found out, the old man had certainly lost his touch.

Deep frown lines creased Samuel's wide forehead as his pale gaze bored into Jonathan. "I thought you should know."

"And I appreciate your tact."

His father's skin turned deep red from his sagging jowls to his scalp, visible through the steely gray crew cut. For a moment, Jonathan thought Samuel might explode, but instead his lips curved into that dreadful smile—the same one he had feared as a child and sometimes saw twisting his own mouth as an adult.

"You always did have a soft spot for trash." The old man chuckled and turned away.

As Samuel left, still snickering to himself, Lara pressed her back against the wall behind one of the Romanesque pillars lining the long hall like silent gray soldiers. She hoped to God he wouldn't see her.

As his footsteps echoed off the marble floor, fear gripped her heart and squeezed until she could hardly breathe.

Jonathan knew. The words drummed again and again in her head. Closing her eyes, she swallowed back the thick bile bubbling in her throat.

How could she be so careless? First she had forgotten to lock the desk and now Richard. She couldn't lose this life. Not after all that she had done to get it. She needed damage control and fast. It would take time to put things in place; she only hoped she had enough left.

A few hours and a hot bath later, Haley wondered if giving the man suspected of murdering her sister an ultimatum had really been such a wise decision. She settled on her ugly, mustard-colored sofa, with a cup of tea cradled in both hands, absorbing the warmth through her skin. Probably not.

Granted, she did enjoy his dumbfounded expression, but waving a red flag before a bull was never a good idea. The problem was, she couldn't quite reconcile Dean with the person who had slit Michelle's throat and buried her in a basement.

Stop thinking about him.

Intent on pushing him from her mind, she leaned forward,

set her cup on the battered steam trunk she used as a coffee table, and picked up the want ads.

Another posting for a bookkeeper in Toronto. Absently, she tugged her lower lip with her teeth. Should she send her resume? She doubted anyone would call. What could it hurt?

But what if someone did?

Her stomach quivered with a combination of excitement and terror. What if they did call? What if they offered her a job? Her heart accelerated when she thought of packing up and leaving, of walking away from the town where she had lived her whole life and being absorbed into the city.

Yeah, right, who was she kidding? She wasn't a kid anymore, or Paige. She couldn't simply walk away from her responsibilities. Hareton Furniture Restoration was hers now, for better or worse. And there was also the small issue of her mother. If Haley didn't look after Mom, she doubted very much that Garret would pick up the slack. Still, the idea of telling them all to go to hell held a certain appeal.

She tore the ad from the paper and set it on top of the other similar clippings in the side table drawer. They were starting to pile up. She should go through them and throw some of the older ones away. Instead, she slid the drawer shut and turned back to the paper.

The sudden pounding on her front door made her freeze. It couldn't be Dean. Not this soon, and not at her house. She went to the window and pulled back the filmy lace curtain.

Garret waited, looking down at something in his hand. God damn it, could she not have a moment of quiet? Haley stomped to the door and yanked it open.

"What?"

"I need to talk to you," Garret said. Not bothering to wait for an invitation, he pulled open the screen door and let himself in. "Here."

Haley looked down at the crisp blank envelope in his hand.

"This was wedged in the door."

"Thanks." She took the envelope and turned it over in her hands.

"What is it?" Garret asked, looking over her shoulder.

She shrugged him off and edged away. "It feels like a card."

"Aren't you going to open it?"

"Later. What are you doing here?"

He sat down on the sofa and glanced at the paper she'd left on the cushion. "Are those want ads?"

"I'm thinking about taking some more courses," she said and scooped up the newspaper.

"What for? You're doing fine at the store." His voice raised an octave.

"The more I can do myself, the less I have to pay an accountant for."

"If you're concerned about money, you should reconsider moving back in with Mom. All of this—" he gestured widely, "—is an unnecessary expense. Besides, after everything that's happened, I don't like the idea of Mom alone so much. She could hurt herself or someone else."

Haley flopped into the armchair opposite him. "My sanity's worth the expense. If you're so worried about Mom, why not have her live with you?"

"We've been through this. I can't have her around the children." He shook his head, his face etched with his well-practiced saddened-by-her-selfishness expression. At one time she would have fallen for it and let herself be sucked in by some misplaced sense of guilt. But not anymore. Garret continued, nevertheless. "Well, if you insist on your own place, at least buy something. A mortgage payment would only be slightly more than what you're paying in rent, and you wouldn't be throwing your money away."

She stifled a shudder. The idea of buying something here, in Hareton, left her feeling like a caged animal. "Look, if you've come here to lecture me about my finances, save it. It's been a long day."

"Longer for some."

"So that's why you're here? You're mad because I left early?"

"No, that's not why I'm here. I do think what you did was selfish—"

"I can give you some examples of selfish."

"A detective Faron will be contacting you."

"Why?" Surprise softened her voice.

"He has some questions." Garret took a deep breath. "Have you heard any talk about Dad?"

Haley thought of Mrs. Yolken's hungry gaze. "Just some ugly gossip."

"Me too."

"Is Dad a suspect?"

"I don't know, but I'm worried. You'll let me know what the detective says?"

Haley nodded and waited for him to get up to leave. When he didn't, they sat in a moment of awkward silence.

"Are you going to open that envelope?" Garret asked at last.

"Why are you so interested?"

"I'm concerned. I understand you were talking to Dean Lawson today."

She narrowed her gaze. "Who told you? Erin or Paige?"

"Does it matter? What were you thinking?"

"I didn't even know who he was." If Garret was this annoyed about a few words exchanged in a parking lot, she could only imagine his reaction if he knew she'd been inside Dean's hotel room.

"What the hell is he doing back anyway?"

Haley shrugged. She should know by tomorrow, but thought better than to tell him.

"When I think of what he did..." Garret's eyes darkened. "He would have gone to jail if Dad hadn't given him a chance. And Lawson thanks him by murdering Michelle."

She swallowed the lump lodged in her throat. It hadn't been her father who had saved Dean from jail, or a juvenile detention center, or wherever troubled sixteen-year-old boys went after totaling stolen delivery vans. It had been her stupid adolescent crush. If she had just kept her mouth shut, Dean would have been sent away. He and Michelle would never have dated. And Michelle would still be alive.

"What did he say to you?"

"Nothing really. I thought he looked familiar, but I couldn't place him. I asked him if he knew Michelle and he said he did. That pretty much sums up the conversation."

"Humor me, open the card."

"For God's sake," she muttered and set the newspaper on the floor. The envelope hadn't been sealed, so she only needed to lift the flap and slide the card out.

On the front was a glossy black and white photo of two little girls dressed in grown-up clothes.

"Who is it from?" Garret asked.

Haley opened the card. "I don't know." She turned it so he could see. "It's blank."

"That's strange."

"It's probably some kind of condolence card."

"Who doesn't sign a card?"

She shrugged. "Someone in a hurry?"

"The whole thing is off." He stood and crossed the room. "I wish you would stay with Mom and Paige." When she started to protest, he interrupted. "Just until Lawson is gone. I don't like you here alone."

"I'll be fine. Paige isn't leaving tomorrow?"

"No. Faron asked her to stay on. He wants to speak to her too."

"Maybe Dad's not the only suspect."

"Anything's possible," Garret said as she walked him to the door. "Keep your doors and windows locked."

She snorted. "I'll see about getting some bars for them tomorrow."

"This isn't a joke, Haley," he snapped.

She gentled her voice. He'd lost a sister too, and she wanted very much to believe that his concern was more than the fear of losing his mother's primary care taker. "I can look after myself. Besides, I doubt Dean's going to come skulking through my windows in the middle of the night."

"I hope you're right. Call me when you hear from the police."

She nodded and said good-bye as she closed the door behind him.

With a frown, she looked down at the card still in her hand. It was a strange condolence card. Where was the typical lily or the "Our Deepest Sorrows"?

Just throw the damn thing out and forget it.

Haley went to the kitchen to do just that, but hesitated over the garbage. With her fingertip she traced the outline of one of the little girls.

The sudden ding-dong of the doorbell made her heart jump.

"Christ, Garret," she muttered. "What now?"

She slipped the card into the envelope before setting it on the windowsill behind the sink. Quickly, she walked to the living room window and peered outside. Dean stood on the porch with his hands jammed in his jeans pockets, rocking back on his heels. A brown legal-sized envelope was tucked under his arm.

So, she'd been right. Dean wouldn't come sulking through her window. He'd boldly ring the bell and wait for her for her to answer.

Chapter Seven

She could pretend to be out. After all, did she really want to deal with a potential killer in her home? Haley sighed. It would never work. Her lights were on and her car was in the driveway. From the window, Haley watched Dean press the bell again, then his eyes met hers through the glass. He smirked. Crap.

She walked to the door, turned the bolt, and pulled it open. "When I said you had until tomorrow, I didn't think you'd show up at my door in the middle of the night."

He glanced at his watch. "It's ten-thirty, hardly the middle of the night."

"It's late," Haley said, rubbing her bare arms. The frigid wind whipped through her thin T-shirt and cotton pajama bottoms as if she wore nothing at all. "What do you want?"

"It's what you wanted. Can I come in?"

"I'm not in the habit of inviting accused murderers into my home."

"This may come as a shock, but I never was actually accused. Questioned. I was questioned and that's all. Never charged, never convicted. For whatever that's worth."

"Only because no one could prove it."

His eyes flashed. "That's right, criminal mastermind that I was, at nineteen I achieved what so many career criminals only dream of. *I* committed the perfect murder."

Haley glared at him through the mesh of the screen door, mildly impressed. He could give Paige a lesson in sarcasm.

"Look—" he waved the envelope at her, "—in the morning I go to the police with this. You can see it now or hear about it tomorrow."

She pushed the screen door open. "Won't you please come in?"

"I thought you'd never ask." He stepped past her into the small foyer, brushing against her as he did. Goose bumps spread over her skin, having nothing to do with the cold. She stepped back quickly and he smirked again.

"You're in. Now, let me see what you have." She reached for the envelope, but he snatched his hand back.

"May I sit down?"

"Sure, why not? Maybe I could get you something to drink, fix you something to eat."

"I'd love a coffee."

"Then you should have picked one up on your way over," she snapped before flopping onto the sofa.

Dean lowered himself into a frayed armchair opposite her and glanced around the small room. Did the battered, mismatched furniture surprise him? Had he expected the beautifully finished antiques that had filled her parents' home? Her father had loved his work. And she wasn't her father.

"What?" she demanded.

He met her gaze. "This is a nice place. Cozy."

"I'm so glad you like it. Are you going to tell me what you're doing here?"

He looked away from her, dropping his gaze to the envelope in his hand. He lifted the flap and tilted the envelope so the papers slid into his palm.

"I didn't kill Michelle," he began. "But I know who did."

Haley leaned back and folded her arms over her chest. "Really? Who?"

He hesitated as if searching for the right words. "I only came to be a suspect because I argued with Michelle in front of half the bloody town the day she disappeared."

"I think it may have been the content of the argument that did you the most damage. When she accused you of stalking her, and telling people that you were still sleeping together months after you'd stopped dating that might have come off as a tad suspicious to some."

"Two things I never did, by the way. I had no idea what she was talking about. Christ, I broke up with her."

That was true. Haley worried her bottom lip. He had ended their short relationship. She remembered standing with Paige, their ears pressed to the thick door dividing the shop from the store, listening to Dean and Michelle argue. Michelle had been furious. Being dumped by someone two years younger than her with his background had probably been quite a blow to her ego. Haley had been secretly pleased. She never liked them together anyway.

"So who sent her all the flowers and started the rumor that you were still seeing each other?"

"Lara started the rumor."

"Lara was her friend."

"She was, and look who she married. I think we can safely assume the motive."

Ridiculous. The whole thing sounded like a bad made-for-TV-movie. "How do you know it was her?"

"I had a nice talk with Lara earlier tonight." He shook his head, almost to himself. "She confirmed everything."

"So, what are you thinking here? Lara killed Michelle so she could marry well and then let you take the blame?"

"No."

She sighed. "I think I'm missing your point."

"The point is, I didn't do it, and without that confrontation, there's really nothing else to implicate me."

"A witness saw the store's delivery van empty on the side of the highway past midnight."

"Lots of people had access to that van."

"But you were the only one who had stolen it before."

"No, I'm the only one who got caught. Your brother and sisters took the van regularly without your father or Nate knowing."

"Fine, you've exonerated yourself in my eyes, but why bother if you know who the killer is?"

"I just don't want you to think that I pulled a name out of the air."

She narrowed her eyes, apprehension tickling the base of her skull. "What name?"

"Your father killed Michelle."

Fury flooded her veins. She leapt from her seat and pointed at the door. "Get out."

"Listen to me—"

"No. Get out!" What had she been thinking, listening to him?

"Haley, by this time tomorrow the whole town will know. Do you want the heads up or not?"

"How could you do this to him? You would have gone to jail, if it hadn't been for him." If it hadn't been for her asking her father to give Dean a chance. "He saved your sorry ass."

"I wanted to be wrong. I never wanted it to be him."

"So you say, but that's not going to stop you from accusing a man who, conveniently, is no longer here to defend himself."

He continued as if she hadn't spoken. "I suspected him almost from the start. When Al called and told me that Michelle had been found, and where, I was certain."

"My grandmother's house?" *The detective.*

He nodded.

"Anyone could have hidden her body there. My grandmother lived with us for nearly a year. She was still living with us when she died." Haley stopped and took a deep breath, while she tried to ignore the tightening in her throat. "Anyone, yourself included, could have gotten into her house."

"Why didn't he sell? It's not like he kept it for the income potential. He never rented the place."

She hated Dean then, for forcing her to make excuses for her father. "He also never believed she was dead." Memories of her father diving for the phone when it rang, even years after Michelle had been gone, assailed her. She took a deep breath and steadied herself. "He hoped that if for some reason she was afraid to come home she would try to contact my grandmother. He didn't want someone else living in the house in case she did. He also kept her phone line active and had an answering machine that he checked three times a day until he died."

"It could have been a cover." Dean shrugged.

She dug her fingernails into her palms. "A cover?"

"Like I said, the house just tied the rest of it together."

"What else is there?"

"The day I was fired I found a bag with his coveralls in it, and they were stained with what looked like blood."

His calm, quiet voice scraped her nerves raw. "You're lying."

"I'm not."

"You have them now?"

"No. I showed them to Nate. He convinced me it was furniture stain and put them back in the crawlspace behind the tool cage. When I looked a few days ago, they were gone."

"You believed Nate then, but not now?"

"I never believed him. I wanted to, but I didn't."

"It had to be stain." It had to be.

"Nothing we worked with smelled like that. Besides why hide the bag? Why not just throw it out?"

"Maybe to get it out of the way."

"Someone took everything out of the tool cage and pulled shelves out because the bag was underfoot? Come on Haley, you were never stupid."

"I don't know about that, I'm still listening to this bullshit. Even if the coveralls were stained with blood, you had access to them. It was you who conveniently pulled them from their hiding place."

He opened his mouth to speak, but she cut him off. "You have yet to tell me something that truly implicates my father. The only thing I've heard so far is an opportunist trying to pin a murder on the only person no longer here to defend himself. So tomorrow you can tell anyone you want about this because there's nothing here that can't be explained or tied to you."

Dean tossed a sheet of paper onto the table between them. "That's a copy of your father's death certificate. His first one."

"I don't understand."

"Look at the date. The year. According to this, your father died when he was three years old."

"Obviously that's a mistake," she snapped impatiently.

"I'm afraid not. Everything your father did was very

deliberate. Especially changing his name."

"What do you mean?"

"Once I realized your father had changed his name, I wasn't sure how to go about finding out who he'd been. Then I remembered Nate and your father endlessly reminiscing about their high school days when I worked for them. So I tracked Nate's records until I found his high school." Dean thumbed through the papers until he found the one he wanted. He slid it from the pile and dropped the photocopy in front of her. "From an old yearbook. Your father's real name was Thomas James."

Before she could say anything else, he added another sheet. "That's a copy of a marriage license with your father's name on it, dated two years before he married your mother."

"My father wasn't married before." Her voice had a strange, almost robotic quality, to the tone.

He set down another photocopy. "This is a copy of a newspaper article about his first wife going missing. These—" more papers on the table, overlapping the others, "—are articles explaining that your father had been questioned as a possible suspect. Nothing ever came of it. Without a body, the police lacked sufficient evidence to move on him. He and I had a lot in common, wouldn't you say?"

The blood drained from Haley's face as she stared down at the photocopies, and Dean wondered if she might pass out or throw up. When her dark bewildered gaze met his, it was like a kick in the gut. He looked away, hating himself.

He'd wanted truth, he'd wanted vindication, and this was the cost. Again he hardened his resolve. The opportunity to clear his name had come, and he was taking it.

"How did you find all this?" she asked, the heat gone from her voice.

"I started at the clerk's office and followed the leads."

Haley lifted the marriage license and slowly lowered herself onto the couch. "This has to be a mistake."

"It's not."

"But this says he lived in Toronto. He never did. He moved here from Ottawa." She set the license down and reached for one of the articles.

Dean shrugged. "He lived there for about two years, working as a loans officer. He met his wife, Eleanor, at the bank where he worked. She'd been a teller there. They'd only been married about five months when she disappeared."

"You learned all that from the clerk's office?" Her brow quirked.

"No." He shook his head. "I spoke to Eleanor's brother. He's still alive and well. Still blames your father for what happened."

"You think this proves my father murdered Michelle?"

"I think he's a much more likely suspect than I ever was."

"Why would he have killed his daughter?"

"I don't know," he told her. "That's the only part I can't figure out."

"Because he didn't kill her. Everything you have here is interesting, but none of it proves a thing." Her hands trembled and she was so pale. His stomach churned. "You're just shifting the blame to get yourself off the hook."

"I was never guilty."

"So you just wildly accuse someone else?"

"No. I accuse the man responsible."

"My father has an alibi, unlike you, and no motive, unlike you."

Temper smothered conscience. "Really? I'd be interested to hear about this alibi."

"He and my mother were at a dinner party. They got home around eleven and went to bed. Together."

He shook his head. "Do you honestly believe that after a party your mother would know if he was there or not?"

"Bastard."

Maybe, but what he said was true. He couldn't remember Claire without a cocktail in her hand. As far as her drinking went, Michelle's disappearance had only sped up the inevitable.

"And as for my motive, no one was more baffled than I was when Michelle accused me of stalking her."

"You think it was all Lara?"

"I don't think, I know. She also agreed to admit it to the police."

His words seemed to give her pause. She stared at him for a long moment then asked, "How long have you been trying to pin the blame on my father?"

"I wasn't trying to pin the blame on him. I was trying to clear my name."

"How long?" she ground out.

"Close to two years."

"Why wait until now to come out with it?"

"I told you, where Michelle was found made me certain."

She nodded slowly as if digesting all that he'd told her.

God, what a bastard he was. Hours ago she'd been attending her sister's memorial and now he was shoving the proof that her father was a murderer in her face. He needed to go, to get out of there. For every minute he stayed looking at her so small and shaken, his resolve eroded a little more. "I'm sorry," he said, getting to his feet. "I really didn't want it to be him."

"I appreciate that." Her voice sounded dispassionate, a million miles away. Then she stood and met his gaze. A faint, vertical frown line marred her forehead just above her nose. He shoved his hands in his pockets to stop himself from smoothing it.

"I wonder if you could do me a favor?" she asked.

"What?"

"Give me a day to prepare Paige and Garret and my mother before you go to the police."

Dean shrugged. "Sure." After twelve years, what was one more day?

Chapter Eight

Lara hurried through the throngs of frazzled shoppers, nearly stumbling over a small boy who had broken free of his mother's hand and ran madly toward one of the mall's over-crowded toy stores. Damn Erin. Of all the places to host her latest melodrama, why a shopping mall two weeks before Christmas? Lara stepped onto the escalator and descended to the food court. The combined odors of grease, vinegar and BO made her eyes water.

As she left the conveyer stairs, she scanned the blank faces of people standing in long lines, or hovering with trays of overflowing fast food, waiting for one of the molded plastic tables to free up. She spotted Erin alone at a table for two, her coat and shopping bags piled on the chair opposite her.

"Where have you been?" Erin demanded as Lara approached.

"Standing in line mostly." Lara draped her coat over the back of the chair after passing Erin her belongings, then sat down. "So what was so important?"

"Dean's back." Erin sipped from her cup, her gaze never leaving Lara's face.

"I know. I spoke to him yesterday." Lara bit her lip to keep from smiling when Erin's eyes widened.

"When?"

"After the funeral. He was waiting for me outside your in-laws'."

"What did he want?" The urgency in Erin's voice sent a chill through her.

"He knows I was the one who told people he was still seeing Michelle. I think he suspected me of killing her."

"Why would he think that?"

"Maybe because the rumor I started had half the town believing he was a murderer and I didn't say anything to the contrary."

"So what did you tell him?"

"That I didn't come forward to defend him because I didn't want to spoil things with Jonathan. That I was young and selfish and so very sorry, and could he ever forgive me?"

"Did he believe you?"

She shrugged. "I don't know, maybe."

"Why did he come back?"

"I think he's trying to clear his name."

Erin said nothing and Lara hesitated before telling her the rest. "I'm going to help him. I told him I would admit that I made everything up."

"Even *you* can't be that stupid." Erin's eyes darkened, her mouth contorting into an ugly scowl. "Nothing's changed. If you tell anyone what you did, who do you think the police will suspect?"

"Is that what you're afraid of? That if anyone knew you helped me, they would think you had something to do with killing her?"

Erin's hands shot across the table, gripped Lara's and squeezed tightly. Painfully. "Did you tell him that?"

"No." Lara shook her head, her heart thundering in her chest. Her knuckles ached where the bones ground against one another.

"You better not have." Erin released her abruptly. A sunny smile lit her features. "And I'd think twice about admitting to anything if I were you. Do you want everyone to know how jealous you were of Michelle? Poor little Lara, living in Michelle's shadow. She had everything and you had nothing. You were invisible when she was in the room and everyone knew it. You showed her, though. You got Jonathan, and Michelle got murdered."

Lara stood and gathered her coat, its image turning blurry

through unshed tears. "You hated her too."

"That's true, but I'm not stupid enough to admit it."

Haley raked her fingers through her hair and let out an exasperated sigh. Nothing. As she stood slowly, her gaze swept the cramped space again. Only ancient bolts of fabric and boxes of forgotten tools. No sign of blood-soaked coveralls anywhere. No sign that anyone had been back there in years, except for smeared footprints in a thick layer of dust.

Not that she had expected otherwise. Still, she couldn't help but feel a weight had been lifted. When she had started pulling out shelves in the tool cage, she'd been afraid of finding something that would give Dean's claims verity.

She stretched her aching back, cramped from hunching over for so long, then turned and started fitting the heavy shelves back into place. As she bent to lift the second to last one, a dark spot on the concrete floor caught her eye. She crouched down and rubbed away the dust until the dark brown splotch nearly glowed against the pale gray cement.

A chill danced up her spine and she couldn't stop the shiver that gripped her body. It could have been anything. The workshop floor had a number of marks from various stains and varnishes. So why did this one, slightly smaller than a quarter, leave her with a sick feeling in her stomach?

"What are you doing?"

Haley stood and turned, sliding her foot over the mark. Paige waited, her arms folded across her chest, on the opposite side of the cage.

"Looking for something. Why are you here?"

"I think it's time we have a little chat."

The hair on the back Haley's neck bristled. "Well, by all means, let me just drop everything I'm doing."

"You do that." Paige moved to lean against the workbench and Haley joined her.

"What do you want, Paige?"

"I understand you're still angry at me for what happened at Dad's funeral, and you have this tremendous need to punish me for it, but enough is enough."

"How am I punishing you now?"

"You took off yesterday. Garret and I got stuck doing everything. You missed an incredibly glamorous moment when our dear mother took a drunken header down the stairs."

"I've seen it before and you and Garret weren't there to help me."

"Well, now we've been taught our lesson," Paige said. "Look, I'm stuck here until that detective finishes with me, but I'm not going to sit back and let you dump Mom on me just because I'm staying there. You're going to have to become involved whether you like it or not."

"*You* are going to lecture *me* on involvement?" Haley asked in disbelief.

"If that's what it takes."

"I can hardly wait to hear this. I'm sure I'll remember it always, and if over time I forget, you can give me a refresher, say in another four or five years when we're all treated to another one of your visits!"

"Enough!"

Both women turned sharply to find Nate standing in the doorway dividing the shop from the store. As the heavy door swung closed behind him, Haley caught a glimpse of Billy with a customer at the counter. Both stared wide-eyed and open-mouthed.

Damn. She closed her eyes and mentally counted to ten, angrier with herself for letting her temper get the better of her than Paige.

"Lower your voices and stop acting like spoiled brats," Nate hissed and turned his angry stare on Paige. "This is your sister's store. For you to come in here and shoot your mouth off is not only—"

"Go play the boss somewhere else, Nate, this isn't your place anymore. Haley and I are having a discussion."

"A screaming match is more like it. I don't know what's wrong with you, Paige. Your sister does everything for you and Garret, and you still have the nerve to demand more."

"Oh, yes, poor Haley." Paige glared at her. "I'm surprised

you can manage to take enough time away from your cross to even run a business."

"You bitch," Haley said.

Nate's face was practically purple with rage. "Get out of here, Paige."

"Gladly, but before I go, I'll finish what I came here to say. I have a meeting tomorrow that I can't get out of, so I won't be there to take care of Mom. You'll have to check in with her. But have no fear, I'll be back the very next day and you can continue sticking it to me until that detective lets me get out of here." Paige pushed away from the bench and stormed out. As the door closed there was no sign of Billy or any customers. Damn.

"Are you okay?" Nate asked.

Haley choked back a bitter laugh. *Oh, I'm great. Everything I knew about my father may be a lie. He's about to be blamed for murdering my sister. Added to that, fighting with my still-living sister just chased away the few customers I had. Things couldn't be better.*

"I'm fine," she said, instead. How many times had she claimed those words in the last week? She should just have the phrase tattooed on her forehead and be done with it.

"Your sister is some piece of work."

The derision in Nate's voice surprised her. "I had no idea you disliked her so much." Not that she couldn't relate. Hell, Paige was blood related and she didn't like her much either.

"There's always been a hard streak in her. A selfishness. She's not like you or Garrett. You both remind me of your father."

Haley didn't entirely agree. She, Paige and Garret were not all that different. Not when she considered Garret trying to manipulate her into moving back in with their mother. And Paige had been right. Haley was trying to *stick it* to her, and had been since Paige arrived home.

Oh, forget it. She had enough on her mind without analyzing her relationship with her siblings.

"I appreciate you coming to talk to me," Haley said, opting for a change of subject.

"I just got your message. I was house hunting this morning."

"You're moving back?"

"Yes. I'd started making plans after Joan passed away. With her gone, there's nothing left for me in Ottawa. My family is here. Being with the girls these past few days has made me realize how much I've been missing. They grow up too fast."

Hope sparked inside Haley. "That's wonderful news. But the store?"

"Don't worry." Nate smiled. "The store is all yours now." The spark fizzled as if doused with cold water, and she forced herself to smile in return. "So what was it you wanted to talk to me about?"

Now, how to broach the subject when she was well aware of the reaction her questions would undoubtedly produce. No point in dancing around it. She had less than twenty-four hours to stop Dean. After everything her family had been through, she wasn't about to stand by and let him destroy her father's reputation. She wouldn't let an innocent man take the fall so Dean Lawson could shirk the blame.

"Was my father living under an assumed name?"

Nate paled and her stomach dropped. Oh, God, it was true. She could read it on his face. "Why would you ask that?"

"I spoke to Dean Lawson—"

"You stay away from him," Nate lashed out, his eyes darkening. "He's dangerous."

You have no idea. "He thinks my father killed Michelle. He has proof that my father was not who he said he was, that he'd been married before. Until his wife disappeared."

"Lawson's done his research." Nate rubbed his chin then added almost to himself, "I never would have expected it from him."

"It's true then?"

"Not the way Lawson's claiming it is."

"My father's first wife vanishes, just like Michelle. That's an unusual coincidence to say the least."

"Eleanor was not the right woman for your father. She didn't vanish. She left him for another man."

77

Hope filled her. "So she didn't just vanish. The police found her, just with someone else?"

"No. As far as I know she was never seen again. Her family tried to imply that your father had a hand in it, but there was no proof that she met with foul play. They just couldn't accept the kind of woman their daughter was, despite the evidence."

"What kind of evidence?"

"Receipts from hotels, witnesses that saw her with another man."

"If my father knew, surely he would have been angry." Could it be true? *No, no, no!*

"Don't think that for even a second," Nate snapped.

"Then why the fake identity?"

"That had been my idea. He could come here and start again. We opened the business together, he met your mother. He was happy here."

"Until Michelle disappeared."

"Yes, until Michelle. All his years he never believed that Eleanor just up and left. He was certain something terrible had happened to her and it haunted him until the day he died. I don't know how Michelle's murder didn't kill him."

"It did," Haley said, softly. "Just not right away."

Nate put an arm around her shoulders. "I know this is hard for you to hear. No matter what your father felt for Eleanor, he wouldn't have killed her. And he would never have harmed one of his children. No matter what they did."

Haley frowned. "What do you mean?"

"Just what I said."

"Had Michelle done something?"

"Of course not. Don't give it another thought. And pay no attention to anything Lawson says. Even if that monster didn't kill Michelle, I can promise you he played a role in what happened to her."

Haley stepped away from Nate and met his dark eyes. He smiled reassuringly, but his expression did little to relieve her unease. He had left her with more questions than answers. Could her father have murdered his first wife in a jealous rage? This time yesterday she would have said no. But he had managed to keep a whole other life hidden from them.

Could he have killed Michelle?

She didn't know, and the realization left her cold.

Chapter Nine

Haley pulled into her mother's driveway and shut off the car's engine. Yellow light glowed from the kitchen window, but offered no warmth or comfort. The idea of another confrontation with Paige made her head ache, but Dean wasn't going anywhere and her twenty-four hours were almost up.

She stepped onto the slippery driveway. The frigid wind flapped the edges of her open jacket like puffy, nylon wings as she started toward the house.

Maybe going to Paige was a mistake. Should she tell Garret first? No, she wanted to stop Dean. Paige was the better bet.

Inside, canned laughter from the blaring TV mixed with her mother's rumbling snores from the den. After a quick walk through the first floor, Haley climbed the stairs and started down the hall. She found Paige leaning in the doorway of *The Shrine*.

Paige's eyes narrowed. "What are you doing here? If you've come to ask me not to leave tomorrow, forget it. Even if I wanted to stay, I couldn't."

"That's not why I'm here," Haley said, unsure how to begin. How many awkward conversations could she get through in one day? *Just blurt it out. This is Paige, after all.*

"I spoke to Dean yesterday."

"I know. I saw you."

"No, after that. He came to my house last night."

"You let him in your house? Have you lost your mind?"

"Look, where I spoke to Dean is the least of our concerns. We've got bigger problems because of him."

Paige paled. "What kind of problems?"

Haley told her all that Dean had dug up about their father's previous marriage, his first wife's disappearance, and his real name.

"Dean's lying." Hot anger shone in Paige's dark gaze, and a strange sort of comfort settled over Haley.

"He had photocopies of the marriage license and the articles about the first wife. He even had Dad's old yearbook picture. When I spoke to Nate, he confirmed everything Dean told me."

"Oh, God." Paige pressed her hand to her stomach. "Have you told Garret?"

Haley shook her head. "I wanted to talk to you first. We have to stop Dean and I thought maybe..." she trailed off.

"You thought I'd be devious enough to come up with something."

"I might not have used the word devious."

Paige actually smiled. "Ordinarily, I'd be only too happy to help, but in the end it won't matter."

"How can you say that?"

"There's nothing Dean found that the police won't eventually uncover for themselves. If they had looked past Dean as a suspect when Michelle first disappeared, they would have learned about Dad's past then."

"So what do we do? Just sit back and let Dean pin Michelle's murder on Dad? We know he didn't do it."

"To clear Dad we'd have to find something concrete to prove Dean did it. I don't know why that's been so hard for the police. I can't believe a nineteen-year-old kid could murder a girl and not leave a shred of evidence behind."

"Unless he didn't do it."

"Don't get sucked in by him. It didn't do our father any good, and it sure didn't do Michelle any good."

"He claims Lara started the rumor about him and Michelle still seeing each other. Apparently, she's going to admit it to the police. Without motive there's nothing left to tie him to Michelle's murder."

"That can't be right."

"He did break up with her. We both heard him."

Paige leaned against the doorframe and slid down until her backside hit the floor. She drew her knees to her chest. "I don't know what to do."

"There has to be something." Haley squatted beside her. "We just need to think. Where would the killer most likely screw something up?"

"You have lost your mind. It's been twelve years, Nancy Drew. Whatever evidence there was would be long gone by now."

"If Mom hears that Dad's a suspect, there will be no living with her. Oh, wait, you'll be living with her. At least until the cops say you can leave."

"And *I'm* the devious one? Okay, the only thing anyone is certain of is where Michelle was buried. This is probably a pointless endeavor since the police would have already gone over every inch, but why don't we check it out?"

"That's a great plan, except someone else is living there now."

"Sarcasm is not one of your better qualities. The house is for sale again, and it's empty. Mrs. Yolken said that the Kearney woman refuses to stay there since Michelle was found."

"That's a tad melodramatic, don't you think?"

"I don't know." Paige shrugged. "Anyway, they didn't replace any of the windows, I bet we could still get in."

Haley couldn't think of anywhere else to look. "It's a start."

They decided to walk. If anyone recognized their cars, it could attract unwanted attention. Besides, the house was only a few blocks away. But with the frigid air seeping through her jeans and turning her legs numb, Haley thought the plan needed work.

Paige fared little better. Her teeth chattered loudly in the quiet stillness, and she hunched her shoulders until her coat collar skimmed her ears. She looked like a frightened turtle.

As they came to the Victorian red brick, looming above them in the darkness, they stopped. Years of Christmases and family gatherings spent in the house flashed through Haley's mind, but they seemed distant and faded. Far removed from the one-hundred-year-old shell before them.

"How are we going to do this?" Haley glanced at the houses around her. No one peered out from the lit windows. At least that she could see.

Paige shrugged. "We just go."

Together, they started up the driveway, leaving a trail of messy footprints in the deep snow. Haley lifted her gaze to the tiny stars glittering in the black sky above. No chance of snow before morning.

"Somebody's going to see these," she said, following Paige to the back of the house.

"As long as nobody notices them until we're gone. Besides, people will think they're from kids being morbid. Look, there's the window."

As children, they had often sneaked through the window with the faulty lock. Every Tuesday afternoon their grandmother had played poker with her friends, and Paige and Haley, with a gang of kids in tow, would creep in and raid her candy jar. Their grandmother had had a sweet tooth to rival any child's.

Paige grunted as she tried to lift the window. "It's not working. I think it's frozen shut."

"Let me try." Haley shoved at the sill until her fingers cramped. She and Paige tried together, but the window hardly moved.

"Maybe they fixed the lock," Haley said, panting.

"No, look." Paige pointed to the bottom corner, where the window had opened a fraction of an inch.

After fishing her plastic lighter from her jeans pocket, Paige knelt next to the sill and ran the tiny flame along the edge of the window.

Haley shivered and glanced around her. "If anyone sees us, they'll think we're trying to burn the place down to hide evidence."

"We'd be the most inept arsonists I've ever heard of, using a disposable lighter and nothing else. I think it's working."

Paige stood back and pushed from the bottom. For a moment, it seemed the window would refuse them entrance, then suddenly it slid up, and Paige went tumbling forward through the opening. Haley grabbed the back of her coat to keep her from falling.

Paige stood straight. "We're in."

Haley didn't reply. Instead, she peered into the darkness. The hair on the back of her neck stood straight while goose bumps stippled her skin. The sense that someone or something waited inside slid over her, and Rhonda Kearney's refusal to stay in the house seemed perfectly reasonable.

"Are you okay?" Paige asked.

"I'm fine." She gave herself a mental shake. "I'll go first."

Haley swung her leg through the opening and leaned sideways, awkwardly straddling the sill. As she turned and swung her other leg through, the frame dug painfully into her backside.

"Damn, it's freezing in here," Paige said, following her through. "I guess they're not heating the place while no one's living here. Wonder if there's electricity?"

"It doesn't matter, we can't risk anyone seeing the light. We're breaking and entering here."

"Technically we didn't break, we only entered."

"If we get caught, remember to explain that to the police. Maybe we'll only get half the jail time."

Paige flicked her lighter again. The small flame glowed in the shadowy darkness. "Should be very comforting once we're in the basement."

Haley shrugged. "Let's just do this."

They crept from the living room to the kitchen. Their shuffling footsteps over the wood floors seemed too loud in the silence.

Paige pulled open the ancient basement door and nausea rolled over Haley in a slow wave. But why? What was wrong with her that she suddenly felt so sick? She swallowed down the bile rising in her throat. Doing her best to ignore the thin sheen of sweat coating her body, she followed Paige down the rickety stairs into complete blackness.

"This lighter's useless. It's too dark," Paige whispered.

Haley couldn't speak. The saliva in her mouth had dried up and her heart pounded as the frigid cold rose up around her. Someone watched. She could feel their eyes on her.

"There's no window down here," Paige said. "I'll try the light at the bottom of the stairs."

As Haley stepped onto the uneven dirt floor, Paige moved away from her. The small lighter's flame appeared to float through the darkness then the room filled with yellow light.

Haley squinted against the brightness. When her eyes adjusted, she lifted her gaze to Paige, standing next to the swinging string from the glowing bare bulb.

"So where do we look?" Haley asked. She wanted to get out of there now.

"There." Paige pointed to the back corner where the floor had been dug up.

Haley walked over to the loose, gray mound, knelt and skimmed her fingers over the surface. The earth was cool and dry. Behind her Paige wandered around the large empty space.

"There's nothing here," Paige said. "Not that I know what we were looking for."

But there was something. A sickening fear that hung so heavy in the air it was practically tangible. Haley took a deep shuddering breath. She was being stupid, letting the idea of what this room had been get to her. She needed to pull it together.

"Let's go." Haley struggled to keep her voice even, but failed, the strange quaver audible even to her own ears.

Paige frowned. "Okay."

Haley moved to the stairs, fighting the urge to run. Then Paige yanked the cord on the bulb, plunging the basement back into a sea of perfect black. Fear, like an icy blade, sliced through Haley nearly paralyzing her.

"I can't see a thing," Paige muttered.

Haley didn't reply as she continued up the stairs, taking each step quicker than the last. Her footfalls thudded against the brittle wood. She needed to get out of there. Now. Panting, she stumbled into the kitchen.

Here, the darkness eased some, helped by the street light outside, but the sensation of being watched intensified. Without a word, she crawled out the window, her feet sinking into the knee-deep snow, and gulped the cold air.

After a moment or two, her heart rate slowed and she managed to get her breathing under control. When she lifted her head, Paige gaped at her. Heat stole into Haley's face.

"What the hell happened to you in there?" Paige asked.

"Nothing. I just got a little freaked." A panic attack maybe? Wouldn't that be just great, if all this crap gave her some kind of anxiety disorder?

"Are you okay?"

"I'm fine. Let's go. I'm freezing my butt off out here."

The experience in the house left Haley shaken. But by the time she got home, she'd managed to convince herself that she had suffered an anxiety attack, brought on by the stress from the past week combined with her sojourn to Michelle's makeshift grave.

For twelve years her sister's body had waited there. Under the circumstances it was not at all surprising that she might experience a moment of panic. And there was no reason to assume she would experience anything like it again.

"I'm not losing my mind," she muttered as she started up the path to the front door. Though talking to herself did little to convince her. And her shaking hands weren't helping either.

Forget it. She was home now and mere minutes away from her bed. Sweet oblivion awaited, but a small dark heap on her porch stopped her.

"What now?"

The little pile made her skin crawl. Leftover nerves from earlier, no doubt. She forced her feet back into motion and stepped onto the porch. A hint of red peaked out from layers of gauzy white tissue paper at her feet.

Roses. She knelt and lifted them into her arms, searching for a card tucked into the folds as she stood. There wasn't one. So who would send her flowers?

Some kind of sympathy gesture maybe, for Michelle's memorial yesterday. Why no card? But she had received a card. Just as anonymous as the flowers she held.

"I know it's late."

Haley jerked, her stomach dropped like a brick off a cliff. She spun around, holding the roses out like a weapon. Dean leaned casually against the rail with his hands in his pockets.

"Christ. You scared the hell of out me," she said, when she could breathe again.

"Sorry. I thought you heard me and that's why you were standing there."

"I didn't. What are you doing here, anyway? Do you have more of my dead relatives you'd like drag through the mud?"

"I wanted to see if you had any luck trying to prove me wrong."

"If I told you I did, would you go away?"

He shook his head.

"I didn't think so." She turned from him, annoyed that she noticed the way the wind ruffled his hair. "Look, I've had a lousy day, so if there's nothing else you want..."

"You mean besides your charming company?"

"Naturally." She shifted the roses in her arms and tried to slip her key into the lock, but her hand trembled badly. Dean moved up behind her, his chest pressed against her back and his warm fingers closed over hers, guiding the key successfully. Her skin tingled where he touched.

"I've got it." She shrugged him off.

"Just trying to help," Dean said. "You seem kind of edgy."

"My, what powerful skills of observation."

"Would you like to talk about it?"

She snorted and pushed open the door. "With you?"

"Would that be so bad?"

"I guess that would depend." She faced him, trying to ignore how good he looked. How the muted light on the porch played over the sharp angles of his face. "On whether or not I actually believe you wouldn't try to use anything I told you against my family."

His eyes narrowed and the muscle in his jaw flicked against his skin. "Of course. I do, however, need to speak to you."

"I'm tired, Dean."

"I won't be long."

"Fine. I need a drink. Do you want anything?" She shrugged out of her coat and dumped it on the armchair in the living room.

"Whatever you're having is fine."

He followed her to the kitchen. She didn't need to look back to know it. His presence practically charged the small room. She dumped the roses on the counter and grabbed a bottle of wine from the rack built into the cupboards.

"Are you seeing someone?"

Haley glanced at him. He nodded to the flowers, his expression inscrutable.

"No. Those are probably because of Michelle."

"Probably?"

"There was no card. For all I know they're for my next door neighbor." Sadly, a distinct possibility. Even though Betty was seventy-eight the woman's social life was far more active than Haley's. But then, nuns had more active social lives than she did.

She dug through the drawer, searching for a corkscrew. "So, talk."

"I wanted to know how you did today. What you found out."

"Why? So you can twist it all around?"

"Is that what you think I would do?"

She didn't reply as her fingers closed around the corkscrew in the far corner of the drawer. When she attempted to push the pointed coil into the cork, Dean stopped her, taking it from her. Her hands still shook, not as badly, but enough for him to notice. She hated that she couldn't stop them. Hated letting him see any weakness.

"I'll do this," he said. "You get the glasses."

She brought two down from the cupboard and set them on the counter. He poured a generous amount into her glass, but was far more conservative with his own. She eyed him suspiciously.

"I'm driving," he replied to her unspoken question. "Besides, you look like you could use it. Actually, you look like you could do with something a hell of a lot stronger."

"I don't have anything stronger." She didn't drink often. The fear of winding up like her mother loomed ever-present.

He nodded and followed her to the living room. She sat on one end of the couch, he on the other. For a moment neither spoke. She lifted the glass to her lips. The smooth, dry wine slid down her throat and pooled in her empty belly. More likely than not, she wouldn't need anything stronger. She had skipped dinner and it wouldn't take long for her to feel the effects.

"What's with you?" Dean asked. He sounded impatient. "Why are you so upset?"

"I'm not upset," she snapped. "But if I was, finding out my father wasn't who he said he was and scrambling to save his reputation might have something to do with it."

"You can't believe I'm enjoying any of this? Do you honestly think I wanted it to be him? I admired your father, looked up to him. You were right, he did save 'my sorry ass'. He gave me a chance when one else would, but he also let me twist in the wind for Michelle when he knew I didn't do it."

She shook her head. "You're wrong."

"Even you have to admit, there are a lot of coincidences where your father is concerned."

"And I would think you of all people understand just how damaging coincidences with nothing to back them up can be."

"Don't try and guilt me. I'm here putting up with your mouth, no easy feat I might add, hoping you found something that would mean I was wrong."

She sighed, thinking of what Paige had said about the police surely learning what Dean had. "Nate confirmed everything you told me. I wish I had something more. We even went to where Michelle had been buried—"

"What do you mean?"

"Paige and I went to my grandmother's house.'"

His lips curled in distaste. "Why would you do that?"

He had good lips. Thin and nicely shaped. He'd be a good

kisser. What was she thinking? *That's it, no more wine.*

"I don't know." She leaned forward and set the glass on the chest. "I guess we thought we'd find something the police had missed."

"Correct me if I'm wrong, but that house no longer belongs to your family."

"I know, but the people who own it haven't lived there since Michelle was found."

"Breaking and entering is still a crime, even when the owners aren't at home."

"Yeah, well, you would know."

"Very funny."

"I did wonder about something." After she had freaked out and all but run screaming from the house. "I couldn't figure out why those people would dig up the floor."

"What did they tell the police?"

"They were doing renovations."

Dean shrugged. "There you go."

"That doesn't make sense. Why would they dig up a dirt floor to start renovations?"

"Maybe they planned to finish the basement."

"The house is over a hundred years old. Only a crazy person would try to finish the basement down there. And if they were that crazy they wouldn't be able to do it themselves, they'd have to hire a professional contractor to dig out the basement."

"Why would they lie about it?"

"I don't know. I do know the house needed a new roof, windows and the floors refinished, so why would anyone start their renovations by digging holes in the dirt floor of the basement?"

"They were probably repairing something structural. With a house that old it stands to reason that something in the foundation might need repairing."

"Maybe." She leaned back, nibbling at the corner of her mouth. Was it coincidence, or had Dean helped things along a little? Could he have told the Kearneys where to look? Or could Dean be right about her father?

No. Her father had loved his family. He never would have hurt Michelle.

"I don't get where you're going with this. Do you think these people knew that Michelle was there?"

"I can't think of any other reason why they would just happen to dig a hole in the basement and find her. Unless someone told them where to look."

"That's not a completely unreasonable assumption." He looked thoughtful, but not threatened.

"So, come with me to talk to the Kearneys."

"What? No. Forget it." His expression was hard to read. He frowned, but he didn't look at all nervous.

"You said you wanted to be wrong. This could be what you need. What we both need."

He didn't say anything, just studied the untouched wine as he swirled it in his glass.

"Before you destroy a man's reputation, don't you think you owe it to him to investigate every possibility?"

His eyes locked with hers. Pale green, and swirling like the sea before a storm. "We're going to look like a couple of idiots."

She smiled. "Billy gets to the store at three-thirty. You can meet me there then. I would do this earlier, but I can't leave Allister alone."

Dean nodded. "I don't know what you think you'll accomplish. I doubt they'll tell you anything they didn't tell the police."

Maybe not, but the real question was, would the Kearneys recognize Dean? "I would feel better if I spoke to them."

"Fine," Dean stood. "I'll meet you tomorrow."

"Thanks. I appreciate it." *Sucker.*

Chapter Ten

Jonathan pretended to read his newspaper while waiting for his wife to put in an appearance. He checked his watch. It was almost eight-thirty. Damn it, where was she? He had a meeting in less than an hour and no time for her stupid games. She was still avoiding him, after nearly a week. About the same time Lawson had turned up.

He drank from his coffee cup, the bitter liquid now tepid, but he hardly noticed. She was probably hiding in her room, waiting until he left.

The cup clattered on the table when he set it down and stood. A slow simmering anger built inside him as he left the kitchen and started up the stairs. Did she actually believe she could avoid him forever? That simply staying out of his line of sight would protect her? And had she honestly thought he wouldn't find out about Lawson?

Outside his wife's room, he rapped loudly on the door before entering. Lara sat at her vanity dressed in a long, sage, silk robe, her eyes wide with surprise.

She was a remarkably beautiful woman, with her smooth, ivory skin and nearly black hair. Fresh from the bath, the still-damp locks curled slightly under her chin.

He admired her as he would a fine piece of art, acknowledging the beauty on the surface. Though, he would likely have felt more passion for a painting than for his wife.

She said nothing, only continued to watch him in the mirror.

"Did you really think I wouldn't find out?" He demanded. She paled and perverse delight filled him. "Answer me."

"I—" she hesitated. "I hoped you wouldn't."

"I'm sure you did. So tell me, what did he want?"

She frowned. "I don't understand."

"Many things," he agreed. Then slowly, as if speaking to a small child, he asked again. "What. Did. Lawson. Want?"

"Dean?" she said, as if joining the conversation at last. "You mean Dean?"

"Yes, Dean. Who did you think?"

She let out a breath and some of the tension left her. "I only spoke to him for a moment."

"I didn't ask how long you spoke to him. I asked what he wanted."

"Nothing, really." She waved her hand airily. To his amazement her features turned cool and inscrutable. "Just to say hello."

Lying bitch! But why? "Is that why he accosted you in your car the day of the funeral?"

"How did you know that?" Her eyes, wide and a little afraid, stared at him from the mirror's reflection.

"What did he want?"

Her hand trembled as she ran it through her hair and she moistened her lips. Was she working on another lie, trying for something more believable this time?

"The best lies, Lara, always hold an element of the truth. So let's start with the truth. Does he know that you started the rumor?"

"I didn't—"

"You did. Does he know?"

"How did you find out?"

"I've always known, but the question at hand is does he?"

"Yes." The word escaped her in a breathy whisper.

"Did you deny it?"

"No. I offered to admit it to the police if it would help clear his name."

Jonathan chuckled. "And why would you do that? Are you seeking absolution?"

"It's the right thing to do."

This time he laughed hard and deep. "Since when have you cared about doing what's right? You take care of you, and you always have. There's no honor among thieves is there, Lara?"

She didn't speak. Good, because she would listen. They all lived in this purgatory together, and she had less right to an escape than anyone—except maybe him.

"You will admit nothing, do you understand?

"I'm not one of your employees."

"No, you're my wife, but if you don't stay away from Lawson, you won't be for long. I'll divorce you. I have grounds, thanks to the way you've been carrying on with Richard." He smirked and added in mock horror, "My own brother?"

"All this time and you knew?"

"You should have been more discreet and taken a lover outside my family."

"I see. But how could admitting what I've done possibly matter to you?"

"I'm late." He turned to leave. At the door he stopped and faced her. "I'm as responsible for what happened to Michelle as you are." *As much and more.*

Dean had just stepped out of the shower and was drying himself with a faded gray towel that may have been white at one time, when a light knock at the door stopped him. He left the bathroom and picked up his watch from the corner of the dresser. Not quite noon. It couldn't be Haley.

The knock sounded again, light and somehow distinctly feminine. He grabbed his jeans from the floor and pulled them on. The denim stuck to his still damp skin. Fumbling with the fly, he opened the door.

"I'm sorry to have disturbed you."

Dean met Lara's pale gaze. A faint smile played at the corners of her lips as she swept an appreciative glance down his bare torso. Struck by the urge to cover himself with his arms, he turned away from her instead, snatching the shirt off the end of the bed and pulling it over his head.

"You didn't. Come in and close the door."

She did as he asked, then lowered herself to the corner of the bed. He folded his arms over his chest and leaned against the wall opposite her.

"I have some bad news," she began slowly.

"Really?"

"I'm afraid I won't be able to help you."

His heart picked up the pace and a slow, seeping anger settled over him. Why did he feel like he'd been had?

"And why is that?" he asked, but he had a pretty good idea.

"Do you mind if smoke?"

He shrugged, pretending not to give a shit when, in reality, he wanted to toss her out on her ass. He grabbed the chipped ashtray from the desk and shoved it at her.

Her finely shaped black brows lifted a little, but she said nothing as he resumed his position against the wall. With almost painful slowness, Lara slipped the cigarette between her lips and lit the end.

"Are you comfortable now?" He didn't bother to hide his contempt, but if she noticed, she didn't let on.

"I am, thank you."

"Good. So maybe you'd like to tell me what's changed in the past few days."

Days that he'd held off going to the police, all to suit Haley. She'd done a fine job stalling him. Now he knew why.

"I've had some time to think, and after careful consideration I think it's best to let sleeping dogs lie."

"You do, huh? Well, I don't. You see, it's my life that you screwed up with your little-girl games. So, we're going to leave here together, right now, and you're going to tell the detective everything."

"I'm not, Dean. I'm sorry, but I can't. There are too many people who will be hurt, whose lives will be disrupted. I'm sorry."

"Lara, I will tell the police what you told me. All of it. You'll look guiltier if you don't come clean now."

"Tell them anything you want. I'll deny it. I'll tell them

you're crazy. I'll tell them I'm afraid of you. And they'll believe me, not you. I'm Mrs. Jonathan Williams and no matter what you're doing these days, you're still Dean Lawson, the man who murdered Michelle."

Hot fury made him lash out. "You keep telling yourself that, because no matter how many fur coats you buy, no matter how much jewelry you own, no matter how many rich men marry you and ignore you, you're still Lara Kramer. You and I come from the same place, and if you think anyone's forgotten that, you're deluded."

"This town may see me as a gold digger, and they'd be right, but that's a long way off from a killer." She squashed her cigarette in the ashtray and stood to leave, but he grabbed her arm.

"Who changed your mind?" He perversely needed to hear her name.

"No one, I just thought—"

"Give me a break, you haven't thought for yourself in years. Someone put you up to this."

"Fine. You're right. A friend did remind me that I have a lot more to lose than you do to gain. Now, if you don't mind." Dean released her arm and she swept out of the hotel room, slamming the door behind her.

He half-sat, half-leaned on the edge of the dresser, not at all certain the brittle faux wood could support his weight. Well, he had to hand it to Haley. While he'd been wracked with guilt, she'd come at him from an angle he hadn't even considered. God damn it, what now?

Haley drummed her fingers on the counter and stared at the door. It was quarter to four and still no sign of Dean. Would he stand her up? *Stand me up? This isn't a date.* Still, the butterflies swooping and diving in her stomach couldn't quite grasp that.

"Do you want me to finish for you?" Billy asked.

She frowned. "What?"

"The invoices." He pointed to the pile next to the computer

and then gestured to the spreadsheet on the screen. "Did you want me to finish entering them for you?"

Despite staring blankly at the screen, she hadn't inputted an invoice in the past twenty minutes. She shrugged. "Sure, that would be a big help."

Provided Dean showed up, otherwise she would have the rest of the afternoon to do it. She checked her watch again. Ten to four. So, where was he?

Holy God, maybe she'd been right all along. Maybe he was afraid the Kearneys would recognize him or give him away. Of course that would make him Michelle's killer, and she still couldn't quite believe it. Not that it mattered because he was going to stand her up anyway.

"Hey." A sharp bubble of pain bloomed in her side as Billy elbowed her in the ribs and whispered, "That's the guy, the one who came to see Al last week. I told you he's out of Al's league."

Haley looked up from the computer to where Dean stood just inside the doorway, and her stomach flip-flopped.

Not a date!

Was she so hard up that trying to prove or disprove a high school crush guilty or not guilty of murdering her sister had become a social outing for her? She needed therapy.

"You're late," she snapped and slid off the stool, but froze in her tracks when she took a good look at him.

His catlike eyes practically glowed from the taut lines of his face. He stood stiff and unyielding, a harsh scowl etched into his expression. The tiny muscle in his jaw flicked wildly.

"Sorry I held you up."

She frowned. "Is everything okay?"

"Everything is just great. Let's go."

"Okay." Her heart rate quickened as she pulled on her jacket. The idea of Dean Lawson as a dangerous man seemed far more plausible.

"I'll drive," she said.

He nodded, following through the rear door to the alley where she had parked, but stopped short as they approached her car.

"Oh, look, a coffin on wheels," he muttered.

She looked at the car as a stranger would. The salt stains and even the wine-colored paint couldn't hide the clusters of rust dotting the doors and hood. The nearly bald tires, about as wide as pizza cutters, looked too small for the heavy metal frame. The whole thing just screamed death trap. One more winter, that's all she asked.

"Just get in," she said, frowning. There was something off with him today. The edge in his voice and that scowl. He was angry about something.

She slid into the driver seat and pushed her key into the ignition.

"Even if I was a murderer, chances of survival in my car would still be better than traveling in this," he said, sitting next to her.

She turned the key and the motor made a strange choking sound, then went silent. She tried again and the same thing. On her third attempt, he snorted, shaking his head.

"Don't tell me," he said, his voice thick with derision. "We can't go."

She stopped battling the engine and turned. "What's going on with you?"

"Are the theatrics really necessary?"

"What are you talking about?"

"You have what you wanted. There's no reason to stall me anymore, and no reason to take this trip. Couldn't you have just called and made an excuse? Saved me coming down here instead of faking car trouble."

Okay, so he knew she was stalling him, but she sure hadn't gotten what she wanted. Yet. "You think I'm faking this? You did look at the car when you got in, right? And that was you who made the, oh-so-clever coffin-on-wheels crack? Or was that some alternate personality? Because, I gotta be honest here, I'm starting to suspect you have a few."

"I spoke to Lara. She's not going to admit to the rumor, but no doubt you know that by now." His eyes were blazing and his voice deadly calm.

"Why would I know that? I haven't done more than smile and nod at Lara in years. I don't think I even spoke to her at Michelle's memorial."

"So it's simply coincidence that you come up with convenient reasons to keep me from going to the police and now Lara's backed out."

"Go to the police if you want. I told you last night that there's nothing you've found that the police probably don't already know by now."

"That's true, but without Lara, I'm still on the block."

She frowned. "I'm missing your point."

"Don't play dumb. You knew your father was a suspect no matter what, but going to Lara and having her refuse to admit anything keeps me as one too."

Haley leaned back in her seat. "Wow, that is a good plan. A lot better than mine."

"You made me feel like crap and all along you were stalling me—" He stopped speaking for a moment, as if her words were only just registering. "What do you mean better than your plan?"

She shrugged. "That going to Lara was a great idea. I wish I'd thought of it."

"You're telling me you didn't speak to Lara?"

"You're catching up. Good."

"What about your sister? Maybe the two of you hatched this plan together."

She rolled her eyes. "Well, obviously, we're so close after all. Besides, I only told Paige last night and she left first thing this morning for a meeting in the city. She had no time to contact Lara."

"Garret?"

"I haven't told Garret. Nate maybe, I spoke to him yesterday, but I'm almost certain I didn't mention Lara."

"So, this is all just a strange coincidence?"

"I think so."

He shook his head. "When I accused her of being incapable of forming her own thoughts, she admitted that a friend told her she had more to lose than I had to gain."

"I'm not that friend." She faced him again. "That's interesting, though. Who else would want to keep you looking guilty?"

"I can't think of anyone. Besides you and yours, of course."

She tugged at her lower lip with her teeth. Very interesting.

"You did have a plan?" His voice intruded on her thoughts.

"Yeah." She sighed. "It wasn't a very good one."

"What was it?"

"To drag you in front of the Kearneys to see if they recognized you."

"What was the point of that plan?"

"If they did seem to know you, it would make sense that you had told them where to find Michelle and that would make you—"

"The murderer," he finished for her.

"Right."

"So if you were right, then you would have been alone with a killer for the rest of the afternoon."

"I told you it wasn't a good plan," she said, wishing she didn't sound so defensive.

They both fell into silence, staring through the windshield. A few big flakes of snow drifted down, nearly touching the glass, before the wind swept them away into the pale gray sky.

"Now what?" Dean asked.

"I'd still like to know why the Kearneys dug up the floor, but I'd also like to know who Lara's friend is."

"We could still go, take my car instead."

Haley turned the key again and the engine roared to life. "Fourth time's a charm."

He smiled at her, and butterflies the size of a hippopotamus rolled over in her belly.

Not a date.

Chapter Eleven

Erin slipped into her mother-in-law's kitchen through the side door, trying to stay as quiet as possible. For a moment she stood motionless, waiting for a sign of what she could expect. A lamp glowed softly from the den, and as she edged closer the unmistakable clink of ice against glass reached her ears. She froze.

Damn. By five Claire should have already passed out. Obviously, Erin hadn't waited long enough. Claire was still awake. Still drinking.

Guilt nagged at Erin. Garret had asked her to look in on his mother throughout the day. With Paige in the city and Haley on a buy for the store, there'd been no one to limit how much Claire drank. Except her.

Erin hated to do it. Hated dealing with Claire's emotional outbursts that spewed venom one moment then collapsed into fits of tears the next. So she'd waited. And for what?

Damn Haley. She couldn't have made the buy tomorrow when Paige was back? Spite. That's what it came down to.

She sighed and started forward, fixing a smile in place. What choice did she have?

"Hello, Claire," she said, her insides tied in tight aching knots.

Claire lifted her head and returned the smile. "Look at my girls." Her words slurred.

Claire held out a photo of Michelle, dressed in her cap and gown, flanked by Paige and Haley, standing in front the high school. Erin remembered the day that photo had been taken. She'd graduated that day too. Who would have guessed then that things would turn out the way they had?

"Aren't they beautiful?" Claire half-sobbed.

"Yes," Erin admitted, her eyes locking with Michelle's. Dark, alive and frozen in time, they bored into her, knowing, accusing. Erin looked away.

"Why would anyone want to hurt her?" Claire asked, weeping. "She never hurt anyone, she was a good girl."

"Have you eaten?" Erin asked. She couldn't look at those pictures any longer.

"Oh, Erin, look," Claire insisted. "Look at her when she was a little girl." She fiddled with the photos until she found one of Michelle when she was no more than two. Her hair a tangle of white-blonde curls, and dressed in a ruffled pink dress. Erin took a step back so she could no longer see.

"I remember when she was born," Claire continued, oblivious to Erin's averted gaze. "She was like a living doll for me. That first day home from the hospital I had her dressed in at least ten different outfits." Claire tried to chuckle, but it was dry and brittle and turned into a sob. "She's dead."

Hot and nauseous, Erin went to the kitchen and prepared a sandwich. She would do what she came to do then she would get out of there.

With the sandwich and a tall glass of milk, Erin returned to the den. Claire looked up, her eyes red rimmed from drinking and crying.

She shook her head. "I can't."

"That's okay," Erin said, setting the food on the coffee table and doing her best to ignore the faces staring up at her from the photographs. "I'll just put this in the fridge and you can eat it later if you want. Maybe you should lie down for a bit. You look tired."

Relief poured over her when Claire nodded and let Erin help to her room. After Claire practically fell into the unmade bed, Erin pulled up the blankets, smoothing them over her shoulders as she would with her children.

"It never goes away," Claire said miserably, her voice flat and dead. "It's like a part of me has been ripped away, and it still hurts as much as it ever did. It just keeps hurting. Paige and Haley don't understand. Even Garret doesn't understand.

But you might. You could understand what it would be like to lose one of your girls."

Erin nodded. She couldn't speak. Her throat had constricted until it was nearly sealed shut.

"I told your father that when he came to see me," Claire said sleepily.

Erin jerked as if slapped. "When did he come to see you?"

"This morning."

Why? What could he have been doing here? Fear, cold and desperate, turned the blood in her veins icy. Claire was already drifting off. Erin considered shaking her back to consciousness and demanding answers, but she was afraid of giving herself away.

What had her father been doing here? Maybe just visiting with his friend's widow. God, she hoped so.

With frigid terror settling over her, the need to act was almost overwhelming. What could she do?

Confess! The word screamed inside her brain like a siren. No, not that. Not now. It was too late for that. Years, too late.

"So, you did have a plan, a lousy plan, but you still intended to manipulate me to get your own way."

Haley's gaze shifted from the road to Dean. He stared stonily out the window. It was the first time he'd spoken to her since they pulled out of the alley nearly forty-five minutes ago.

"He was my father," she turned her attention back to the dirty salt stained highway. "I know he didn't kill Michelle. What did you expect me to do? Sit back, smile and nod while you went ahead and ruined him?"

"Oh, yes, let's keep a dead man's reputation intact, but the living breathing man, let's make sure he keeps looking guilty."

"Just because he's dead, doesn't mean that having him blamed for a murder he didn't commit will have no effect. Besides, for all I know you could have done it."

"You know I didn't."

"How do I know that?"

"You wouldn't be in the car with me if you thought I had actually killed Michelle."

"That's not proof. I just want to protect my father's memory since he's not here to do it himself."

"The evidence points to him." Dean turned and looked at her, the tiny muscle in his jaw flicking wildly. "I didn't wake up one morning and say, 'Gee, I don't really like the idea that everyone in my hometown thinks I murdered my old girlfriend, I know I'll accuse her father, he's dead anyway'."

Throwing up his hands, he sat back in his seat. She glanced from the road to him and then back to the road. "Why did you? I mean, why bother coming back to try and clear your name? You moved away, built a new life. No one could have known about Michelle."

Could he hear the envy in her voice? If he did, he didn't let on.

"You'd be surprised. You just never know when and where your past will pop up to give you a kick in the ass."

"When did yours?"

"About six months ago. I had a new client, when I went to his home to do some measuring his brother and sister-in-law were visiting. The sister-in-law was Tanya McPhail. She used to sit in front of me in tenth grade science."

"Oh, God, did she say something in front of everybody?"

"She didn't recognize me right away, but she kept staring at me, like she knew me from somewhere. And the longer I'm there, I know it's just a matter of time before she's going to figure it out. I couldn't leave fast enough. Needless to say, the guy canceled the next day."

With a quick glance in her rearview mirror, Haley signaled and changed lanes as they approached their exit.

"You know," she said. "Tanya may not have recognized you at all. Her brother-in-law could have canceled because you were in such a hurry to leave. Besides, what are the odds that you'll ever run into anyone from Hareton again?"

"Everybody knows somebody. How many people do you suppose that guy told that he almost hired a contractor who had murdered a girl, but thank God his sister-in-law eventually remembered him from a high school science class?"

"You may have a point. Still, if I were to leave, I don't think I'd ever come back."

"Easy for you to say, no one thinks you killed anybody."

For the rest of the trip neither spoke. The beginnings of a tension headache tightened the muscles in her shoulders and at the base of her spine. A dull but steady pain throbbed behind her eyes.

With a crude map that she had drawn pinned beneath her thumb on the steering wheel, Haley maneuvered through the suburban side streets. At last, she found the house she was looking for.

"They moved in with her parents," Haley said as she pulled up against the curb.

"How did you find that out?"

"You know Karen who runs the Java Joint?"

He nodded.

"Her sister is their listing agent for my grandmother's house. I asked Karen, Karen asked Darlene, and voila, address and phone number."

"You have a knack for this."

"Are you impressed?" Grinning, she turned to face him, but the smile fell away as soon as her eyes met his.

"Extremely," he said. His expression serious and his gaze hot. Again that flutter in her lower belly. She looked away quickly, pretending to be absorbed in carefully refolding her badly drawn map.

"So what now?" he asked.

She opened the car door. "We knock."

They stood shoulder to shoulder on the concrete porch while they waited for the front door to open. Dean jammed his hands in his pockets and leaned back. There was no car in the driveway and no sound beyond the closed door. *Nobody home,* he thought, relieved.

He put his hand on Haley's arm and opened his mouth to speak, but the clunk of the bolt turning stopped him. The door opened about three inches and a tall, thin woman filled the space.

"Can I help you?" She pushed her reddish brown curls out of her face.

"Rhonda Kearney?" Haley asked.

The woman nodded, her hazel eyes narrowing. "I know you," Rhonda said, her voice filled with accusation. "You and your brother sold us that house."

"That's right," Haley took a step back.

"What do you want?"

"Um—I—this is going to sound strange." Haley hesitated. The other woman's hostility seemed to have shaken her.

"Why doesn't that surprise me, coming from you?" Rhonda snapped.

"I beg your pardon?"

"I've got nothing to say to you." Rhonda started to push the door closed, but Dean stepped forward and blocked it with his forearm. Fear flickered in the woman's eyes so he backed off a little.

"If you could just talk to us for a minute, then we'll go."

"What do you want?" she asked again.

There was no point in dancing around the issue, no time to finesse answers from her. "Why did you dig up the floor in the basement? What happened that made you dig where you did?"

Rhonda chuckled, a brittle sound, and again looked at Haley. "Like she doesn't know."

"I don't have a clue what you're talking about." Haley crossed her arms over her chest and stuck out her chin. Her eyes practically glowed with simmering fury.

"You sold us a house with a body in it, and God knows what else," Rhonda accused. "We sunk every dime we had into that place and now we'll never be able to sell it for what we paid. You're lucky we're not suing."

"You can't possibly believe we knew she was there. Christ, she was my sister."

"But I do believe it, and I'm not the only one."

Dean stepped between them, trying to regain control of the

conversation. "But how did you know she'd be there?"

Rhonda scowled. "You want to know? Ask Sandra." She slammed the door in their faces with a hard thwack.

With her head high and her hands closed in tight fists, Haley turned and marched down the newly shoveled drive, the black pavement a stark contrast against the brilliant white snow. Dean sighed inwardly and followed a few steps behind. The ride back should be pleasant.

"That could have gone better," he said, sliding into the passenger seat. Haley didn't reply, seeming to concentrate on starting her motorized deathtrap instead. "You have nothing to say?" The engine caught on her second attempt and coughed to life like a cranky old man after a nap.

"What can I say?" She shrugged. "She thinks Garret and I knew Michelle was down there all along."

Dean watched her lean back in and press on the gas, revving the engine. Her teeth tugged at her bottom lip

"Are we—"

"Why in the hell would she assume Garret and I knew that our sister was buried in her basement?" she demanded, cutting him off. "That doesn't even make sense."

Dean hesitated before replying, searching for the right words. She'd obviously missed the implication. "I think she believes you and Garret were protecting someone."

"Let me guess, my father. Isn't that convenient for you?"

"I'm sure he's a suspect, but people know the police have made Paige stick around, maybe they think she's a suspect. Maybe your brother. Hell, maybe even you."

Still gnawing at her lip, Haley seemed to consider what he said. At least there was no sharp retort.

"Are we going?" he asked.

She nodded and shifted into drive, pulling away from the curb. As they wove through the snow-lined streets, making their way back to the highway, she remained quiet, lost in thought. He turned his attention to the dirty gray sky and snow-blanketed lawns that made up the bland scenery.

"It must have been hard for you," she said once on the highway and headed toward Hareton.

"What?"

"Being a suspect, being blamed and no one believing you when you said you were innocent." She didn't look at him when she spoke. Her gaze remained on the fast-moving highway, flicking occasionally to the mirrors.

Uncomfortable, he shifted in his seat. He hated thinking about that period in his life, never mind actually talking about it. "It was hard."

"I'm frustrated out of my mind and so far people are just speculating that my father was responsible. I can't imagine what it'll be like when someone actually points a finger and says 'he did it, he's guilty'. Or if someone did that to me."

"You move on." Just like he wanted this conversation to. He tried for a change of subject. "How did you end up with the store?"

She snorted softly. "Things kind of fell apart once Michelle had been gone a few months. I think deep down everyone knew she wasn't coming back. Except my dad. He was obsessed with finding her. He used up most of their savings hiring private investigators. It's ironic really, they followed leads as far as Mexico when all along she'd never left Hareton."

Doubt nagged his conscience and he didn't like it. "Didn't anyone try to stop him?"

"Garret tried talking to him a few times, but he wouldn't listen. Besides, Garret was getting married and had other things to think about. Anyway, I worked at the store after school, putting money aside when I could so I could go to university. If Paige could disappear that way, why not me too?"

"But you stayed."

"I stayed." She nodded. "My grandmother had a stroke and died about two months before I graduated high school, so I had to be around more to help my mom. A couple of years later Joan was diagnosed with ALS. She and Nate moved back to Ottawa so she could be close to her parents and sister. There was no one left to run the store. My father hadn't actively done anything with it, probably since he fired you. So I ran the place, hoping that eventually my parents would pull themselves together."

"And when they didn't, you stayed behind and took care of

them."

"To make a long story short."

Annoyed, he tapped his finger absently against the car door just below window. But who annoyed him more, Haley or her parents, he couldn't say. "You shouldn't have stayed if you didn't want to."

She shot him a scathing look before turning back to the road. "And what should I have done? Left them to go bankrupt?"

"Yeah, but I doubt it would have come to that."

"Wow, thanks for your expert opinion on my family situation. Quite impressive how you managed work all that out in only a matter of days, but I guess coming from such a tight family unit yourself, you'd have some real insight." Her words were hard and jagged, but before he could respond she apologized. "I'm sorry, really, that was low."

He shrugged, unperturbed. "Maybe, but true."

"I shouldn't have said it, I'm sorry."

Memories of that shitty house in the south end of town and his mother, barely there, were faded now, as if those days belonged to someone else. Maybe they did. He felt so far removed from that lonely, bored teenager.

From time to time, he saw traces of that surly, smart-mouthed boy in the reflection staring out at him. Small reminders of who he'd once been.

Funny, looking back at all the things he would have done differently, of all the things he'd change, he never once regretted stealing the Carling's delivery van with his friends. Or taking it off-roading in a field outside town. Or having the police find him passed out in the back, deserted by his friends, the following morning.

When Carling had offered him the chance to work for him and pay off the damages rather than pressing charges, he'd changed Dean's life.

Darren had been a tough taskmaster, but a patient teacher. He'd been fair. Or at least Dean had thought so at the time. He never would have guessed that Carling could murder his own daughter, and then let Dean take the blame.

"So, is Nate a silent partner now?" Dean asked, doing his best to shove the memories away. No point in dwelling on a past he couldn't change.

She shook her head. "No. Shortly after my Dad died, Nate needed to sell. I had some money put away, and he let me pay off the rest."

"Why'd you bother? I mean if it's not what you wanted to do?"

"My father worked hard to build that store."

"That he couldn't be bothered to run."

"Maybe we shouldn't talk about this anymore."

"Maybe," he agreed, still annoyed. He turned back to the window.

They drove a ways in silence. The dreary gray sky outside darkened to blue twilight. Christ, it had been a long day.

"What do you think Rhonda meant when she told us to ask Sandra?" Haley asked. "Who's Sandra?"

He shrugged. "I don't know. The name doesn't ring a bell."

"It did for me." She frowned. "I feel like the name's familiar."

"It's a first name and not uncommon. No doubt you've heard it before."

"Still, it's the only lead we have."

"We? When did we become we?" he teased.

Even in the pale light from the dash he could see her roll her eyes. "With Lara backing out, you've lost your chance to clear your name and I'm still trying to find away to clear my father's. Sandra is the only clue we have."

The town's lights brightened the dark sky as they drew closer.

He sighed. "I think you're grasping at straws, but what the hell, that's all we've got. Drop me off at my car and I'll grab us something to eat, then meet you back at your place."

Haley left Dean at his car across the street from her store then started home. The name Sandra still played through her brain. Why did it sound so familiar? Where had she heard it before?

Absently, she nibbled at the corner of her lip. The only thing more perplexing than the name tickling her memory was her uneasy alliance with Dean. Who would have guessed he would become a strange sort of ally in all this? Ally or not, Sandra wasn't a whole lot to go on, for either of them.

She pulled into her driveway and got out of the car. Her muscles had stiffened from the long drive and an air of defeat seemed to have settled over her. Maybe after she ate something she'd feel better.

She followed the narrow cement walk to her doorstep, digging for her keys in her purse. They jingled maddeningly just out of reach as she searched blindly, through the receipts, gum wrappers and ATM statements. She needed to clean this crap out.

At last her fingers closed over the cold metal, but as she reached out to push the key into the lock she realized she didn't need it. The door stood open. Barely a quarter of an inch, but open just the same.

Her heart rate tripled as she pushed the door the rest of the way, fisting her keys in her other hand so that each one stuck out between her knuckles. A vague recollection from a self-defense class in high school phys-ed.

Maybe she should call the police. She shook her head as if answering herself. What if she just hadn't closed the door properly when she left that morning? She'd look like an idiot.

From the small front hall, the pale kitchen light spilled into the living room. Had she left that light on this morning? She struggled to remember, but came up empty as she ran her hand over the switches for the light overhead and the lamp next to the couch.

Nothing moved, or seemed out of place in the sudden brightness. The house was silent except for the familiar tick of the furnace and the ever-present hum of the refrigerator. She stepped farther into the house, half expecting someone to jump out at her from the dining room, but no one did.

With her heart pounding in her ears, she went into the kitchen. Everything was as she left it. From the dregs of coffee still in the pot, to the mug, plate and knife on the counter, to the crumbs next to the toaster. But then, what had she expected? That an intruder would break in and tidy her kitchen?

She considered grabbing one of the serrated knives from the wooden block on the counter, but rolled her eyes at her own foolishness. She'd probably forgotten to turn off the light in the kitchen this morning. God knew she'd been a touch preoccupied lately. The door probably hadn't closed properly behind her when she'd left for work. And the only reason she was climbing the stairs to make sure everything was how she left it was simply for her own peace of mind. Just so she could say "I told you so" to her overactive imagination.

Her breath locked in her throat as she reached the small hallway at the top of the stairs. Soft, pale light flickered through the narrow gap between the wall and her partially closed bedroom door. With feet that felt as if they were made of stone, she dragged herself forward and pushed open the door with one trembling hand.

Her stomach dropped and a strange sound escaped her lips, something between a whimper and a gasp. The room glowed as if on fire. Candles of every shape and color flickered on her dresser, vanity, and on the floor surrounding the bed. Someone had pulled back the bedspread as if in invitation and scattered dark red rose petals across the sheets.

She covered her gaping mouth with her hand and took a step back. Who could have done this? And more importantly why?

A dull thump from below made her freeze where she stood. Someone was in the house. She should have brought the knife.

Chapter Twelve

Another thump, then footsteps crossing the floor below. Haley remained still as if her every muscle had seized. More movement in the kitchen, then footsteps coming toward the stairs. She could hide, but where?

"Haley?"

Dean. Relief swamped her like a tidal wave, making her knees weak. Just Dean, thank God. She opened her mouth to call out, but only an odd sounding squeak escaped. She cleared her throat and tried again. "I'm here. I'm up here."

He frowned as he came to stand beside her. His gaze swept the room, the flickering candlelight dancing over the planes of his face.

"What is this?"

She shook her head. "I don't know. Someone must have broken in. The front door was open when I got home."

He edged past her into the room and bent to study one of the thick pillar candles on her dresser. "These haven't been burning long. The wax is only just starting to run down and pool." He blew out the flame. "Are you certain whoever did this is gone?"

"No." The terror that had gripped her when she heard Dean downstairs still fresh in her mind.

"Call the police then go wait in the car while I search the house."

His words pricked her temper. "I don't think so. I'll call the police and then we'll look together."

"Don't be stubborn."

"Don't be stupid," she shot back. "And don't order me around in my own house. Do you expect me to hide in the car like a simpering female, while the big strong man searches my house for scary bad guys?"

His lips quirked. "You think I'm big and strong?"

She rolled her eyes. "Your ego maybe."

As he blew out the tiny flames on her dresser, she turned and did the same to candles on her vanity, then moved on to the ones circling her bed. He knelt on the opposite side, extinguishing the tiny flames. They followed the wide semi circle until they met in the middle.

Without the candles, the room was dark except for the faint glow from the hall light. She glanced up at the bed and shuddered. The idea that someone had touched her covers left a cold, sick feeling in the pit of her stomach. What else had her intruder touched? Had he rifled through her clothes? Her personal things? Everything in her room seemed contaminated.

"Don't touch anything else," Dean said. "Not until you talk to the police."

She nodded and followed him downstairs to the kitchen. As she lifted the phone from the cradle on the wall next to the fridge, she hesitated then hung it up.

"Kind of a strange coincidence don't you think?"

He frowned. "How so?"

"Lara backs out on the advice of a friend, we speak to Rhonda Kearney and now this. Maybe someone's trying to scare me off. Keep me from helping you."

"Up until four o'clock this afternoon you were still trying to find a way to pin the murder on me. How is that helping? Besides, who else knew where we were going?"

"Maybe it's not where we were going, but that we were together. Maybe someone saw Paige and I last night."

"So? No one knows for sure why you were there. You could have broken in to say good-bye. Closure."

"Why would we do that? Her body is in some morgue somewhere."

"You're missing my point."

"No, you're missing mine. We've both been so fixed on our

own agendas we're not seeing the big picture. While you're trying to prove my father did it and I'm trying to prove he didn't, maybe we're close to figuring out who really did kill Michelle. And that person isn't too happy about it."

His eyes held hers, but his expression remained impassive. "You think that what happened in your bedroom was a kind of warning? An attempt to scare you?"

She shrugged. "Until I started looking for answers about Michelle, no one had ever turned my bedroom into a bizarre kind of altar."

He seemed to consider what she said. "Call the police, and then let's check to make sure we're actually alone."

Dean helped himself to another cup of coffee as Haley walked the two policemen to the door. All the while he tried to tamp down his slow, bubbling anger. The two bonehead cops had taken their statements and done little else once they made the connection between his name and Michelle's.

At first, they'd implied that perhaps it had been Dean who had set up Haley's room that way. When Haley pointed out that he would have needed superhero powers to be in two places at once, they changed theories. Maybe someone who knew they'd been spending time together had taken exception. Either way, the overall impression had been she'd gotten what she deserved.

"Young lady," the older one, Beckette, who, unfortunately, remembered Dean from his less than law-abiding youth, had said, "When you keep the company you do, you have to expect this sort of thing to happen."

It had taken everything Dean had not to pop the condescending bastard. But even his anger couldn't thaw the tight ball of fear lodged in his gut like a chunk of ice.

Was Haley right? Was Michelle's killer trying to send them a message? The cold inside him spread, stippling his skin with goose bumps. What if she'd come home earlier? What if the intruder came back? What if she vanished like Michelle? And all because of him. If he had just moved on with his life, Haley wouldn't be searching for answers to questions she hadn't had before he returned.

"Well," Haley said, sinking onto vinyl seat of the chrome kitchen chair. "There's three hours of my life I'm never getting back."

"Come back to the motel with me," he blurted out.

She quirked a single brow.

"That's not what I meant. We don't know who did that to your room or why. You shouldn't be here alone."

"Does the I'm-afraid-for-your-life line usually work?" she asked, her lips curving into a smile.

"I'm serious."

"I know." She got off the chair and opened the pizza box he'd left on the counter after he arrived. "The thing is, I don't think I'm in any real danger. I'm nearly certain that what happened up there was a warning."

Frustration throbbed inside his skull. "Let's say you're right. Michelle's murderer is trying to warn you off. That means someone who has killed and managed to get away with it for over a decade was wandering around your house. He got in once, he could definitely do it again."

"So what am I supposed to do? Move out?" She bit the tip off her slice.

"Isn't that cold?" His stomach turned at the sight of the thick congealed cheese, housing tiny pools of grease.

"I like cold pizza."

He shuddered. "Just for one night. Until you've changed the locks."

She shook her head. "I'm not sleeping there, and actually, I don't know how you can. Besides, I think you're overreacting. I'll check the windows and doors before I go to bed, make sure everything is locked up tight."

"You're being stubborn again."

"I'm not being stubborn," she snapped. "This may come as a shock to you, but I'm not fifteen anymore. I'm twenty-seven. I run a business, pay taxes, vote, all the things grown ups do because I've grown up, in case you hadn't noticed."

"I noticed." He'd have to be blind not to.

"Then try to understand. I don't need you to protect me or rescue me."

"I'm spending the night."

"Did anything I say sink in?"

"Yes, but unfortunately I don't think anything I've said has had the same effect on you."

"Where did you plan to sleep?" she asked taking another bite of pizza, then added around the mouthful, "I'll be in the guest room. I won't be sleeping in my bed until I've had a chance to burn the sheets."

"I'll sleep on the couch."

She turned to the living room. He followed her gaze, to the ugly, lumpy corduroy. When he turned back, she was smiling at him.

"If you wake up tomorrow miserable with a sore back, I want you to remember this was your idea."

He'd remember all right. How could he forget?

Paige cracked the car window a half inch and lit another cigarette. The thin line of bluish smoke streamed steadily through the narrow space into the dark night. She glanced in her rearview mirror by habit more than anything else. She hadn't seen another car for at least an hour.

What had she been thinking, driving back to her mother's after midnight when she could have been asleep in her own bed in her own apartment like a sane person?

She knew why. The thin web of apprehension that had clung to her most of the day, leaving her edgy and anxious had led her here. Alone on an empty highway, jittery from what was undoubtedly too much caffeine.

She rolled the window down enough so she could fit her hand through. The frigid wind whipped at her bare skin as she flicked the cigarette away. She lifted her gaze to the rearview mirror in time to see tiny orange sparks spiraling, then vanishing into the black.

A row of thick pine trees rose up on the far side of the highway as she passed the Williams' place. Another twenty minutes and she'd be home. A shudder passed through her. Not home, her mother's house. That red brick shell hadn't been home in years.

God, when would she be free? Maybe she could demand that the detective deal with her. She had a life to go back to, after all. And a career. But if she wasted much more time here at the ends-of-the-earth, she may not even have that. Especially, with Lucy taking credit for her work. If she did make it back in time to salvage her career, she'd toss that little bimbo and her collection of ridiculously short skirts out on her ear.

The image made her smile and gave her at least some sense of control over her life no matter how fleeting. She turned up the volume of the radio and tapped her fingernail on the steering wheel to Cher's rendition of "Walking in Memphis".

What if Michelle's murder did end up getting pinned on her father? A dull ache throbbed in her chest. The mere possibility left her cold. At least she wouldn't be there to deal with the whole mess on a day-to-day basis.

Paige did her best to ignore the guilt wiggling into her brain. Despite what Garret and Haley both thought of her, she did have a conscience. At the same time, she'd chosen to build a life away from Hareton, her family and Michelle, and she wasn't about to be dragged back in. That Haley and Garret stayed was their decision.

Tough talk for a woman driving back in the middle of the night because she had a bad feeling.

She reached for the half-empty pack of cigarettes on the dash. She had bought them just before leaving the city. How to give yourself lung cancer in a month. A wry smile touched her lips, but fell away as her eyes lit on a slight figure trudging up the shoulder of the road.

A chill swept through her body and she dropped the forgotten pack onto her lap. What kind of person wandered highways in the middle of the night? And where had they come from? She hadn't seen a car, parked or moving, since forever.

She pressed a little harder on the gas. Whoever would be walking along a highway in the middle of nowhere past midnight in December was clearly crazy. And Paige had a strict policy of not picking up insane people from the side of the road.

Still, she let her gaze drift back to the rear mirror until the weirdo was out of sight. Relief seeped into her stiff muscles. Almost there.

Movement ahead evaporated the small relief, and her heart started to pound as she came across another highway walker, remarkably similar to the one she'd only just passed. Long blonde hair whipped out from under the figures hood and Paige's mouth went dry.

She slowed the car, pulled onto the shoulder and stopped. Crazy. What was she doing? She needed to pull back onto the road and drive like mad until she reached her mother's. But she didn't move. Instead, she kept her gaze fixed on the mirror and the woman jogging up to the car with painfully familiar movements.

Paige's fingers trembled as she plucked a cigarette from the pack still in her lap, then slipped the filter between her lips. She needed both hands to light the stupid thing, one to hold the lighter, the other to keep the first from shaking.

At the light tap on the passenger window, she lifted her gaze. Her sister peered through the glass. Michelle. But not the way Paige remembered her. With pale skin and sunken eyes, Michelle's light blonde hair flailed crazily around her head.

The cigarette fell from Paige's gaping mouth, landing on her nylon-clad thigh, burning through the sheer fabric and into her flesh.

"Son of a bitch," she cursed, brushing it off her leg. The ember sparked and landed on the floor at her feet. She crushed the smoke into the mat with the heel of her boot and when she looked up, Michelle was gone.

Her insides quivered as Paige climbed out of the car into the frigid air. Clutching herself around the middle, she circled the vehicle, but there was no sign of Michelle. Or that she'd ever been there. Not even footprints in the snow.

"Michelle," Paige said softly. Her voice sounded creepy in the quiet. "Michelle." This time she yelled and cringed at the noise.

No one answered. She was completely alone.

Chapter Thirteen

A muffled pounding thudded behind Paige's eyes, stretching out through the rest of her body until even her fingertips reverberated. With a groan, she buried her head under the pillow and willed the noise to stop, but the banging continued.

Not morning already, not possible. She felt as if she'd only just fallen asleep minutes ago. Lifting the pillow slightly, she opened her eyes. Hard morning sun seeped through the slats in the blinds, striping the navy bedspread. She rolled and glanced at the clock next to the bed. Eight-thirty. God, she'd only been asleep for four hours.

Her experience on the highway had kept her awake and sitting in the den, watching infomercials, for hours after she got home. Somewhere between an ad for a revolutionary exercise device that looked like a bunch of Bungee cords and another for a microwave omelet maker, she managed to convince herself that she'd imagined the whole thing.

Was it any wonder? Everything in her life right then was about Michelle. And she had been exhausted. Her diet had consisted of little more than cigarettes and coffee. Hallucinating her dead sister on the side of the highway shouldn't have been wholly unexpected.

She closed her eyes and snuggled deeper under the heavy duvet, waiting for sleep to reclaim her, but the banging didn't stop. What was that, and why wouldn't it go away?

Had her mother locked herself out after an early morning trip to the liquor store? No, too early. Maybe the old witch kept a secret stash outside since both Paige and Haley had been watering down the bottles in the den. Not only was it possible, but very likely that her dear mother had gone outside to collect her hidden bottle—from the garage, or under the porch, or buried in the snow—and while she was out there had somehow managed to lock herself outside. Now she beat on the door with one bony fist.

At last the pounding stopped. She'd finally frozen to death. When Paige finally crawled out of bed, she would undoubtedly find her mother on the back stoop dressed in her dirty, pink robe, her colorless hair still matted with sleep, frozen in place with tiny icicles clinging to the tip of her nose and earlobes. One arm would be raised in mid-pound and a bottle of rye tucked under the other. Not a pleasant image.

Paige forced her eyes open and flung back the covers. Her body ached as she stood, her muscles stiff and sore from lack of sleep. A special kind of crappy feeling similar to a hangover. She changed from the silky, gray nightgown she wore to a pair of sweatpants and a T-shirt.

"She's not here." Her mother's loud and annoyed voice boomed despite the closed door.

Well, at least she isn't frozen on the back step.

"She won't be back until later today," her mother continued.

"Her car is in the driveway." Paige cringed at the sound of Erin's voice. As if she didn't feel lousy enough, now she had to deal with her sister-in-law.

She opened the bedroom door and stepped into the kitchen. "Good morning." Though she expected anything but.

"I need to speak to you," Erin said, her expression ridiculously somber.

"About what?" Paige stifled a yawn and the urge to roll her eyes.

"I need to speak to you," Erin said again, opening her eyes wide. She tilted her head and nodded toward Claire, bobbing her head like chicken with a stroke. Paige wanted to speak to Erin like she wanted a bikini wax, but the sooner Erin said whatever she'd come to say, the sooner she'd leave.

"Mom, why don't you go get dressed while I make your breakfast."

"It's about time," her mother muttered. "I thought I'd starve to death before you thought of me."

Wonderful, the old woman had woken reasonably sober and miserable. Paige took the bread from the fridge and popped a couple of slices into the toaster while Erin stood with her head cocked, listening to Claire climb the stairs. After a few moments, Erin peeked around the corner to make sure she was out of earshot. Satisfied, she turned back to Paige.

"I was at the girls' gymnastics class when I heard something terrible," Erin said.

Paige's hands stilled and she waited for the inevitable, that her father was now a suspect in her sister's murder.

"I rushed right over as soon as I heard," Erin continued. "There's only twenty minutes left in the class so I need to be quick."

"Just say it." Her voice sounded flat.

"Someone broke into Haley's house last night."

"Oh my God." Paige turned to face Erin, her insides tight with fear. "Is she all right?"

"Last I heard she was okay. She wasn't home when it happened."

Paige relaxed a little. "Was anything stolen?"

"Nothing," Erin said. Her skin was pale and her eyes wide. "Whoever broke in had left all kinds of candles burning in her room and flowers in her bed."

"What kind of creep would do that? Did you speak to Haley?"

"No, I haven't seen her yet. I heard it from Patty-Sue Sullivan. Her brother-in-law was one of the cops who followed up on her call. And as if the break-in wasn't bad enough, do you know who was with her when she got home, and who was still there when the police left?"

Paige had a sick feeling she did know, but shook her head anyway.

"Dean Lawson." Erin said. "He seems to have taken a real interest in Haley."

Paige nodded, only half listening. Anger thick and blinding spilled over her until her hands shook with it.

"She's usually so down to earth. I can't imagine why she would have anything to do with him. I would talk to her myself, but I don't think she'd listen to me. Are you going to talk to her?"

Paige nodded. Oh, she'd talk to Haley all right. Dean may not get the chance to kill her, because as angry as Paige was, she might just do the job herself.

"I've got to get back," Erin said. Her color had returned.

"Fine. Thanks for telling me."

Erin smiled. "We're family. We have to look out for each other."

Again Paige struggled to keep from rolling her eyes. Once Erin had gone, she fed her mother, showered, and dressed in record time.

"I've got to go out for a couple of hours," Paige said, before slipping out the door. Her mother didn't bother to tear her gaze from the television screen. "I'll be back before lunch."

"Don't hide my car keys again," her mother snapped, still staring at the flickering box. Paige shook her head and left.

Haley scrambled through the deep snow, barely able to see past the falling flakes. The cold made her shiver and drained her of strength, but stark terror forced her on. Something hunted for her in the dark, hidden behind the fluttery white curtain.

With gasping breaths, she struggled to move faster, but the snow grew deeper, almost swallowing her up to her hips. Half-panting, half-sobbing, she forced her legs forward, each small step costing her precious seconds and strength.

The gurgling snarls of her monster rose above the howling wind. So close. She clawed at the snow, pulling herself free.

As she gained her footing once more, the snow lessened, and through the tiny flakes, her grandmother's house rose up against the black night like a beacon. Warm yellow light shone from the windows and she knew that if she could make it there, she'd be safe inside.

Hot breath tickled the back of her neck as she clambered

up the steps to the porch. She gripped the door handle and pressed down with her thumb, but nothing happened. The door was locked.

Panic welled inside her as she pushed repeatedly on the handle, beating against the door with her fist. She screamed and begged almost incoherently, and all the while the snuffling grunts of the beast chasing her grew louder in her ears.

Suddenly, the door gave, sending her stumbling forward. Michelle stood in the dark hall, pale and drawn. She leveled her empty black eyes on Haley.

"He used to bring me flowers."

Something sharp dug into Haley's shoulder—

Haley sat straight up in her bed. Her heart skittered against her chest and an icy sweat slicked her body. A dream. Just a dream. She panted as if something really had been chasing her over some generic snowy expanse.

Clutching her covers tightly to her chest, she looked around the guestroom, memories of the previous night rushing over her. After searching for her sister's killer and having her house broken into, no wonder she'd had a nightmare.

The candles and rose petals bothered her more than she'd let on. Too intimate and too personal. And too close to receiving the anonymous card and roses.

Should she tell Dean about them? No way, he'd move in if she did. Bad enough he'd insisted on taking up residence on her sofa for the night. No need to encourage him to make the arrangement permanent.

Haley threw back the covers and did her best to ignore the flutter in her belly at the thought. Just because the man was not a psychotic killer, that didn't make him datable. She was a decade over her adolescent crush, and wouldn't be falling back into it anytime soon.

Once downstairs, she started the coffee then quietly went to the front door and collected the newspaper from the porch. As she started back to the kitchen, despite her better judgment, she tiptoed nearer to the couch.

Dean lay stretched out on the flattened corduroy, one arm thrown over his head, the other on his chest. In sleep, the lines of his face seemed smoother, more relaxed. His lips parted slightly and again she found herself thinking how nicely shaped they were.

When she had been fifteen, and he had flashed that slightly wicked grin, her insides had quivered. Just as they did now while her gaze drifted over the smooth flat muscles of his chest and followed the line of crisp black hairs between contours of his stomach, until it disappeared beneath the blanket at his narrow waist.

She lifted her gaze back to his face and locked with his smoky green eyes. Oh, crap. Heat instantly burned her cheeks. He smirked and sat up a little.

"I made coffee," she muttered and turned away, unsure what words were appropriate when caught ogling a man in his sleep.

The coffee had finished brewing when she returned to the kitchen. She could hear the rustle of fabric from the living room as Dean pulled on his jeans.

"Haley," he said as he came to stand beside her.

"Here's yours." She slid a chipped mug with a Gary Larson cartoon on it toward him. "I don't know how you take it."

"Black."

He hadn't put his shirt on.

"Easy to remember." She dumped three spoonfuls of sugar into her own mug. "I'm going to clean the mess upstairs, then head to work." Why did he have to stand so close to her? Like she wasn't embarrassed enough. His body heat practically radiated from his bare skin. Avoiding his gaze, she moved toward the fridge for the cream.

"Wait a second, would you?" His hand closed over hers. "Look at me."

She tried to pull her hand away, but he tightened his grip. "Could we not make a big deal about this?"

With his other hand, he cupped her face and tilted her head up. She met his gaze, bright and hungry, before his mouth closed over hers.

Heat pooled low in her belly, her eyes closed as she wrapped her free hand around his neck, pressing herself against the hard length of him. Sinking into him. His lips, the same lips she had fantasized about since she had been a love struck teenager, devoured hers, better than anything she had ever imagined.

"Well, isn't this a sorry sight."

Paige's disdain-filled voice washed over Haley like a bucket of ice water. She stepped away from Dean as he turned around. Paige stood in the dining room, hands on her hips and eyes filled with fury.

"Good morning Paige," Dean said. "Coffee?"

Chapter Fourteen

Paige practically shook with pent up anger. "Get away from my sister."

Sensing the impending explosion, Haley moved so she stood in front of Dean. "What do you want Paige?"

"A word, if you wouldn't mind?"

"Fine."

Haley followed Paige to the hall by the front door, wishing she didn't feel like a traitor. She shouldn't. Dean wasn't responsible for what happened to Michelle and, hell, she was a grown woman. She could kiss any man she wanted to in her own home. Or anywhere else, for that matter. Still, that didn't extinguish the guilt that flickered inside her when she saw betrayal in Paige's eyes.

"I cannot believe you're sleeping with him." Paige rounded on her as soon as they were out of Dean's line of vision.

"Keep your voice down," Haley snapped with a harsh whisper. They may have been out of sight, but they were no where near out of earshot. "I didn't sleep with him. He spent the night on the couch because he didn't want me here alone after my house got broken into." She gestured to the blanket and pillow lying in a forgotten heap on the sofa.

"How noble. What was that I just walked in on?"

"None of your business."

"He murdered Michelle," Paige said, throwing her arms in the air and no longer bothering to keep her voice quiet.

"He didn't, but we're close to figuring out who did." She told Paige everything. The card, the flowers, the break-in and Lara.

"I think whoever killed Michelle is feeling threatened."

"Are you out of your mind?" Paige demanded. "Don't you find it strange that from the first moment you talk to Dean you start receiving weird little gifts? I mean how is an unsigned card or a bundle of roses threatening? You said yourself that at first you thought they were condolences."

"I know he had nothing to do with what happened to Michelle."

"I'm sure the girlfriends of most serial killers say the same thing. Oh wait, no they don't, because they're dead!"

"I can't talk to you about this. You're being ridiculous." Haley turned to walk away.

"Think about this." Paige grabbed her arm, almost desperately. "Your house gets broken into, and then he generously offers to spend the night. He's playing you, and you're letting him."

"He was with me all day yesterday. There's no way he could have broken into my house."

"Haley, I remember the way you used to moon over him."

"I've never mooned a day in my life."

"Oh, you mooned. When Michelle was dating him, she thought it was funny. We all did."

Heat stole into Haley's cheeks. God, Paige could be a bitch. Had she actually thought for one second that they could have some kind of relationship?

"I think you should leave."

"If I knew and Michelle knew, wouldn't it stand to reason that Dean knew too? You need to ask yourself what he's hoping to get out of you. The way I see it, the best case, he's trying to find out what the police know. Worst case, he's searching for his next victim."

"I can't talk to you now." A slow simmering rage boiled just below the skin. "You need to leave." She walked away, leaving Paige standing alone.

"You have the worst taste in men," Paige called then slammed out the front door.

Haley still seethed when she walked into the kitchen. Dean leaned against the counter and drank from the mug, his expression inscrutable, but the tic in his jaw gave away that he'd heard most of what Paige said.

She wanted to pick up where they'd left off. To feel his mouth on hers again, his arms wrapped around her. And to forget.

"Maybe it's best if we stop all this," he said, his voice low.

"No," she told him, and meant it. "I've never been so close to finding out what happened to Michelle, and I'm not stopping now."

"I heard everything."

Great. "Then you know I think we're onto something."

"I know that since I came into your life again someone's been watching you. And now I'm alienating you from your family."

She snorted. "My family spends more time alienated from one another than anything else. Until Michelle was found, I hadn't spoken to Paige in nearly four years."

"Why is that?"

"It doesn't matter. The point is, I'm not giving up on this. Whoever killed Michelle took more from me than a sister, and I need to know why. I'll do this with or with out you."

He sighed. "Fine. What did you have in mind?"

"I have to go to work today, but while I'm there I'll try and find out who Sandra is. Maybe you could talk to Lara, find out who persuaded her to keep quiet."

"I don't know how far either of us will get."

"We have to try. They're the only leads we have."

He nodded, lifted his coffee to his mouth and drained the mug. When he lowered the cup, a smirk twisted his mouth. "So, you used to moon over me?"

She couldn't have stopped the blush rushing to her cheeks if her life depended on it. "I suppose it was too much to hope that you hadn't heard that."

"Oh, yeah."

"I stand by the claim that I have never mooned over anyone."

"That's too bad. I kind of like the idea." He bent his head

129

until his lips were only inches from hers.

"You would," she said, her mouth suddenly dry. "What with your giant ego."

His lips brushed hers softly, playfully teasing. Her mouth tingled, the sensation spreading throughout her body as he deepened the kiss.

She stepped back. "I need to clean the mess upstairs and get to work."

"I'll help you."

She nodded and waited as he shrugged on his shirt from last night, her gaze on the rippling muscles in his back.

Not mooning. Admiring. Big difference.

The speed at which gossip traveled never ceased to amaze Haley. Yesterday her store had less than a dozen customers all day, today she had that many browsing at any given time.

She knew she was being gawked at. She could feel their gazes on her as she rang in orders and accepted pieces for refurbishing. At times, she caught people whispering out the sides of their mouths or behind their hands, all the while looking at her with a mix of pity and contempt.

As the day progressed, her mild irritation turned to full anger. What business was her life to anyone else anyway? Sometimes she hated this town. What she wouldn't give to live a life outside the fishbowl. Where her every move, decision or family tragedy wasn't fodder for town gossip.

By the time Billy arrived to start his shift, she was practically crawling out of her skin. She couldn't wait to retreat to the workroom, away from the scrutiny and speculation. She still hadn't had the chance to look into who Sandra was. The sudden surge in business hadn't left her with the spare time she'd hoped for.

"Busy today," Billy said, coming behind the counter to stand beside her.

"I'm going to get some work done in the back," she said, keeping her voice low. "Will you be all right out here on your own?"

"I think so."

"If you get swamped, let me know and I'll send Al out to help you."

"I'll be better off on my own."

He probably would be. She nodded then slipped into the back room.

Al, his face hidden behind a respirator, scraped the waxy finish off a large, square dining table. The chemical stink of wood stripper stung her nostrils and burned her eyes. Even with the steel door open to the alley, the frigid air did little to alleviate the heavy fumes.

Haley lifted a respirator from the workbench and fit the molded plastic over her nose and mouth.

"Are these ready?" she asked, pointing to the row of six chairs, seats removed, lined up against the far wall.

"Should be."

She nodded and took a stack of newspaper from the pile next to bench. As she spread the paper on the floor, a familiar headline from last week's paper caught her eye. "BODY FOUND." Instinctively, Haley started to turn the sheet over so the article would be face down as she worked and she'd see only benign advertisements for Christmas savings, but she stopped. The name Sandra stood out from the article as bold to her as the headline itself.

"Brian and Sandra Gallagher, present at the time the remains were discovered, also declined comment."

That had to be the same Sandra Rhonda had mentioned. Haley fought the urge to do a little happy dance.

With her foul mood forgotten, she rushed back out into the store, yanking off the respirator as she went. She set it on the counter and bent to dig her planner from her purse. She flipped through the pages until she came to where she'd scribbled Dean's cell phone number that morning.

"Everything okay?" Haley asked Billy, as she dialed. Only three customers wandered through the cluttered aisles. The fewest she'd had all day.

"Fine. Mostly just browsers left."

"Hello." At the sound of Dean's voice, Haley turned away

from Billy.

"Hi, it's me."

"Hi me, how's your day?" His deep, almost melodic voice had her stomach tightening. How could five little words have that kind of effect on her? *Stop being stupid, you're not fifteen, anymore.*

She snickered. "It's been interesting."

"That bad, huh?"

"Well, actually, business has picked up. I wondered if you might be available for some appearances this time next year."

"Cute."

"Anyway, that doesn't matter, I found Sandra."

"Where?"

"In an article from last week's *Gazette*. Her last name's Gallagher. She and her husband were there when Michelle's body was found. I'm not sure how we'll figure out where they live. Maybe I could call whoever wrote the article."

"They might not tell you anything to protect her privacy. Try the phone book."

"Have you had any luck with Lara?"

"A woman keeps answering, I'm assuming she's Lara's housekeeper, and telling me she's not home. The woman might be telling the truth. I've called three times, pretending to be someone else each time, and got the same answer. This last time, I told her I was from the credit card company, and I needed to speak to Lara regarding some strange activity on her account. I left my cell phone number. Who knows, she might actually call me back."

"I'll see if I can track down the Gallaghers."

"Good. Why don't I pick you up at the store after you're done?"

"No need. It makes more sense to meet you at my place."

He was quiet for a minute. "Make Al walk you to your car."

"I'm sure he'd be a big help if someone was in the alley waiting for me."

"Humor me?"

"Fine. I'll make him walk me to the car," she lied.

"Good. Call me when you know more."

"I will."

After a quick good-bye she hung up and turned around. Nate stood on the opposite side of the counter, his dark eyes boring into her. God help her, not another lecture.

"Let me guess, you'd like to speak to me." She tried to keep her voice light and even smiled faintly.

He didn't return her smile, only glared. "Was that him?"

A woman, running her fingers over the smooth surface of a dark wood secretary, glanced over. Her eyes met Haley's for just a moment then she looked away.

"I don't have a lot of time for lectures right now. Could we do this later?"

"Your father would be rolling in his grave if he knew what you were doing."

"I guess not," she said more to herself. To Billy she said, "I'll be in the back."

She didn't say a word to Nate as she yanked open the door, but she knew he followed. His quick, angry footfalls on the cement floor covered the sound of Al's scraper on the wood. The air still stunk heavily of chemicals and she'd left her respirator out in the store so she continued out the open back door into the alley.

Nate, perhaps believing she was trying to escape him, grabbed her arm as soon as they were outside. His long fingers sank painfully into her flesh.

"That hurts," she snapped, wrenching her arm away.

"So is he worth it?" Nate demanded, his face turning red and blotchy.

"Worth what?"

"What you're doing to your family."

"What am I doing to my family?"

"Your brother and Erin are worried sick that something will happen to you."

"I'm sure they are. Who would look after Mother?"

"Why don't we discuss your mother? What do you think she'll do when she discovers her youngest daughter is sleeping

133

with the man who murdered her oldest?"

Haley's insides tightened instinctively at the thought. God help her if some do good neighbor like Mrs. Yolken decided to fill her mother in. Forget it, Yolken could never get past Paige. There were times having a pit bull for a sister helped.

"Dean didn't murder anyone."

"He must be a phenomenal lay to be able to manipulate women the way he does."

The fury simmering just below the surface exploded in her head. "Shut up, Nate. I'm not answerable to you. I don't need to listen to any of this. Go home."

"I'm not finished with you."

"Too bad. I'm finished with you."

Without a backward glance, she walked into the shop as composed as possible, but her hands shook as she pulled the door closed behind her.

"Hey, I need that open," Al said, looking up from the table.

"Just wait a few minutes and then you can open the door again."

She went back out to the store. The eavesdropping lady had gone and so had the secretary.

"Did she buy it?" Haley asked, collecting her respirator from the counter.

Billy nodded, staring at her warily. Did she look as furious as she felt?

"That's good."

She slid the respirator into place and went back to the shop. Al had opened the door again, but there was no sign of Nate. Nausea swirled in her belly. How could he have talked to her like that? And how could she have told him to shut up? She got to work on the chairs and tried to push the incident out of her mind.

Chapter Fifteen

At half past six, Haley set the alarm and slipped out the back door. She clutched the scrap of paper with Sandra Gallagher's address scribbled on it while trying to formulate the best way to approach this woman.

She didn't have a clue. She could try showing up at Sandra's front door. Though, that plan hadn't worked very well with Rhonda.

As she crossed the narrow strip of pavement from the door to her car, the hair on the back of her neck prickled. Nothing moved in the alley. The few cars parked behind the other stores were still and lifeless. A row of trees formed a natural barrier between the alley and the houses backing onto it. Their bare branches made a dry clicking sound in the wind that sent a shiver down her spine.

This was Dean's fault. In all the time she'd worked there, she'd never once been spooked going to her car after dark. But he'd made such a big deal about having someone walk her out.

After fishing her keys from her purse, they slipped from her trembling fingers, landing on the pavement with a jingle. The sound was ominous in the quiet.

She bent and scooped them up in one fluid motion. As she straightened, something moved in her peripheral vision. She turned sharply and froze.

Nothing. She waited, keeping her body absolutely still, her eyes glued to the rusted Dumpster and her ears strained for any sound. The cold metal of the keys dug into her palm.

After a few minutes, she released her breath then quickly unlocked the door, slamming it shut once behind the wheel.

She slapped down the locks on both sides of the car.

Ridiculous. Still, panic fluttered through her as she struggled to start the car.

"Please, please, please," she chanted and turned the key a fifth time. The engine choked and coughed then caught at last.

She threw the car into gear and started forward, not bothering to give the motor a chance to warm up. If the pile-of-junk stalled on the way home she didn't care, so long as she was away from the alley.

"None of that would have happened if you just let Al walk you to your car," Dean said.

Haley leaned back against the passenger seat with a sigh. Why had she mentioned the incident at all? "None of that would have happened if you hadn't made such a big deal about it and freaked me out."

He glanced at her briefly, before turning his attention back to the road. The streetlights reflected off his glasses and kept her from seeing his eyes. "Maybe you should be freaked out. If you're right, this is Michelle's killer we're dealing with, and he feels threatened."

"I have no problem being cautious, but I don't plan on jumping at shadows." Well, not again anyway. "Besides, I don't see anyone walking you to your car."

She waited, a smug grin in place. How would he respond and not sound like some macho male chauvinist? His lips pressed together in a thin straight line. Then he smiled. "No one has broken into my home or left me creepy gifts."

"You're good," she admitted. "With all that diplomacy you should become a politician."

He snorted. "That'll be the day. I'm serious, though, if this is Michelle's killer you need to be careful."

"You do too. You're as much a threat as I am. And don't think that just because you're a man you're somehow exempt from danger. The killer could club you over the head from behind. You never know."

"Fine. Point taken. I'll be careful too."

"I might be better convinced if you didn't sound like you were humoring me."

"I've been trying to think of suspects," Dean said, clearly opting for a change of subject. "Given all that we know."

"And what do we know?"

"The store's delivery van was seen on the side of the highway at about eleven-thirty the night Michelle disappeared. Days later I found a pair of your father's coveralls with blood on them in the crawl space."

"You could have been wrong. That was a long time ago, maybe it was stain."

"It was definitely not stain."

A sudden, desperate panic bubbled inside her. They were supposed to be on the same side. "We know my father wasn't involved. He's dead and obviously couldn't have been the one to break into my house."

"What about his first wife? We can't ignore that. Whoever did that to your room last night could be someone who's as eager as you are to keep your father looking innocent."

"Or, Michelle's actual killer."

"I'm not disagreeing. I just think we should keep an open mind and look at everything as a whole."

"Fine." He could look at whatever he wanted. As far as she was concerned, her father was innocent. "So who had access to the van, the store and my grandmother's house?"

"Your family, Nate and his family. Al and I had access to everything except your grandmother's house."

"Her place was hardly Fort Knox. Anyone who wanted in could have gotten in with a minimal amount of effort. Paige and I did two nights ago."

He nodded. "So consider motive."

"Excluding your alleged obsession."

He turned and scowled at her.

"I said alleged."

"Who else?"

"Lara? She tried to make Jonathan believe that you and Michelle were still seeing each other. Would she have killed her because of him?"

He opened his mouth, but hesitated for a moment. "I don't think she has the brains to kill anyone and successfully get away with it for over a decade. What about Jonathan? He was the last person to see her before she disappeared."

"The police ruled him out before looking at you. Jonathan had an alibi. The housekeeper saw Michelle leave and he didn't go after her." Haley stared out the windshield at the rows of red lights from the cars ahead of them on the highway. "We need to know what was going on in her life before she went missing."

He glanced at her again and hesitated before speaking. "Who would she confide in?"

"Her friends. Maybe Erin or Lara."

"I don't think Lara's going to be much help. What about Paige? She was closer in age than you are, did they talk?"

"They fought, but I don't know if they had many sisterly heart-to-hearts."

"This is our exit," Dean said, nodding to the sign on the right. "Maybe Sandra will solve everything for us."

"Wouldn't that be nice."

Haley read off the directions while Dean steered down the dark streets. He pulled up to the curb in front of a small town house. White Christmas lights dotted the eaves and green floodlights cast an eerie glow on the small porch. A black SUV stood in the driveway, and light seeped out from around the blind on a window upstairs. A good sign.

"Looks like she's home," Dean said as he climbed out of the car.

Haley nodded as she stepped onto the driveway, pushing the door closed behind her.

"Do you know what you're going to say?" Dean asked when they reached the front porch.

She shook her head. "Nope. But after yesterday, I'll just be happy if she doesn't slam the door in our faces."

After a deep breath, Haley knocked. Tiny silver bells, dangling from the wreath on the door jingled with the vibration.

A loud clatter rose up from inside followed by two ferocious barks. Haley automatically took a step back, certain some kind of vicious hellhound with matted fur and glowing red eyes waited for them.

The door opened and a small woman with dark hair struggled to hold back a large barrel-shaped dog. The yellow Lab lifted his big, grinning face and barked, his backside wiggling wildly. After successfully blocking the dog with her leg, the woman lifted her head, smiling apologetically, but her smile melted away when her gaze fell on Haley.

Dean must have noticed too. He stepped forward, moving in front of Haley.

"Sandra Gallagher?" he asked.

Sandra nodded.

"I'm Dean Lawson, this is Haley Carling."

"You're related to the girl we found?" Sandra asked.

"She was my sister."

Again Sandra nodded as if struggling to comprehend. Behind her, the dog whined, his wagging tail banging and rattling the mirrored closet doors.

"We were hoping you wouldn't mind talking to us," Dean said.

Sandra hesitated a moment, then nodded. "Of course, come in."

Haley stepped past Dean as she entered the house and met his gaze. He shrugged.

"For a minute," Sandra said, holding the quivering dog by the collar. "The way the floodlights hit, I thought... You look like her."

Haley didn't think she looked anything like Michelle, but she didn't contradict the other woman. At least she hadn't slammed the door in their faces. Already this was going better than their visit with Rhonda.

"Settle down Cooper," Sandra said. The dog ignored her and tugged free of her grasp, bounding first to Dean then to Haley, his tail wagging with wild abandon. Haley chuckled and rubbed the short fur on his side. His eyes closed and he groaned in ecstasy while slowly sliding down her legs. As soon as he hit the floor, he rolled onto his back, exposing his belly.

"He'll never leave you alone," Sandra warned.

Haley rubbed the dog's pink tummy. "I don't mind."

"Come on, Cooper, out of the way." Sandra snapped her fingers and pointed down the hall. With a huff, Cooper rolled back onto his stomach, stood and ambled away as dignified as possible.

"Come on in," Sandra said. Haley and Dean followed her down a narrow hall that opened into the den. A man sat on the sofa, his feet propped on a square, wooden coffee table, his gaze glued to the large TV on the opposite wall. A playpen tucked in the corner of the room sat empty except for a few forgotten stuffed animals.

"Brian," Sandra said.

He looked away from the screen and offered them a bewildered smile.

"This is Dean Lawson and Haley Carling. Haley's the sister of the girl we found."

He muted the TV with the remote and exchanged a quick, questioning glance with his wife. "Please, sit." He gestured to the loveseat on the far wall.

Haley sat next to Dean, her cheeks warm. God, she felt foolish, descending on these poor people in their home. For a moment no one spoke, the soft hiss from the baby monitor on the side table the only sound in the quiet room.

"We appreciate you speaking to us," Dean said at last. "We saw Rhonda Kearney yesterday. Did she tell you?"

Haley shot him a quick look. Why bring her up? He ignored her.

"I haven't spoken to Rhonda since—" Sandra hesitated. "Well, in a while."

"What did she tell you?" Brian asked, frowning.

"Not a lot," Dean admitted. "We wanted to know what made her dig up the floor, and she said we should ask you, Sandra."

Sandra paled and sat next to her husband.

"This will be hard to believe," Brian said. "You'll probably think we're crazy or liars, but I swear every word is true."

Brian launched into a story about how they picked up a girl hitchhiking on the highway who disappeared from the backseat of their car. As he spoke, Haley's patience ebbed away. Who was this ghostly hitchhiker supposed to be? Michelle? What a load of crap. She glanced at Dean. His expression was stoic, but the tic in his jaw made her suspect he felt the same way.

"Once the body had been identified, we saw your sister's picture in the paper. It was the same girl we picked up in the snow storm."

Of course it was. "But how did you know she would be buried there?"

"I saw it," Sandra said, her voice trembled when she spoke. She was quite the performer. "Because of the weather we had to spend the night. I guess I walked in my sleep. The whole thing felt like a dream."

"What did?" Haley asked, her tone sharper than she had intended. Brian's eyes narrowed slightly.

"I was in the basement, watching someone bury her."

"Who?" Dean asked.

"I couldn't tell. I could hear the shovel, but whoever was digging stood in the shadow. All I could really make out was a bundled blanket with strands of her hair, poking out the top." Sandra shivered. "When I woke up, I was digging. I knew she would be there."

What drove people to make up things like this? Had Rhonda done this for some kind of sick revenge for the house she couldn't sell or live in? Or was this a cover, to protect whoever really told them where to dig?

Haley tensed, ready to stand, but Dean gripped her hand. She relaxed, turning to him.

"This phantom hitchhiker, did she say anything?" he asked.

Brian shrugged. "We asked her what she was doing out there by herself, and she said she'd had a fight with her boyfriend. Nothing too strange." He frowned then added. "But when Sandra said something about her boyfriend leaving her out there she said it was okay because someone always stops. That did strike me as kind of weird."

I'm sure it did. "Well, thanks for talking to us," Haley said with a tight smile as she and Dean stood.

Sandra walked them to the door while Cooper plodded

behind them. As Haley was about to step outside, Sandra touched her arm and stopped her.

"I know you don't believe us," Sandra said slowly. "I wouldn't either, but she said something else, just before she disappeared. 'He used to send me flowers.' Does that mean anything to you?"

The blood drained from Haley's face and the air sucked from her lungs as if she'd been kicked in the stomach. She shook her head dumbly. Those words did mean something to her, she just didn't know what.

How could Sandra have known what Michelle had said in Haley's dream? Standing on the glowing green porch, cold reality set in. She couldn't have.

Chapter Sixteen

He used to send me flowers.

Haley stared into the darkness. The words played over and over in her brain like an audiotape caught on an endless loop. There was something horribly invasive about hearing the words from her nightmare spoken out loud. How could Sandra have known?

There had to be a reasonable explanation. Haley didn't believe for one moment that Michelle was some phantom hitchhiker, haunting the road into town. Nor did she believe Michelle's ghost had shown Sandra where to find her grave. It was crap, all of it.

He used to send me flowers.

A line from a movie, or a song maybe, that had seeped into her subconscious. It was sheer coincidence that Sandra would choose the same line for her bogus ghost story.

Haley was grasping, and she knew it.

"Are you okay?" Dean asked.

She nodded. "I'm fine."

"You're quiet."

"I'm thinking."

"They were full of shit, Haley." He kept his gaze on the dark road ahead of them. "The things people will do for their own sick amusement never cease to amaze me."

"They didn't look like the kind people who would do something like that."

He turned his head sharply. "You don't believe them, do you?"

143

"No." How could Sandra have known?

Dean nodded and turned onto 25. Haley held her breath and peered into the darkness, searching for anything that remotely resembled a person on the side of the road. There was nothing but the wide expanse of snow-covered fields stretching out like a great white sea.

When they reached Hareton, instead of turning toward her house Dean continued straight through town.

Haley sat up straight. "Where are we going now?"

"The Mountainview," he told her as the green neon sign advertising 'M TEL' came into view.

"I told you I didn't want to stay there."

"I know, but I have to go to the city tomorrow and I need a change of clothes."

"You're planning on sleeping on my couch again?"

"Did you get your locks changed?"

"No."

"Then yes, I plan on sleeping on your couch."

He parked in front of his room and left the motor running. "I won't be long."

She nodded, but didn't say anything.

Dean had found her unusually quiet for the most of the drive. He didn't like her this way. Pale and withdrawn. He'd rather be faced with her sarcasm than deal with her monosyllabic replies all night. She was keeping something from him.

As he stepped onto the wooden walk, dusted with a thin layer of fresh snow, he dug his room key from his jacket pocket and unlocked the door.

A cool draft closed around him like icy fingers as he moved into the dark room. He flicked the light switch on the wall. Nothing happened.

The bulb? No, something felt wrong. He leaned back so he could see Haley. She was fiddling with something on the dash. Probably the radio. Turning back to the dark room, he reached his hand around the corner, flipping the switch in the bathroom.

White light spilled out the doorway, illuminating the apocalyptic mess in the rest of the room.

"Shit."

Dean kicked a path through the clothes and bedding dumped on the floor. The lamp that had once sat on the end of the dresser now lay in pieces on the stained carpet. Certainly explained why the switch hadn't worked. The mattress, stripped of covers and pushed askew, teetered on the edge of the box spring. The desk had been toppled and the chair broken beneath it.

"Someone smashed the bathroom window too."

Dean jumped at the sound of Haley's voice. "I thought you were waiting in the car."

"I wondered what was taking you so long. What happened?"

"The room's been ransacked." He sighed. "I'm going to lose my deposit."

"What was taken?"

"It's hard to tell with all the mess. My laptop, which is all I have of any real value, is in the car." He moved to the desk. "The articles about your father are gone."

"Taken by someone determined to keep you looking guilty? The same someone who spoke to Lara?"

"Could have been Lara."

"Why do you think so?"

"Whoever did this couldn't be overly bright. Those articles were copies. Not only could I get them all again, but anyone could. Unless our thief planned on stealing the originals from the clerk's office, I'd say this was a waste of their time. And my two hundred dollar deposit."

"Did you want to call the police?"

"Because they were so helpful last night?"

Haley grinned. "Now that your room's been broken into, I'd say you might be in a whole lot of danger. You better sleep on my couch where I can protect you."

He knew where he'd rather be sleeping, but kept that thought to himself. "Let me just get my things off the floor."

"Coffee?" Dean asked, setting his bag down in the hall.

Haley nodded as she struggled free of her coat, dropping it in a pile on the floor and flopping onto the lumpy couch. If the day could have been longer, she didn't know how. Between the store, Paige, Nate and the Gallaghers, she felt like she'd been through an emotional gauntlet. She closed her eyes and lay there for moment, letting her tense muscles sag.

The banging and clattering of Dean rummaging through her cupboards forced her to open them again. She should help him, but she couldn't quite bring herself to move. Besides, her kitchen was small; he'd find what he needed—eventually. She closed her eyes once more.

"You're not going to sleep on me?" Dean asked, emerging from the kitchen.

She shook her head and forced her eyes open. "No. Just resting."

"If you say so." He smirked and sat next to her. "Long day."

"And unproductive."

He frowned. "I wouldn't say that."

"The Gallaghers' ghost story was hardly helpful. We're no further ahead than we were last night."

"We still have to talk to Lara."

Haley sat up a little. He had a point. Lara knew more than she was saying, and while she wasn't talking to Dean, maybe she would talk to Haley.

"And maybe Erin," Dean continued.

"Why Erin?"

"She was Michelle's friend. She might know what was going on in her life when she disappeared."

Haley nodded. "Jonathan too. He may have an alibi, but he was the last person to see her alive."

"I wouldn't put too much stock in his alibi. I'd be curious to know if his housekeeper received any substantial bonuses that year."

"What were you doing the night she disappeared?"

He turned sharply.

"I'm curious," she said, holding her hands up in mock surrender. "Not accusing, just curious."

"I was home, watching a movie on TV and drinking beer. Pissed off at your sister because she embarrassed the hell out of me, and sulking about it."

"Your mom wasn't home?"

"No, it was Saturday night. She didn't get home until around two the following afternoon. Just in time to see the cops cart me off for questioning."

"Do you ever get angry at her, for never being around, or at your father for leaving?"

His gaze fixed on her face and he looked at her a long time until she had to look away, afraid he could see inside her and read her every thought.

"When I was young maybe. Not so much now." He shrugged. "My mother wasn't cruel. She worked hard to keep a roof over our heads, but she wanted her own life. As for my father, I was so young when he left I don't remember him at all."

"You don't think they owed you a little more than a roof over your head?"

"Would I raise my kids the way they raised me? No, but I'm not going to waste my life resenting them for it."

"They had responsibility to you."

"Are we still talking about me?"

"Yes," she snapped. Were they? "Did you want a cup of coffee?" As she started to stand, Dean took her hand and pulled her back down to the couch beside him.

"Are you angry at your parents? Your mother for giving up and your father for leaving?"

"Don't be stupid. My father died, he didn't leave." She didn't want to talk about this. "When did you start wearing glasses?"

"Abrupt subject change."

She shrugged. "I think we've got enough to worry about, without psychoanalyzing our families."

"You brought it up."

"Do you only wear them for driving?"

His smile was slow and a little sardonic. It made her heart thud. "Driving, movies, TV. Anytime I need to see distances."

"How long have you had them?"

"Almost a year. I got them the day before I turned thirty."

"You're thirty-one next month right?"

He nodded.

"I thought the age gap between you and Michelle was bigger. I didn't realize it was only two years."

"She would have been thirty-three October fifth."

"You remember that?"

"I remember."

He used to send me flowers.

The words popped into her head and she shivered. God, she wished she would stop hearing them in her mind.

"Are you okay?" Dean asked.

"I'm fine." And she wished to never utter those two words again. "Stop asking me."

Dean frowned, his mist green eyes centered on her face. She dropped her gaze to his mouth. The smooth line of his lips. What would it be like to have them pressed against hers? To feel their heat? To have his hands on her? To melt against him? To stop thinking about Michelle, the Gallaghers, her family, the store? To do something just for her?

With her heart thundering against her chest, she leaned forward and rested her palm against his cheek. Invisible stubble scraped her skin. She lifted her gaze and met his eyes, bright and hungry now.

He wanted her. Maybe as much as she wanted him. The realization surprised her. Thrilled her.

Lightly, she brushed her mouth against his, a soft feather of a kiss, barely more than a whisper against his lips. Yet even his slightest touch made her quiver. Made her wet.

She started to move away, but his hand slid behind her head and he pulled her back to him, capturing her mouth with his. No gentle taste this time, but a searing, mind-numbing kiss that sent her senses spinning. She moaned, wrapping her arms around his neck, sinking into him.

His big hands slid over her sides. The heat from his skin penetrated through her sweater. She wanted to tear her clothes away, and his, too. She wanted the skin-to-skin contact.

He gripped her hips and a dark internal quivering filled her, but rather than pull her close, he pushed her back, tearing his mouth from hers. She bit her lip against the scream of frustration bubbling in the back of her throat.

"What is it?" Her voice sounded deep and throaty, even to her.

He lifted his gaze, his eyes wary and as turbulent as the sea. His breath ragged when he spoke. "I don't want to be a mistake."

Her heart trembled and swelled. Did he honestly believe he would be?

"I'm a grown woman, Dean, and I know exactly what I want." She stood and faced him, tugging her sweater over her head and tossing it to the floor.

He licked his lips, and a shiver raced through her.

"Are you sure—" He cleared his throat and tried again. "Are you sure this is what you want?"

"I'm undressing in front of you. I don't know how much more obvious I can be."

She started to unbutton her jeans, but his hand closed over hers and he pulled her toward him until she stood in the V of his legs. He popped the button then drew down the zipper with painful slowness.

Heat pooled in her belly, spreading out to her limbs. Her every nerve ending came alive as his fingers curled around the waistband of her jeans. He pressed his mouth against the smooth skin of her stomach. Her breath clogged in her throat. Lower. She wanted him lower, easing the ache between her thighs.

"Don't regret me," he murmured.

She could barely form words. "Never."

Chapter Seventeen

Dean tugged the jeans over her hips, dragging them down her legs until they lay in a heap at her feet. She stood over him slender and pale, the ends of her dark hair curling over the slight swell of her breasts above her bra. She was incredible. Everything he'd ever imagined, and yet so much more.

His mouth went dry as he ran his hands up the backs of her smooth, firm thighs then cupped her bottom and pulled her closer. He closed his mouth over her, tasting her through the creamy silk of her panties. A tiny whimper escaped her lips, filling his brain with raw primal hunger. He wanted to feel her come. To drive her to the edge and send her over. He held her tighter, his tongue working her through the flimsy material.

"Oh God," she gasped, her fingers tangled in his hair. Tiny spears of pain stung his scalp and fed the raging need inside him.

He wanted to roll her beneath him and bury himself deep inside her, but couldn't tear himself away from her musky scent and the taste of her wet heat.

Her leg muscles stiffened and she cried out. His grip on her backside locked her in place while his mouth drove her over the edge until she shuddered and went lax against him. But he wanted her as hungry and as desperate as he was.

He dragged her onto his lap, so her legs straddled his thighs and her apex rubbed his aching erection straining against the confines of his jeans. Starving, and unable to get enough of her, his hands roamed her body, following her every line.

He cupped one pert breast, kneading the small mound

through the smooth fabric of her bra. She groaned as he pulled down the edge and bent his head, capturing the tip with his mouth.

Haley could barely think. The remnants of her orgasm still quivering through her, yet Dean's hands and mouth continued drive her higher. His teeth tugged at the already tight nipple and she gasped and jerked at the sharp sensation then melted into the soothing strokes of his tongue.

She could feel it again. The tight spiraling, low in her belly and the throbbing ache between her legs. She rocked against the hard bulge in his pants. The wet material of her underwear slid easily over his jeans.

"Wait," he murmured against curve of her neck.

Was he kidding? "What is it?"

He leaned back and let out a frustrated sigh. "Protection. I don't have anything."

Of course. How could she not have thought of that before now? With need humming through her body like a slow gathering charge, she knew exactly how. Still, didn't she have a box of condoms from when she'd been with Jason? She sure as hell hoped so.

"Hold on, I think I have some."

She eased off his lap and hurried upstairs to her bedroom.

"Please, please, please," she muttered, yanking open her underwear drawer. She dug through the tangle of silk panties and bras until her fingers closed around a smooth box. Yes. But how long were those things good for? She turned the box in her hands until she found the expiry. They still had another six months.

She rushed back down to the living room. Dean was waiting for her on the couch.

"Found them," she said and handed him the box.

"You have no idea how glad I am to see those," he told her, taking her hand and pulling her back onto his lap.

"I think I do."

She caught his mouth with hers, tugging at his lip with her teeth. He growled low in his throat, his hand tangling in her hair and his mouth devouring hers. His fingers expertly unhooked her bra and pulled the thin straps over her shoulders, leaving trails of heat along her skin. He cupped both breasts in his hands. The hard calluses on his skin scraped her sensitive nipples, and she whimpered for more.

Desperate for the feel of him against her, she struggled with the buttons of his shirt, but her fingers trembled and the process seemed to take forever. Finally, she gripped the edges and yanked, sending buttons shooting off in different directions.

He lifted his head and looked down at her. A wolfish grin curved his mouth, sending renewed fissures of heat zigzagging through her. She pressed her hand against his chest and pushed him back on the sofa, letting her fingers explore the hard, flat contours of his body.

She had wanted this, wanted him, for so long. A teenage fantasy come to life. She kissed him again, while his fingers trailed her ribs, making her hot and shivery all at once.

She moaned when his arms wrapped around her, crushing her against him. Desire streaked through her blood like liquid fire as his teeth scraped at the delicate skin of her throat. She couldn't still her trembling. How could she feel so hot and tremble like this?

A wild throbbing pounded at her core. She needed more. She needed all of him against her, inside her. Her hands fisted in his hair as her mouth hungrily found his. His callused fingers slid over her back and curved around the edge of her panties.

"God yes," she murmured.

He groaned and tugged at the flimsy fabric, his big hands sliding under the smooth satin and cupping her bottom. She shifted so he could pull them off of her then yanked open his jeans, freeing his penis and running her hand over the hot, hard flesh.

"Christ, Haley," he gasped. "Hold on a second."

He took one of the condoms from the box, tore open the package. She watched, transfixed, as he smoothed the rubber over his swollen erection. Then he was gripping her hips and helping to guide her over him. She lowered herself gradually, taking him one exquisite inch at a time as he stretched her, filled her. The sensation fed her need like dry scrub to a brush fire. Never in her life had she experienced want like this. The desperate need to possess, and be possessed.

She rode him slowly, savoring the feel of him inside her. His hands moved up her body, cupping each breast, then he closed his mouth over the tip of one. He caught her nipple between his teeth, sending a jolt to her core. She gasped, her entire body trembling as she teetered on the brink of orgasm.

With a low growl, he gripped her hips and thrust deep inside her, setting his own pace. He drove into her, hard and frantic. Their sweat-slicked bodies moved together, filling the air around them with the slap of damp flesh against damp flesh, and their nearly desperate panting. He suffused her senses like no one had before. All she could think of, all she could feel was him. She gripped his shoulders and cried out, spiraling into the sweet abyss of her climax. Spasms rippled low and deep inside her. She clung to Dean while he pumped into her hard and fast, until he thrust a final time, groaning his release.

Breathless, Haley collapsed against his chest, the aftershocks of her orgasm still shuddering through her body. Holy God, where had all that come from? She hadn't realized she had wanted him that badly, but as his arms wrapped around her, one hand trailing fingers down her spine and the other tangling in her hair, the sharp tightening in her belly told her she'd barely whetted her appetite.

A small tremor of panic rippled over her. She felt too much, wanted too much for a brief affair. No, she'd be fine. The strange feeling of expansion in her chest was just the thrill of being with a teenage crush, and the aftermath of really good sex following a dry spell. More like a drought of biblical proportions, but why dwell.

She closed her eyes and pushed the confusing thoughts from her mind, concentrating instead on the rapid thud of his heart against her ear. The denim of his jeans rubbed against her thighs. She hadn't even managed to get him completely undressed. At least he had seemed as desperate as she was. A slow smile curved her lips.

"Something funny?" he asked.

"You're still wearing your pants."

She sat up and looked at him. With his head back against the sofa, his features relaxed, he watched her through hooded eyes. Her heart skipped a beat.

"A situation I intend to rectify. I have to get up first though."

"Right." She shifted so he could stand.

"I'll be right back," he told her before going upstairs.

Once alone, she reached for his shirt and pulled it over her shoulders. She felt little conspicuous sitting naked in her living room by herself. Above, the toilet flushed and Dean's foots steps thudded on the stairs as he came back down.

"You look good in my shirt," he said, moving to stand in front of her. He reached down, took her hand and pulled her to her feet. "Why don't we continue this upstairs."

"You just didn't want to spend another night sleeping on this lumpy couch."

He smirked, drawing her against him. "Who said anything about sleeping."

She chuckled and snuggled against his chest, closing her eyes and relishing the feel of his body next to hers. But the muscles beneath her cheek hardened, the arms holding her went stiff.

"What is it?" she asked, trying to sit up.

"Wait here," Dean said, moving away from her and never taking his eyes off the wide front window.

Cold slick fear curled in her belly. She bent, snatched jeans from the floor and dragged them on. "What's wrong?"

"I thought I saw someone outside."

She glanced at the window, hidden behind long, white sheers. The idea that someone may have been watching them made her sick, but surely a peeper couldn't have seen more than shadows through the drapes.

"Where are you going?" she demanded, following him to the door.

He pulled on his boots. "I'm going to take a look. Wait here."

"I don't think so. Have you never seen a horror movie before?"

"I'm not kidding, Haley."

"Neither am I. The man goes to investigate on his own, leaving the woman alone. The man of course never comes back, and the psycho killer murders the woman."

Dean pulled open the door. "I'm just going out on the porch."

"Then I will just stand in the doorway and watch."

"Fine." He stepped outside.

"Fine." She leaned outside, wrapping her arms around her middle to protect against the frigid cold. A set of messy footprints in the snow led from the narrow walk to the window. Dean followed the prints until he stood where their peeper had.

"How much can you see through the window?" she asked, through chattering teeth.

"Enough."

"I think I'm going to throw up."

He glanced at the lawn buried under the pristine layer of snow. "When did it snow last?"

"A few inches late last night. I had to shovel the driveway and walk this morning."

"Let's get back inside before we freeze," he said, coming to join her. He closed the door and slid the bolt into place. "Check all the windows and doors, make sure everything is locked."

She nodded and together they checked the first floor.

"Like Fort Knox," she said, meeting him at the bottom of the stairs. "Do you think it was our would-be killer out there?"

"I don't know. Could be some perv who just got a free show."

"Here comes that nauseous feeling again."

He pulled her to him, his arms warm and strong. She could have let herself melt against him, absorb some of that warmth, draw on his strength, but that would have been a mistake. As good as he felt, there was only now in his embrace. And when he was gone, she'd be back to relying on just her.

Lara, Erin and Jonathan. Haley underlined each name on a sheet of paper. These were Michelle's closest friends and boyfriend. Her confidants and the last person to see her alive. Were any of them the one peering in her window last night as she and Dean made love?

"Are you going to help stain this?" Allister demanded, dabbing the intricate grooves of the dining room chairs with a thin paintbrush. "Burland is supposed to be picking the suite up tomorrow."

"In a second." She really should help him. They were behind already and she prided herself on never missing a deadline. Hadn't she argued the point with Dean when he insisted she stay home?

"Just one day. Stay home and call in sick," Dean had said, backing her against the kitchen counter and nuzzling her ear.

"I'm the boss, I can't call in sick."

He caught her earlobe in his teeth, and tiny darts of lust raced over her skin. "Yes, you can. Just one day, while I'm in the city."

She laughed and shoved him away a little. "What are you planning to do when you get back? Stand guard?"

"Maybe."

"Life goes on, Dean," she told him seriously. "That's the one thing I learned when Michelle disappeared. Bills need to be paid, inventory must sell, and Ed and Nancy Burland's dining room table needs to be ready for pick up tomorrow. That's just how it works."

"I could cancel with Matt," he considered.

"No, you can't. You have work that needs your attention, and so do I. We can't hide inside until we figure out who killed Michelle. What if we never do?"

Saying the words aloud terrified her. Two weeks ago she had accepted Michelle's death and the anonymity of her killer. Now, she hunted for the murderer with a growing fury. An obsession that snowballed daily. And why? What would knowing the truth really change?

Would her mother's drinking stop? Would she and her siblings develop a renewed closeness? Not likely. Dean would be exonerated in the eyes of the town, and while that would be very nice for him, it wouldn't affect her life. So why then? Why this compulsive need to know what happened? And why did she feel like if she knew, she would be free?

Haley turned back to the piece of paper on the bench. One of these people had to know what was going on in Michelle's life when she disappeared, surely one of them could help her.

Lara seemed the obvious choice, but not only was she not returning Dean's calls, she wasn't returning Haley's either. Erin was her next best bet, but speaking to Erin would have the same effect as speaking to her family as a whole. Erin would no doubt blab, and Haley had no desire to explain her actions to anyone right now. Jonathan? Would he even speak to her?

Haley tore the paper from the pad and turned away from the workbench, ignoring Allister's impatient sigh as she stepped into the store.

Let him do the work for a change.

The glowing green numbers on the register told her it was nearly four p.m. Jonathan would likely still be at the mill. She knelt and pulled the phone book out from under the counter then flipped through the flimsy pages until she found an ad for Williams Family Textiles. Producer of quality work gloves since 1952. Hareton's only real industry.

Shifting from one foot to the other, she waited for Billy to finish taking down an order over the phone. As he hung up, she nudged him out of the way, lifted the receiver and dialed.

"Helen Campbell wants a quote on a desk. Today, if possible," Billy said as Haley waited for someone to answer.

"Give me a sec," she told him.

"Good afternoon, Williams' Family Textile," a perky voiced receptionist said.

"Jonathan Williams, please." She used her best phony professional voice.

"May I ask who's calling?"

"Haley Carling." Maybe she should have lied.

"One moment please." The receptionist put her on hold and a disturbing Muzak version the Rolling Stones' "Satisfaction" filled her ear. A moment later the music cut out and the receptionist returned. "I'll transfer you now."

He was going to speak to her? She actually hadn't expected him to take her call. What would she say? She barely had time to think as Jonathan picked up before the first ring concluded.

"Haley," he said, his voice smooth and deep. "This is a surprise."

"I'm sorry to bother you at work," she told him, still trying to script what she planned to say in her head.

"Not at all. I didn't have a chance to speak to you at Michelle's memorial, and I wanted to let you know how sorry I am that things turned out as they did. For you and your family."

His attempt at earnest sincerity had the opposite effect, sounding smarmy to her ears. "Thank you," she said anyway. "I did call because of Michelle."

"Really? How so?"

He didn't sound surprised. Not by her phone call, or the topic of conversation. Had he been expecting a call? Did he know that she and Dean were looking for answers?

"I was wondering if you might be able to speak to me about her. I was very young when she disappeared and the age gap didn't leave us very close. I'm trying to get an idea of the person she was when she went missing. You and she were an item for a long time, I thought maybe you might be able to help me."

"I'd be happy to. When would you like to sit down?"

"The sooner the better."

"I'm here until six tonight. Would that be convenient, or too last minute?"

This was way too easy. "I can be there in a half hour."

"I look forward to seeing you."

Haley hung up the phone, her stomach curling in knots. Something was off, maybe she should call Dean. Her hand hovered over the receiver, but she stopped herself. She could manage on her own. She didn't need him to do anything for her.

With a few quick instructions to Billy, and an angry scowl from Al, she grabbed her purse and left. As she hurried to her car, she couldn't shake the gnawing sense that something was wrong.

Chapter Eighteen

Snow fell softly from the darkening sky as Haley pulled into the gravel lot next to the old warehouse. After zipping her coat and grabbing her purse from the passenger seat, she climbed out of the car and started toward the large, crumbling brick building.

She pulled open the front door, a hundred scenarios playing in her head, but she had no idea how to word the questions she needed to ask without sounding accusatory.

Too late to turn back now.

Inside a cramped foyer, a notice on the wall indicated the office upstairs. She climbed the worn wood steps until she came to a security door at the top, then pressed the buzzer on the wall. After a moment, the lock clicked and she pulled the door open.

To her surprise Jonathan sat on the edge of the reception desk, alone in the empty office space. Dressed in a dark suit, his black hair, peppered with gray, cut short and neat, he could have stepped off the pages of a *GQ* magazine.

"Are you the only person here?" she asked, a flicker of apprehension tickling the length of her spine.

"It's after five, most of the office staff has left." His smile was wide and reminded her of a shark. "I didn't think you'd mind. You're here to see me, aren't you?"

She smiled her own fake smile. "Yes. I'm not keeping you from getting home, am I?"

"I'm in no rush. Come in and sit down."

He led her past a row of dreary gray cubicles, made more so

159

by the pale fluorescent lights overhead. Behind the desks a wall of windows opened onto the factory below. His office was at the end of the hall. A big square room, with ultramodern furniture.

"Have a seat." He nodded to the low chrome and leather chairs in front of the glass and chrome desk.

She did, taking in the stark white walls, broken only by floating ebony shelves. He lowered himself into a throne-like leather chair.

"You look surprised."

"Your office isn't what I expected," she admitted.

"You were expecting something more traditional?"

"Less sterile, actually."

He shrugged. "My home is very traditional. I wanted something different for work, but you didn't come here to discuss decorating themes."

"No, I didn't. I wanted to ask you about Michelle."

Again that toothy smile. "Ask away." His indulgent tone irritated her.

"What happened between you the night Michelle disappeared?"

"No dancing around the issue for you."

"I wish I could say the same."

The smile faltered and anger flashed in his pale blue eyes. "I gave my statement to the police years ago. You'd be better to read that, over time I'm sure my memory of that night has turned a little hazy. I've probably forgotten a detail here and there."

Condescension dripped from his saccharine voice, igniting a slow fire inside her. "Why did you fight that night?"

"Because she was sleeping with Lawson and I was not impressed."

Another question burned in her brain, but asking it would give credibility to the fear lurking inside her. The hell with it. "Did you send her flowers before she went missing?"

"No." He frowned. "Lawson had been."

Another layer to the lies and rumors Lara had been spreading? Or was Jonathan lying?

"I understand why you're asking these questions," he said. "I suppose finding Michelle has renewed your interest in discovering what happened to her, but I doubt there's more to be learned after all this time."

Haley's fingers tightened around the arms of the chair until her knuckles ached. "You say that like I lost interest somewhere over the years, as though I forgot. Let me make this very clear, for the past twelve years not a day went by when I didn't wonder what happened to her."

"Of course," Jonathan said. The smile was gone, and for the first time since she spoke to him on the phone, the overly sweet sincerity left his voice.

"Did you know that there was nothing between Michelle and Dean back then? Lara spread the rumor, I suspect to get close to you."

"Sweet Lara," he said. "Is that what Dean told you?"

"Yes. She'd actually agreed to go to the police and admit it to help clear his name, but backed out at the last moment."

"Convenient. Has it occurred to you that Lawson's lying?"

She shook her head, refusing to get caught up in defending Dean. "Nope."

"Really? That's interesting. When I heard that you two had become an item I suspected he was working his way through sisters. Maybe he'll move on to Paige next. That might be embarrassing for you, though. A case of history repeating itself."

She bit back on the choking anger, and fought the urge to storm out. Jonathan was intentionally being crude, and bringing up Jason was a strike meant to sting. Instead of smacking the smug expression off his face, as she would have liked, she merely chuckled, feigning indifference. "Low blow. Did I touch a nerve? Maybe you know more about what happened to Michelle than you're letting on."

"How could I? My housekeeper saw her leave and will tell you that I didn't go after her. Just like she told the police."

"I wonder how hard it would be to look for a pay off, or if she would admit to being intimidated by her employer."

His smile evaporated and his eyes suddenly blazed. "I don't like what you're implying. This isn't a game you're playing, I will not have my business and reputation affected by being

161

connected to your sister's murder simply so you can justify a fling with Lawson. If you don't drop this, I can, and will, make you very sorry."

"Don't you threaten me," she snapped, her anger peaked. "You might be impressive in a crappy little town with a population under ten thousand, but outside Hareton you're as much a no one as I am."

Rather than angering him further, he laughed. "My God, I think you hate this town almost as much as I do. I know why I stay, why do you?"

"I'll tell you if you tell me."

"Maybe another time." He pretended to check his watch. "I'm afraid I really must go. I have another appointment."

She didn't believe him. "One last thing."

He nodded.

"Why didn't you go after her? It was cold and snowing, it would have taken her hours to get home walking, she could have frozen to death."

"I assumed someone would pick her up, offer her a ride back to town." He looked away.

"Someone probably did," Haley agreed as she stood. "And that same someone killed her."

He lifted his gaze and met her eyes, his face void of emotion. A chill settled over her. "As I said, I have an appointment."

"Thanks for seeing me."

She left his office and worked her way through the maze of cubicles to the security door. The conversation, combined with the events of the past few nights, had left her exhausted. She turned the knob, but the door remained locked.

"Damn it," she muttered, studying the combination box beneath the doorknob. Now she would have to go back and get Jonathan to open the door for her. She really didn't want to speak to him again.

Maybe she wouldn't have to. He'd buzzed her in from the reception desk. She went to the high rounded counter and searched for a button to let her out.

"You have to know the code."

Her heart skipped a beat and she jerked her head up. Jonathan's younger brother, Richard, leaned against the wall next to the door. Unlike Jonathan, whose appearance was rigidly neat, Richard had a casual arrogance, from the curly dark hair in need of cutting, to the loosened tie and rolled up shirtsleeves.

"How did Jonathan let me in?"

"There's a button on the switchboard, but it only works when someone's buzzing in."

"Okay. Could you please open the door for me?"

"What were you doing with Jonathan?"

She rolled her eyes. "None of your business."

"I wondered if you were following in big sister's footsteps. First Dean, and now a play for Jonathan."

God, was there anyone in this stupid town who didn't know her every move. "Just punch in the code."

"Let's play a game." He pushed off from the wall and took a step toward her. Alarm bells jingled in her head. "I'll ask a question and for every answer you give me, I'll press a number for the code."

"I have a better game. I ask you to open the door and every time you say no, I kick you where it hurts."

He laughed a low almost menacing chuckle and the alarm bells turned to wailing sirens. The silver glint of scissors jammed in a cup with different colored pens caught her eye. She grabbed them and gripped the plastic handle tightly. He laughed again, the sound grating her nerves.

"Open the door, now."

"You're not at all like your sister are you?"

"Just do it."

"She was a real slut, did Jonathan tell you that?"

Fear turned to incredulous fury almost instantly. "What is wrong with you? Were you dropped on your head as an infant?"

"My poor brother found out the hard way," Richard continued, ignoring her question. "When she gave him all the proof he ever needed."

"Open the damn door!"

"What are you doing, Richard?"

They both whirled to face Jonathan, his features drawn into a furious frown. How must it look? Richard slowly advancing, and her holding out a pair of scissors. Not that she cared, she'd never been so glad to see anyone in her life.

"I was just helping Haley with the door, but you're here now." Richard started down the hall, but turned to wink at her before disappearing into one of the offices.

A shiver raced up her spine. She could very easily imagine Richard peering in her window while she and Dean made love.

"Sorry about that," Jonathan said, punching in the code. "Can I walk you to your car?"

She snorted as she set down the scissors. "No thanks, I'll manage."

He nodded and held the door open. With her stomach twisted in tight knots, she hurried down the stairs to the parking lot, eager to get home.

Dean pressed the small cell phone to his ear and slowly paced the wide veranda. The icy wind whipped around him, penetrating his thick sweater and adding to the numbing cold spreading inside him. The ringing in his ear stopped and Haley's voice instructing him to leave a message after the beep played again.

Where was she? For the better part of an hour he'd been trying reach her. At the store, and at home. Still no answer.

How could she not have a cell phone? Who, in this day and age, did not carry a cell phone?

"Good news," Matt said, joining him on the porch. "They've narrowed it down to two colors."

"That's good." When he got back to Hareton, he'd buy her a cell phone then super-glue the damn thing to her hand.

"You okay?" Matt asked.

"Hmm?" Dean looked up. "Yeah, I'm fine. I've just got my mind on something else."

"Why don't you head out? I can handle the rest."

"You've been stuck handling everything while I've been away. The least I can do is bully these people into committing to a paint color."

Matt snorted. "Not to worry. Once you're back, I plan to take a nice long vacation."

"You've earned it after helping that woman choose bathroom fixtures."

"The longest afternoon of my life."

Dean turned the cell phone over in his hand and glanced at the time on the screen. 6:47. Where in hell was she? He ran his free hand through his hair then clipped the phone to the belt loop on his jeans. He had to get back to Hareton. He had to see that she was okay. "Let's hurry these people up."

He followed Matt back inside the house. The smell of sawdust and primer made his nose twitch. A surge of pride welled inside him as he passed through the front hall to the roughed-in kitchen at the back of the house.

The ground-up renovation had turned out amazing. And having managed to keep from murdering two of the most indecisive homeowners he'd ever met showed he'd reached a new level of patience.

As the project neared completion, only the finishing touches remained outstanding. Unfortunately, this couple dragged their feet, and changed their minds about everything. From tiles, to fixtures, to moldings, and now, paint color.

As he approached, the Lintons stood comparing two paint chips under a bare bulb hooked on a stepladder. Shelly looked up. "Maybe you can help us decide, Dean." She turned the chips so he could see. "Dreamy Avocado or Forest Sage?"

They looked exactly the same to him. "The avocado. It'll go better with the granite on your counter."

Shelly nodded and turned to her husband, Fred. "He's right. Maybe we should rethink the granite."

"No, no," Dean said quickly. Next to him Matt tensed. "Both colors work. I personally like avocado. It's warmer, but if you're looking for something a little more formal then go with sage." Every word out of his mouth was bullshit, but if the decision would be made quicker for it, and he could get back to Hareton and Haley then the lie was well worth it.

"He's right," Shelly said again. "What do you think, Fred?"

Fred scratched the spiky white hair on his head. "I like them both."

Pick! Dean wanted to shout.

"Maybe we should take these chips home and think about it some more."

"We really need a decision tonight so we can book the painters. It's only a week until Christmas. People will be going on holiday, if they haven't already. You need to decide now if you want the house to be ready by the end of January."

"Okay." She sighed. "The sage."

"Good," Dean plucked the chip from her hand and passed it to Matt. "Now, the floor guys are coming Thursday. I would like to meet you here to confirm the stain." Just the thought made his head throb.

"Yes, good. What time?"

"I'll call them tomorrow then let you know."

Shelly nodded.

"I'm glad that's resolved." He fixed a smile he didn't feel in place. "The house is coming along great, but I've got to get going."

"So soon?"

Soon? He'd been dealing with these people since three o'clock, the past hour and half discussing the paint color alone. As guilty as he felt leaving Matt to fend for himself with the Lintons, he had to talk to Haley.

After a short good-bye, he slipped out the front door and got into his car. He dialed Haley's number as soon as he climbed behind the wheel. Her machine picked up again. Where could she be?

Fear, dark and edgy, consumed him as he drove. He did this. He brought this on. If he had stayed away, let sleeping dogs lie, she'd never have started looking for Michelle's killer. If he had kept his hands off of her, she'd be safe at home now.

Memories of her body moving against him, her soft skin beneath his touch, her eyes like warm whiskey locked with his, fired his blood. Not even twenty-four hours later and he wanted her as badly as he had last night. More even.

Beyond the sex, wrapped in his growing fear, was something he didn't want to dwell on for too long. A longing and an ache that went beyond the physical.

He dialed her number again. Answer, damn it. But her machine came on again. He snapped the phone closed and glanced at the clock in the dash. 7:10. With a sigh, he accepted what had to be done. He had no choice.

Ten minutes later he pulled into the driveway of his house, climbed out of the car and unlocked the front door. The air smelled heavy and still from being closed off for so long. His boots thudded against the wood floor as passed through the hall into his office, flipping lights on as he went.

A quick call to information and he had the phone number he needed. He dialed. Maybe Haley would be there, but deep down he knew this would be the last place she would go. A woman's voice answered midway through the first ring.

"Paige, is Haley there?" Dean asked.

"No. Who is this?" she demanded, but judging from her tone, she already knew.

"Don't hang up."

"I knew it was you."

"I can't reach your sister," he said quickly, before Paige could cut him off.

"What do you mean you can't reach her?" Fear crept into her voice. Good. Why should he be the only one worried sick?

"I've been trying to call her all night and she's not answering."

"Where are you?"

"I'm home, in the city."

"Have you tried the store? Maybe she's working late."

"I started calling around five-thirty and nobody answered."

"She doesn't close until six," Paige said slowly, the hostility disappearing from her voice.

"Look, I would have started back sooner, but I got stuck in a meeting. I need you to go to her place and see if she's okay."

"How do I know you're not trying to set me up?" Paige asked with renewed suspicion.

"What?"

"Sending me over there alone. How do I know you're not just trying to lure me out of the house to kill me?"

First the Lintons and now this. How he didn't pop a blood vessel in his head was a miracle. "Because," he muttered through gritted teeth, "I'm two hours away. Take Garret, take your mom, take the whole God damn police force, but go and see if your sister's all right." Silence greeted him on the other end. Had she hung up? "Paige?"

"I'm here. When are you coming back?"

"As soon as I hang up."

"Fine. I'll meet you at her place."

The line went dead and Dean set the receiver back in the cradle. It rang again almost immediately.

Let it be Haley. "Hello?"

"Just making sure you're where you say you are," Paige said.

"Satisfied?"

"For the moment. Do you have a cell phone?"

"Yeah."

"Give me the number."

Dean did as she asked.

"Good, I'll call you when I get to Haley's."

"Wait." Concern flickered inside him.

"What is it now?"

"Don't go alone. Take someone with you."

She chuckled. "I'll consider it."

She wouldn't, of course. Just like Haley insisted on going to work, and wouldn't let anyone walk her to her car. What the hell was wrong with the women in that family?

Chapter Nineteen

Haley spotted the car in her driveway as soon as she turned onto her street. What now? Exhausted, the last thing she wanted was a visitor. As she drew closer, she could see the make and color of the car. Her heart sank. Paige.

Sighing, she pulled against the curb in front of her house so as not to block the Mustang. She wasn't up to another round with her sister.

As she climbed out of her car, Paige did the same and came to meet her on the sidewalk.

"Where have you been?" Paige asked, a note of hysteria tingeing her voice.

"Why?" Haley frowned. "What are you doing here?"

"When your boyfriend couldn't reach you, he asked me to make sure you were okay."

"My boyfriend?"

"Dean."

"And when I wasn't here you waited?" Haley started up the walk to the front door. "How long have you been here?"

Paige fell into step beside her. "Too long."

Haley unlocked the door, and Paige followed her inside. After flipping on the hall light, Haley shrugged her coat off and tossed it onto the armchair.

"No. You're not staying," Haley said when Paige unzipped her own jacket.

"Yes, I am." Paige smiled sweetly and dropped her coat on top of Haley's. "I'm not leaving until you tell me where you've been. What has our diligent Haley closing the store early this close to Christmas? What could be such a big secret she didn't even tell her precious Dean?"

"You sound like a ten-year-old. And I didn't close the store early."

"Dean tried calling the shop around five-thirty and no one picked up."

"Damn, Allister. I bet he closed early just to spite me."

"Probably. So where were you?"

Haley flopped onto the sofa. Memories of last night flooded her and her cheeks heated. She stood quickly and went into the kitchen before Paige noticed.

"I don't understand what you're even doing here," she muttered as she started to make coffee.

"God, this house is freezing." Paige rubbed her arms briskly. "While your boyfriend was stuck in the city and couldn't get a hold of you, he called me to check on you."

"Well, as you can see, I'm just fine. You can go now."

"Actually, I can't." Paige smiled sweetly. "Dean asked that I stay with you until he gets here. He'd just turned onto 25 so you're stuck with me for at least another twenty minutes. Longer if you don't tell me where you've been and what's going on."

Haley filled the pot with water and poured it into the machine, doing her best to ignore the prick of jealousy, but failing. "Since when do you listen to Dean? What, are you best friends now?"

"He was really worried about you," Paige's dark eyes bored into her, as though she could see inside her. Haley looked away.

"Is it serious between you two?" Paige asked.

"If I say yes, you'll probably to want to make out with him."

"Thanks."

Haley sighed. "I was kidding." Sort of.

"I am sorry about Jason."

Surprised, Haley looked up from the decaffeinated grounds she was spooning into the basket. "Paige apologizing? Is it a full moon?" Haley never believed she'd ever hear those words from Paige.

"I'm serious. I know sorry is kind of inadequate, and I don't have an excuse. He kissed me, caught me off guard, and I was so mad at you that day."

"You were mad at me?"

"If I had to listen to one more person at that funeral talk about poor, sweet Haley, and how much Dad had loved you... Anyway I'm sorry for what I did, and I've regretted kissing him everyday since."

Haley nodded slowly. Paige's words were only slightly less out of character than her almost pleading expression.

"He was a jerk anyway." Haley shrugged and finished with coffee before turning on the machine. "You did me a favor."

"I said the same thing to Garret, and he yelled at me."

Haley smiled and shook her head. "I'm going upstairs to change."

"You still haven't told me where you were," Paige reminded her as she followed. "Why is this house so damn cold? Can't you turn up the heat?"

Haley froze in the middle of the stairs. Paige was right. The house was cold, especially where she stood. An icy draft circled her like an invisible shroud.

"What is it?" Paige asked.

With a quick shake of her head, Haley continued forward. The fear of what she would find when she reached the top dried her mouth and made her heart pound. She flipped the light switch in hall as she came to the last stair. The soft light poured through the open door into her bedroom, across the bare mattress, and dresser. She hadn't used the room since finding the candles. Nothing appeared out of place.

She crept farther down the hall to the guestroom, where she and Dean had slept the night before.

"There's a draft in here," Paige said. "Like you left a window open. Did you?"

Unable to produce sound, Haley shook her head and surveyed the chaotic state of the room. With trembling fingers she reached for the switch. The wall sconce knocked sideways, flickered then shone brightly over the mess.

"My God," Paige murmured beside her.

171

Tiny white feathers from the shredded duvet buried the smashed and broken pieces of furniture like a blanket of snow. A frigid wind rushed through the open window.

Paige pushed past her, stepping over glass from the broken lamp. She bent over the bare mattress and ran her fingers over long gaping tears in the fabric. "Someone slashed your mattress? My God, Haley, what have you and Dean been doing?"

"Someone broke in again," Haley said, her voice dispassionate.

"Obviously, but why?"

"I told you before. I think Dean and I are closer than we realized to Michelle's killer."

Memories of Richard and his parting wink filled her head. Had he done this? Was he her killer? Or Jonathan? Or Lara? Or any one else in Hareton? She didn't have a clue. If these break-ins were scare tactics, they were a wasted effort. She didn't even have an educated guess as to who killed Michelle.

"Haley? Paige?" Dean's voice drifted from downstairs.

"Up here," Paige called.

Haley winced and considered trying to head Dean off. She didn't want him to see this. His protective instincts were already on overload, but she couldn't hide this kind of vandalism.

"What happened?" he demanded.

"Another break in," Haley muttered, tugging her bottom lip with her teeth.

He grabbed her hand and pulled her against him. She pressed her cheek to the solid wall of his chest and closed her eyes when his arms wrapped around her. She should move away. Moments like these were coming too often, and she could easily get used to them. But it had been such a long day.

"So, Lawson, would you like to tell me what you've gotten my sister into?"

Dean lifted his head and Haley stepped out of his embrace, wishing Paige would go home.

"I'd be happy to. Let's call the police first."

"Why bother?" Haley yawned. "They're just going to blame to you again."

"We'll see," Paige muttered.

Dean made a mental note. Should he ever have to deal with the police again, he would have Paige do the talking for him. Her short responses and harsh criticisms had Beckette's young partner stuttering and Beckette agreeing to speak to the neighbors in the morning. Whether he actually would, Dean doubted.

Now that they were gone, she leaned back in the armchair and exhaled a thin blue stream of smoke to co-mingle with the cloud hovering over her head. Dean sneezed twice, went to the front window and slid open the glass. Cigarette smoke had the same effect on him as dust. The allergy being the only reason he hadn't taken up the habit during his misspent youth.

Outside, the night was quiet and still. The flurries he had driven back in had tapered off and the streetlights glittered off the fresh snow. No sign of last night's peeper.

"Is the smoke bothering you?" she asked as he sat down next Haley on the sofa.

"I'll be fine."

"It's bothering me," Haley said.

"Tough." Paige leaned back and put her feet on the corner of the trunk, crossing her legs at the ankles and carefully balancing the blue china saucer she was using as an ashtray on her lap. "I did an excellent job handling the police for you. The least you can do is not force me to smoke outside in the elements."

Dean slid his arm around Haley's shoulder and drew her against his side, relishing the feel of her soft warmth. He'd never known fear like he had on the drive to Hareton. What would he have done if she'd vanished, knowing that he had been the catalyst? Bad enough, he'd been responsible for her break-ins.

"So, Haley." Paige ground the cigarette butt in the makeshift ashtray. "Where were you tonight?"

Dean shifted so he could see Haley's face. She quirked a brow and glared at her sister. "It's not a secret. I went to visit Jonathan Williams at his mill."

He sat up. "Why?"

"We did want to know what had been going on in Michelle's life before she disappeared. He was the last person to see her alive and he seemed an obvious choice."

"You could have waited for me. What did he say?"

Haley relayed her meeting with Jonathan, but nothing she said came as a shock. "I also saw Richard while I was there. We might want to add him to our list of suspects.

"Why?" Paige asked

Haley shrugged. "He tried to intimidate me."

Dean tensed. "What did he do?"

"He was a jerk, but it's not a big deal. I will tell you this, though, right before I left he turned and winked at me, it was the creepiest thing. He could easily be our peeper."

Richard. Dean had never considered him. He could have influenced Lara, but why would he have killed Michelle?

"Okay," Paige said, leaning forward. "You two are talking in code. Let me get this straight. You don't think our father did it anymore?"

Dean hesitated. "Let's just say that I agree there are other avenues worth investigating."

Paige nodded and turned to Haley. "And you don't think it was Dean."

"No," Haley said. "I don't."

"Well, I've spoken to the detective," Paige said. "And while town gossip is pointing a finger at Dean right now—your break-in the obvious proof apparently—the police are after Dad."

Haley paled nodded. "What did they say?"

"Not a lot. Faron asked me about a million questions. I would have liked to have done better, but the whole thing happened so long ago, some things I just couldn't remember."

"He hasn't contacted me yet," Haley said.

"He will. He's talked to Garret and Mom."

Haley rubbed her eyes with her fingertips, her body rigid. Dean wanted to ease things for her, but didn't know how.

"How was she?" Haley asked.

"Pretty drunk," Paige admitted. "I kind of hoped she

wouldn't be coherent enough to understand the detective. That his questions wouldn't sink in."

"But they did?"

"She was furious and afraid. She didn't know about Dad's first wife, either."

"Maybe she just forgot. Drinking the way she does, she forgets things all the time."

"Haley, I am telling you she had no idea. When Faron told her, I thought she was going to physically attack him."

"Dad couldn't have done it. Why would someone go through all the trouble of breaking into my house twice and Dean's hotel room?"

"To keep me looking guilty and to protect your father's memory," Dean said.

"Who would do that?" Haley snapped. "The only people who my father's memory matters to are my family. And none of us would let you take the blame if we believed you were innocent."

"She has a point," Paige interjected.

"Who are you kidding?" He understood the desire to believe in her father's innocence, but she was letting emotion cloud her judgment. "Until now, Paige thought I was guilty, and she's probably still not convinced."

"Ooh, now he has a point."

Haley rolled her eyes. "Thank you, you've been very helpful."

"Well, you both make a good argument. Besides, I don't really see what either of you have done that would make a murderer feel threatened."

Haley sighed. She wished Paige would go home so she could climb into bed. Then she remembered the state of her guestroom. Looked like the couch tonight.

"We've been to see Rhonda Kearney, the woman who bought Nan's house, and Sandra Gallagher who was at the house when they found Michelle's body."

"You've been busy. What did they tell you?"

Haley shrugged and repeated Brian's ghost story. As she spoke, the color drained from Paige's cheeks.

"What is it?" Haley asked.

"Do you believe anything they said?" Paige asked, her voice hoarse. Her hand trembled as she lit another cigarette.

"Do you?"

With a harsh exhale Paige shrugged. "No."

"You're lying." Haley's heart rated quickened. "Tell me what happened."

"Nothing."

"Would you tell me if I told you something strange happened to me?"

Paige leaned forward. "What happened to you?"

"You first."

"You'll think I'm crazy."

"No crazier than I am."

Paige drew hard on the cigarette. "When I was coming back two nights ago I saw her, Michelle, on 25."

Haley's insides tightened and turned cold. "What do you mean?"

"Just what I said. I passed the same person on the highway twice. The second time I stopped. When I looked out the window, Michelle was looking in at me. I dropped my cigarette and when I looked up again she was gone. I got out of the car to look, and there was no trace of her. Not even footprints in the snow. I thought I had lost my mind. Now you."

"I dreamed about her."

"That's not strange," Paige snapped.

Haley swallowed hard. "Let me finish. In the dream she said 'He used to send me flowers' and when I asked Sandra if the girl they picked up said anything, she told me Michelle had said the same thing. 'He used to send me flowers.' How could she have known what I'd dreamed?"

"You didn't tell me that," Dean said.

For a moment Haley had nearly forgotten he was there. Heat climbed into her cheeks. "I thought I might be going crazy and wasn't real eager to share."

"So do you believe our sister is a ghost, haunting the highway into town?" Paige asked.

"I don't know," Haley admitted with a shrug. "But it's so strange."

Paige nodded. "But why now? Why would she start appearing now after all these years?"

"She wanted to be found," Dean said. "At least that's what it seems like. She appeared to Sandra, and she found the skeleton. She's appearing to you and Paige, so what does she want from both of you?"

"I don't know," Haley whispered.

Paige stubbed out the cigarette. "Me either, but I do know I'm tired and I want to go to bed. I'll worry about this tomorrow with a clear head."

"That's probably a good idea," Haley agreed, barely stifling another yawn.

Paige stood and pulled on her jacket as Haley and Dean walked her to the door.

"You're leaving me with your sister alone?" Dean asked, in mock horror.

"Yes, I am," Paige said. "If anything happens to her, I'll blame you, and there will be no where in this world you can hide from me."

"Gotcha." A slow smile curved his lips.

"I'll come by the store tomorrow and we can talk about this some more."

"Yeah, okay," Haley said, opening the door. "I've got a customer coming in first thing..." The words died on her lips and her stomach leapt into her throat. A tissue wrapped bundle lay in the center of the porch.

Paige knelt and scooped them up. "Roses. Here's the card."

Haley took the small square envelope and removed the tiny white square, the words "I'm Sorry" printed neatly.

"Maybe whoever had been sending Michelle flowers killed her, and maybe that same person is sending you flowers," Paige said, her lips curled in disgust.

"Our peeper was back at the window," Dean said. "Those prints are new."

Haley clutched the roses. How could someone have been right there and she not notice? Sick dread turned her insides cold. "Call me as soon as you get home. And make sure the doors and windows are all locked, okay?"

Paige nodded. "I will, but I'm more worried about you."

"I'll be okay."

Haley stayed where she was until Paige drove out of sight. With a gentle tug on her arm, Dean pulled her back inside, closed the door and turned the bolt.

"I have to throw these out." She held the roses away from her as if they were contaminated.

"I'll do it." Dean took the bundle and disappeared into the kitchen.

With a trembling sigh, Haley leaned back against the closed door. Tired as she was, sleep would be a long time coming.

Chapter Twenty

Haley squinted against the bright shaft of sunlight, stretching from the gap in the drapes, over the floor and up the side of her bed. Closing her eyes, she snuggled against Dean. His lean, hard body curved around her, his arm tight around her middle.

Last night, after throwing fresh sheets and coverings on the bed, they had made love into the early morning hours. She'd drawn comfort from his strong hands and gentle kisses. And even then, craving the security he wrapped around her like blanket, she had known accepting what he offered was a mistake. Soon he would be gone, and she would be on her own again.

With that dismal thought, she opened her eyes. Time to get up. So much light spilling into the room meant she had slept too long as it was.

Carefully, she eased away from Dean, trying to lift his arm without disturbing him. His grip on her waist tightened and his lips pressed against the back of her neck just below her ear. She shivered.

"Don't go," he murmured his breath hot against her skin.

"I have to. I'm already late." Her voice trembled a little when she spoke and her resolve slipped as his fingertips moved feather soft over the curve of her hip. His hand trailed down her thigh then back up, lightly skimming the gentle dip of her waist. Goose bumps formed beneath his touch as he brushed over her ribs and cupped her breast, rolling the taut nipple between his thumb and forefinger. Tiny jolts rippled through her system.

Still, she fought for responsibility. "I'm meeting a customer this morning."

"Please." His voice was rough and pleading. His teeth scraped her neck, and his erection, hot and hard, pressed against her buttocks. "Just a little longer."

A slow ache pounded inside her. She wanted so much from him, and what she felt terrified her.

His hand splayed her belly, sliding lower until he cupped her, his finger slipping inside.

"Dean." Pleasure, fierce and overwhelming, streaked through her. Her hips rocked forward into his hand, as if of their own accord, driving his probing fingers deeper and bringing her to the thin edge of her control. His free hand eased beneath her side, cupping and kneading her swollen breasts.

Desperate for more of him, she reached her arms back. Her fingers tangled in his hair, gripping tightly as if to keep from being swept away by the torrent of sensation raging inside her.

She cried out as the first orgasm exploded inside her, like an invisible land mine, sending hot shards of shrapnel spiraling through her shuddering body. And still his hands and mouth drove her on.

"I want all of you," he said, his voice a harsh whisper. His beard-roughened jaw scraped the soft skin on her shoulder.

Even that tiny sensation sent her already jangled nerve endings into overdrive. With aftershocks of her orgasm still surging through her, her greedy body sought more. Her hips moved to the pace Dean set instinctively. She arched back giving him better access to her heavy breasts, and her heart seemed to swell in her chest from the fierce emotions assailing her.

"All of you," he said again, nudging her legs apart with his knee.

"I can't," she half-moaned half-panted.

He lifted her leg high with his. She heard the crinkle of the condom wrapper then the blunt end of his penis pressed against her sex.

"You can," he ground out and drove inside her, filling her.

White-hot need coiled low in her belly, growing tighter with his every thrust. His fingers continued to manipulate the soft folds of her flesh, and with her leg over his she had no choice but to follow his hard, furious pace. Each deep plunge sent her soaring higher and higher. She cried out as her orgasm burst and swept through her, fierce and fast like a flash flood, leaving her clinging to him.

With a final thrust, Dean gripped her hips and pulled her tight against him. His ragged gasp filled her ear as he came in his own shuddering release.

For a moment, Haley stayed as she was, her leg draped over Dean's and her fingers gripping his hair. Oh, God. What had just happened? She'd had sex before, and she'd come before. But nothing like this. Nothing so powerful and all-consuming. Her heart thudded against her chest and her skin tingled where he had touched her.

Dean shifted and rolled her gently onto her back. His face hovered over hers, his smoky gray-green eyes bright with emotion. Her throat tightened and she was filled with an almost terrifying need. When he opened his mouth to speak, she drew his head down pressing her lips to his and keeping him from saying something neither of them could live up to.

"Good morning." He lifted his head, a half-smirk playing at the corners of his mouth. "I'm sorry if I made you late."

"No, you're not." She ran her hand over his smooth chest. She might never get enough of touching him. "But then, neither am I."

"Why don't we forget everything else and stay like this for the rest of the day?" His smirk widened as his hand gently smoothed her hair away from her face.

The idea was tempting. Too tempting. "I can't," she groaned and wriggled out from under him. "I need to take a shower and get to work."

Dean watched her cross the room naked, his appreciative gaze running up and down her small, lithe form. Her hair fell just past her shoulders, curling slightly inward over the swell of her breasts. She pulled on her robe, covering her nakedness.

After she slipped from the room, he fell back against the tangled blankets, the memory of her body moving with his still fresh in his mind. And her eyes, dark and swirling, looking up at him afterward. He could have drowned in them, drowned in her.

The feelings he had for her were growing and becoming more complex by the moment. Eventually, he would have to go home to the life he'd built, and she would stay here, in the life she lived.

He got up, discarded the condom and cleaned himself up, then yanked on his jeans and sweater from the night before, thoughts of the future too grim to dwell on for long.

Once downstairs, he started the coffee and waited for it to brew. He'd left his computer in the backseat of the car last night in his rush to make sure Haley had been okay. He hoped it was still there.

He made his way down the hall, shoved his bare feet into his boots and stepped outside. The sun glared from the cloudless blue sky off the stark, blindingly white snow. The frigid wind lashed cruelly at the bare skin of his face and hands, blowing through his clothes as if he wore nothing at all.

He jogged to his car parked on the opposite side of the road from Haley's house. With his head bent against the wind, he turned his key in the lock. The black bag sat on the floor, wedged between the front and backseat, just where he'd left it. Thank God, half his life was on that thing. He'd been pretty stupid to forget it outside, but then lately his mind wasn't where it should be.

He grabbed it from the back seat, slung the strap over his shoulder then slammed the door shut. As he started back to the house, something caught his eye.

Slight impressions half-buried in the snow and running up the side of Haley's house. Dean walked along the shoveled sidewalk. Footprints, he realized as he grew closer, partially hidden by yesterday's flurries.

The snow glittered under the sun's brilliant glare and small clouds of powder, like curls of smoke, twisted and danced in the wind. Leaving the sidewalk, he stepped into the footprints to keep from sinking in the deep snow as he followed them to the door off Haley's kitchen. He tried the knob, but it wouldn't turn. Locked.

Tiny rivulets of snow spilled into his unlaced boots, freezing his bare feet. He squatted to inspect the lock. This had to be how the intruder was entering Haley's house, but from where he stood, there was no evidence the lock had been tampered with.

The door swung inward, making him jump.

"What are you doing?" Haley asked.

He didn't answer right away. Again he looked closely at the lock, moving inside and kneeling on the kitchen floor to study both sides. He ran his finger over the smooth metal. No sign of scoring, or anything else that would have forced the mechanism.

"Damn my feet are freezing," he muttered, stepping out of his boots and closing the door. He set his computer on the floor beside him.

"What were you doing out there?" Haley asked, frowning.

"When I went to get my stuff from the car, I saw footprints in the snow next to the house."

Her face paled. "What does that mean?"

"I don't know for sure, but if I were to guess, I think whoever is getting into your house is using this door."

"Not good."

Oh, it gets worse. "And unless your intruder is an expert lock picker, he has a key."

"This is too much," she said, folding her arms over her chest. He moved to pull her to him, but she stepped away. A tiny ripple of fear stirred inside him, but he ignored it.

"So whoever is doing this is someone I know."

"You can't be certain of that."

"How else would he be getting in here? My mother and brother are the only other people who have a key to my house."

"You're renting, right? Your landlord would have a copy. And I bet the locks in this place haven't been changed in years. Previous tenants could still have keys. Just because someone is unlocking and locking this door doesn't mean it's someone you know."

Haley nodded slowly. He wanted to touch her, sooth her, but he was afraid she would move away from him again.

"While you're at work I'll pick up new locks and install them. Until we've got this mess figured out, don't give a copy of the new key to anyone."

She nodded. "I'll give you some money."

He wanted to shake her, tell her to forget the money, but he didn't. She was trying to put distance between them, and maybe that was best. Even if the idea scraped him raw.

"Don't worry about that now. Wait until I'm done."

"Thanks. I've got to get going. I'm really late."

He nodded. She pulled on her jacket and slipped out the front door. A heaviness settled over him. He didn't want to leave her, but he knew he would. And so did she.

Haley parked next to Al's car in the alley behind the store and did her best to ignore the sick feeling sitting in the pit of her stomach. She didn't care what Dean said, someone she knew had been breaking into her house, peering into her windows and vandalizing her bedrooms.

As if having her sister's killer stalking her wasn't bad enough, she'd hopelessly complicated her life by falling in love with a man she couldn't have. And it was love. No matter how she tried to convince herself that everything she felt was simply the result of really good sex, even she wasn't buying it anymore.

What had she been thinking, letting this happen? She had been relying on him too much, depending on him. That had been her mistake. She knew better than to rely on anyone else. It left her open to disappointment. Once inside, she'd call Dean and tell him not to bother with the locks, she'd pick them up herself.

She climbed out of the car and hurried to the back door. She was nearly forty-five minutes late. Al had made it in before her for once. Maybe he'd already taken care of the Burlands. Not likely. As she had driven down Main, she noticed the closed sign still in the window and the lights off in the store.

God forbid Allister show a little initiative. Do something without being told. She yanked on the door, toppling a small drift of snow at the base.

Inside, the room was dark. "Christ Al," she muttered, turning to the alarm then remembering Al would have at least already entered the code. "What are you doing sitting in the dark..."

The words died on her lips. Something permeated the air stronger than the combined chemical odor of solvents and stains. A stink like rancid meat.

No more.

The words screamed in her head, but she flipped on the lights anyway. Her stomach rolled and the spit in her mouth dried instantly. She might have screamed, except her voice had vanished.

Al lay in a dark, red puddle in the middle of the floor. At least she assumed the body, beneath the clotted mess of flesh, bone and hair was Al. He wore the same clothes Al had been wearing when she left last night.

OhGodohGodohGod!

The sound of her pounding heart filled her ears with a rush as the blood drained from her face and cool sweat slicked her skin. She scrambled into the bathroom, emptying her meager stomach contents into the toilet.

Once the waves of dry heaves passed, she pushed herself up, trembling. Her cheeks damp with silent tears.

What next? What do you do when you find a dead man in your shop? The police. She would call the police.

Wiping her face, she forced her feet to move and stumbled out of the bathroom. Careful to keep her toes from disturbing the wide puddle, she edged around the corpse and slipped through the door into the store.

With the mutilated body out of sight, she let out a trembling breath. That couldn't be Al, not that poor, battered creature. It had to be a fake. Not real, just something to scare her. But the thick, meaty smell, hanging heavy in the air killed any hope of falling for her own explanations.

Her hand shook as she lifted the phone to her ear and called the police. How could any of this be happening? How could everything have turned so badly so quickly?

Chapter Twenty-One

Dean waited as the gray Lincoln pulled out from the gap in the wall of pine trees edging the highway. As soon as Lara's car turned onto the strip of road, he followed, hanging back so she wouldn't notice. Even with a car or two between them, keeping track of Lara was easy. While dirty brown and white stains from the snow and salt covered most vehicles, Lara's gleamed spotlessly in the hard winter light.

She led him to the shopping mall well away from Hareton's downtown and he managed to find a parking space not far from hers. As she walked toward the main entrance, Dean fell into step beside her.

"Stalking me now?" Lara asked, walking a little faster. "What will people say?"

Dean did his best to clamp down on his growing anger. "Don't flatter yourself. We need to talk. Let's find somewhere to sit down."

"I thought when I didn't return any of your phone calls, you'd get the hint. I'm not interested in talking to you."

"Let me make something perfectly clear." He grabbed her arm and stopped her in her tracks. "I don't give a shit what you're interested in. I want answers, now."

"I'll scream."

"No, you won't. You don't want to do anything that would lead your darling husband to think you're still talking to me."

The color in her cheeks rose. "What do you want to know?"

"There's a restaurant over there." He pointed to the diner on the far side of the lot. "I'll buy you breakfast."

"I've eaten."

"Well, then a coffee at the very least."

"I don't want to be seen with you."

He bared his teeth a little and gripped her elbow, pulling her across the parking lot. "Then you shouldn't have lied to me in the first place."

Inside the diner, the pungent aromas of bacon grease and disinfectant tickled his nostrils and, combined with the Christmas carols blaring out the speakers over the counter, aggravated the steady throb behind his eyes. He and Lara found a booth at the back of the restaurant, away from prying eyes and big ears. Although none of the morning crowd gave them a second look, and for that, at least, Dean was grateful.

After ordering coffee from a gum-snapping waitress who couldn't be more than sixteen, Lara leaned forward and glared. "I'm here. What do you want know?"

"Who told you not to help me?"

She gave him a coy smile. "A friend."

"Cut it out, Lara. People's lives are involved. Someone has been breaking into Haley's house and watching her. If something happens to her because of your stupid games..." He didn't finish the sentence.

"First Michelle, now Haley. What is it about the women in that family? Are you hoping to marry up?"

"No, Lara, that's your thing."

Her eyes narrowed and she lowered her voice to a furious whisper. "What do you know about it? Who are you to judge me? You don't know what I come from."

"You grew up two doors down from me." Dean rolled his eyes. "Our lives were remarkably similar."

"Not even close. You're mother didn't bring home a string of men. Didn't let them use her and hit you."

"Is that why you married him?" Dean asked. Sympathy he didn't want to feel touched him. "So you wouldn't end up like your mother."

"None of your fucking business." She started to stand, but he put his hand over hers and held her in place.

"We're not done here. Who told you not to help me?"

Her eyes bored into his. "Jonathan."

"Why? What does he care?"

She shrugged.

"Haley went to see him yesterday."

"Really?" She looked about the diner, pretending disinterest.

"Really. He implied that he still believes that Michelle and I were seeing each other while he was dating her. But here's what I don't get; when you know that isn't true, and he's keeping you from admitting what you know, why would he still claim that Michelle and I were together?"

"How should I know?"

"He was also very angry when Haley suggested his housekeeper might be lying for him. Did he go after Michelle that night?"

"You'll have to ask him."

"Maybe I will. I'll swing by the mill and tell him you sent me."

"Do you think you can scare me?"

"Yes. What about Richard?"

Her eyes went wide. "How do you know about him?"

"Haley had a run-in with him yesterday too. He said some rather unflattering things about Michelle."

"He's very jealous of Jonathan."

"Could he have killed Michelle?"

"I don't know."

"God damn it, Lara, give me something."

"I don't know anything, I truly don't. I don't know why Jonathan won't let me come forward for you. He knows you and Michelle weren't together then."

"So somehow it benefits him if I look guilty. Takes the spotlight off him? Do you think he killed Michelle?"

"I don't know. Really, Dean, I don't."

He sighed and threw a couple of dollars on the table before standing. "All right, I give up." What a waste of time, at least he could pick up Haley's new locks at the hardware store in the mall.

"Dean."

Lara glanced around her as if to make sure no one was listening. Her gaze met his and she lowered her voice. He had to lean in closer to hear.

"Erin didn't want me to speak up for you either."

"Erin Johnson—I mean Carling?" he corrected automatically.

She nodded. "Erin also helped spread the rumor about you. She was always jealous of Michelle."

"Erin?" He asked again, still not really believing what he was hearing. "Nate's daughter? Garret's wife?"

"Yes, but don't tell her I told you." She slid out of the booth. "I'm leaving now and I don't want to be seen leaving with you."

Dean rolled his eyes, only half listening. "Whatever, go. I'll count to twenty before I leave." Erin? Would she have killed Michelle? He hardly knew her.

For Carling's kids, the shop had been a second home, but Erin rarely came by to see her father. And, except for the few months he and Michelle had dated, Dean and Erin had traveled in very different social circles.

Dean had run into her at a party once. He had only gone because Michelle had nagged him. Garret hadn't been there and Erin had had too much to drink. She'd said something about Michelle slumming it with Dean, and kept calling him Michelle's boy toy all night. More embarrassed for her than annoyed, he'd chalked the whole incident up to far too much alcohol. Maybe Lara was right. Looking back, he hadn't been Erin's target at all. Michelle had been.

Erin could easily break into Haley's home. Haley herself said that Garret had a key, giving Erin plenty of access.

When he left the diner, Lara was long gone. He walked over to the hardware store. He'd get Haley her new locks and when she got home from work, he'd find out what she knew about Erin and her relationship with Michelle.

Haley was already home when he got back. She was sitting

on the couch, pale and shaken, her arms wrapped around herself as if she were freezing, her eyes wide and haunted. Paige sat in the armchair across from her. Just as pale and just as shaken. Fear clutched him in its boney grasp.

"It's only one o'clock, why are you home? What happened?"

Haley's eyes met his and she swallowed hard. "Al's dead."

A strange, sinking sensation enveloped him. He set down the plastic bags he was carrying onto the floor. "How?"

"Bludgeoned I believe is the term." Her voice was hoarse and low. She ran a trembling hand through her hair. "No one would say for sure, but his head looked crushed. I thought I could see bone."

"You saw him?"

Haley met his gaze, her eyes glassy with unshed tears. "I found him."

"My God, why didn't you call me?" He started to move toward her, but she stood and backed away.

"I overheard someone say that it probably happened last night. I guess when we thought he'd closed early, he was actually being murdered."

Her voice rose and she spoke too quickly. He wanted to do something to take that terrifying edge from her tone, but he was afraid to move closer. Afraid she would shatter if he tried to touch her.

"I was worried about Billy, but the police said he was okay. Al let him go early. Do you think that had he worked until his shift ended he would have been killed too, or do you think that Al letting him go early left Al vulnerable? I keep wondering about that."

Her voice hitched and Dean moved toward her again, but she held her hand out to him, palm open. "No. Don't." She swallowed. "I'll be fine. I just need a minute by myself."

She turned her back to him and went into the kitchen. When he would have followed Paige blocked him with her leg. He looked down at her and she shook her head. "She doesn't like for anyone to see her cry. She never has, even as a kid."

"Did she call you?" Dean asked, trying not to feel hurt.

Paige scowled and shook her head. "Yeah, right. God forbid

she call anyone. Remember I said I would swing by the store?"

He nodded.

"When I get there, the police are all over the place and there's Haley answering their questions. She didn't call me, or you, or Garret, or anyone else."

Al dead, left for Haley to find. "I did this," he muttered. "I brought all of this on. To Al and Haley."

"Don't kid yourself. If this is Michelle's killer we're dealing with, this has been coming for awhile."

Dean didn't buy it. He'd wanted to clear his name and from the first moment Haley talked to him things started to happen. If someone hurt her... Not an option. From now on he was her shadow. Wherever she went, he would be there. Whether she liked it or not.

"Okay," Haley said, wiping her damp cheeks with the heels of her hands. "I'm better now."

Her voice still shook, but that wild edge had gone.

"I want to get this bastard." Haley looked at Paige. "Whoever did this has taken so much from us and he keeps taking more. I want him to pay."

"So let's get him," Paige agreed.

"Al is dead," Dean snapped. Couldn't they see what was happening around them? "Haley has someone coming and going from her house, vandalizing her bedrooms, spying on her through her windows. No more. Let the police do their jobs. Paige go home and Haley come back to the city with me."

"Come on, Lawson," Paige said, narrowing her eyes. "Don't wimp out on us now."

Dean locked his gaze with Haley's. "I don't want anything to happen to you. Either of you."

"He took my sister and destroyed my family in a single blow. He took things from me and Paige that we'll never even know. And he took from you. Hell, you came here to clear your name. Don't you want justice?"

"Not at the expense of your life, Haley."

Paige stood up between them. "Let's do this. Why don't we sum up all that we know and if we feel like we're getting somewhere we'll go to the police."

"Fine." Dean sighed. "I can live with that."

Haley nodded.

"Okay, then. I'll need a pen and paper," Paige said.

"Why?" Haley asked. "Will there be a quiz after?"

"You must be feeling better."

"In the kitchen."

Paige stood and left the room. Once she had gone, Dean reached for Haley's hand. She took it and gripped hard.

"I'm sorry I yelled at you," he said on a sigh, the fear and fury still too fresh to make his apology more gracious. "But I can't stand the idea of something happening to you."

"I know." She squeezed his hand and drew in a sniffling breath. "Don't look at me like that or you'll set me off again."

Haley tried to swallow the tight ache in her throat as Dean released her hand. Exhausted, she would have liked nothing better than to crawl into bed, preferably with Dean. His body curved around her like it had been that morning. No. She had to remember her resolution to take care of herself, and if meant nailing the bastard who killed Al, that's what she would do.

"Okay," Paige said, returning with a pen and paper in hand. She dropped onto the armchair, crossed her leg and balanced the notepad on her thigh. "So, where do we start?"

"I spoke to Lara," Dean said.

Haley turned sharply. "When?"

"This morning." A faint smile touched his mouth as if he had a private joke that no one else in the room knew. "I ran into her at the mall."

"And what did she tell you?" Paige asked.

"Jonathan told her not to admit anything for me, but she doesn't know why."

Haley frowned. Her head felt muddled and slow to work things out. "That would mean everything he told me wasn't true."

"Surprise, surprise," Paige muttered.

"So we're back to square one." Haley flopped back onto the couch and Dean sat down next to her.

"Not quite," Dean said. "She also told me Erin didn't want

her to come forward and that Erin had helped to spread the rumor."

"No way. Erin and Michelle were friends." Erin couldn't know anything. "She's married to Garret for crying out loud."

Dean shrugged. "Lara said Erin was jealous of Michelle."

"I told you Erin was a big fake," Paige said. "And she was jealous of Michelle. Every time Michelle left the room, Erin would make a dig."

"Do you really think Erin could have killed Michelle and then married Garret?" Haley asked, not buying it for second.

"Yes."

"She had access to everything," Dean pointed out. "The delivery van, the store, your father's coveralls. She knew your grandmother's house would be empty and her father was helping with the upkeep."

"Why have we never considered Nate?" Paige asked.

"This is a serious attempt to find our sister's killer, not Paige's private witch hunt."

"I'm being serious. He had access to all the things Erin did, and the strength to carry a body down to the basement."

"That's a good point, he also knew your father's first wife. Still, he had no motive for killing Michelle," Dean said. "And we haven't ruled out Jonathan and Richard yet."

Haley sat up. "Yes we have. I was with both of them at the time Al was murdered." A shudder rippled up her spine as the image of his shattered skull popped into her head. As if sensing her thoughts, Dean absently rubbed her back.

"He's hiding something or covering up," Dean said. "He lied to you, and me looking guilty benefits him somehow. Now, you saw Richard when you were leaving. Could he have killed Al and then returned to the mill in time to catch you before you left?"

"That's a possibility," Haley said. She really could imagine Richard as a murderer. "But how would he have got a hold of my father's coveralls and hidden them in the shop?"

"Anything's possible, if you want it bad enough."

"Maybe whoever killed her had planned to frame Dad, and when Dean wound up being accused he or she never needed to," Paige said.

Haley threw up her hands. "That's possible too. My God, all we've done is establish that anyone and everyone we know could have killed Michelle. We're getting nowhere. We need to know what was happening in her life right before she was murdered. Lara won't tell us anything, neither will Jonathan, and now we're considering Erin a suspect."

"There is one way to find out," Paige said, leaning forward and lowering her voice. "Her bedroom. Nothing's been touched since she went missing."

Haley went cold at the thought. No, nothing had been moved since Michelle disappeared, and Haley didn't want to be the one to do it now.

Chapter Twenty-Two

"The police already searched her room and they didn't find anything," Haley said. The idea of crossing the threshold into *The Shrine* had about as much appeal as spending some one on one time with Richard.

"But they had been looking for something to connect Dean. We might find something that they missed," Paige said. "It's the only way I can think of to get inside Michelle's head."

"That's not a bad idea," Dean said.

The idea was a good one, unfortunately. Haley wished to God there was another way. "Mom will go crazy if she sees us."

Paige glanced at her watch. "It's almost four-thirty, she's probably passed out by now."

Haley sighed. "Fine, we'll try it."

As she stood so did Dean.

"You can't come," she told him.

"No, you definitely can't," Paige agreed. "That would be incredibly bad."

"After what happened to Al, I don't want you going anywhere alone."

"My mother will go ballistic if she sees you. Besides, I'll be with Paige."

He opened his mouth as if to argue then closed it again, turning instead to one of the bags he'd left on the floor. He bent, pulled out a box and handed it to her.

"What's this?" she asked.

"It's a cell phone." Paige spoke slowly, over enunciating

each word. "It's kind of like a normal phone, but you can use it anywhere."

Haley ignored her. "I don't need you to buy me a cell phone."

"With that pile of junk in the driveway you're practically the poster girl for cell phones," Paige chimed in again.

Dean continued to hold out the phone. "Just humor me."

"If I wanted a cell phone, I would have bought one." She didn't need him or anyone else to take care of her.

"I know that."

"Good." She turned away from him and his phone. "Let's go, Paige."

"I'll call you when she leaves," Paige murmured.

"Thanks," Dean said.

Did they think she was a child to be cared for between the two of them? "I'm not five years old. I can take care of myself."

"You're being stalked," Dean said, bluntly. "One of your employees was murdered. Take the damn phone."

"How do you know I'm the one being stalked? Your hotel room was broken into. Any time we've found evidence that someone had been watching me, you've been with me. Just because you're male doesn't make you exempt. Al was a man and someone murdered him. You don't get to keep tabs on me because you think I'm weak and helpless."

"First of all, I don't think that. Second, if you want to keep tabs on me feel free. Call me on my cell phone anytime you want. Use this one." He shoved the phone at her.

Haley turned abruptly and stormed out of the house. She didn't care if Paige followed or stayed behind, making plans with Dean for her poor little sister.

What a joke. Dean takes off for more than a decade, Paige hadn't been back in four years, and yet they hovered over her like doting parents. How do they think she managed before they came back?

Or would again once they left?

As Haley and Paige slipped into the kitchen, muted voices from the TV mingled with her mother's dry snores. And Haley's last hope that this crazy search would have to be called off died.

Resigned, she followed Paige upstairs, but stopped as if by an invisible barrier just outside Michelle's door. Paige flipped the wall switch and flooded the room with soft light. A nervous flutter danced in the pit of Haley's belly as she took her first step into the mass of pale pink ruffles and frills.

The room, silent and untouched, seemed to close in around her, and a sense of intrusion nearly sent her running back into the hall. Was this what archeologists felt when entering a tomb to dig up the secrets of the dead?

Haley crept closer to the big white dresser and the aged photos jammed into the wood frame of the mirror. Faded and yellowed, images of Erin, Lara, Jonathan and Michelle's other friends smiled back at her, all younger than Haley was now.

"Hurry up." Paige's harsh whisper made her jump.

Haley nodded. "Watch for Mom."

"Fine. Just be quick." Paige shifted from one foot to the other like a toddler in need of the bathroom. "If Mom catches us..."

"I know, I know." Still she hesitated. Years of living with The Shrine had been ingrained on her. Don't touch! The words practically glowed like neon inside her head.

With a final deep breath, she squared her shoulders and dived in. She opened the first dresser drawer, dug through a pile of neatly folded sweaters, trying to disturb as little as possible.

Nothing in the first drawer. Not that she really knew what she was looking for. Some kind of diary or journal would have been ideal. Better still, if she could find an entry that read, "I've been feeling threatened by..." or "I think so-and-so wants to kill me." But life was never that easy.

She moved on to the second drawer then the third. Who were they kidding? She wasn't going to find anything. If there was something here, the police would have already discovered it.

From the doorway, Paige glanced over her shoulder and drummed her fingertips on the frame. The rhythmless noise went through Haley, making her grind her teeth.

"Cut it out," she snapped.

Paige folded her arms over her chest. "This is going to take all night."

"I'm working as fast as I can." She moved to another drawer. How many pink sweaters could one person own?

Paige sighed and left the door, moving into the closet on the far side of the room.

"What are you doing?"

"This is taking too long. She's going to wake up soon. I haven't fed her since this morning."

"You make her sound like a pet." Oh God, Michelle's underwear drawer. There had to be something sacrilegious about routing through her dead sister's delicates.

"She ties you down like one," Paige said over the din of wire hangers scraping the metal rod. "Only without the loyalty and affection."

Haley sighed. "Do you think we could get through one task without arguing?"

"I'm not arguing, I'm simply stating fact. Taking care of a rabid pit bull would be more rewarding than looking after her."

"She's our mother."

"Then she should act like it."

Haley closed her eyes and counted to ten. She could do this. She could spend a few hours with her only living sister and not be drawn into a fight. Of course, if said sister were not so damn provoking that would make her resolution a little easier to live up to. "She has a disease, Paige."

"A disease you enable."

Screw resolutions! "You waltz in here after four years without so much as a phone call and lecture me like you suddenly have all this insight. What? Have you been watching Dr. Phil in your time off?"

Paige poked her head out of the closet. "Why didn't you take the phone?"

Just like Paige to change the subject when she might lose the argument. "Because I'm a grown woman and I can buy my own damn phone."

"You're going to blow it with him."

"Was that not you, standing in my house two days ago ranting about my taste in men?"

"I was mistaken. He's a decent guy, he's hot and, for some reason I've yet to figure out, he actually likes you."

Something tight and bitter gripped her heart. "We have our own lives. Whatever this is between us is just for now."

"He has his own life. You're living Mom and Dad's."

"You have been watching Dr. Phil." Haley stood and rubbed her eyes with her thumb and forefinger. Why couldn't Paige shut up? Things were complicated enough. "What would you have me do? Leave, like you did?"

"Yup." Paige stepped toward her. "What that woman is doing to herself is not my problem. Or yours."

"How can you say that? She's your mother."

"Yes, she is, but she makes her choices and I will not have my life dictated by them. And neither should you. It wasn't fair for Dad to expect you to take care of Mom like a nursemaid, or for Garret to ask you to do it now. And it wasn't fair for Dad to have you running that store while he was out playing detective."

A lump formed in Haley's throat. A knot of anger, hurt and resentment all tangled together. "He wanted to find Michelle. He never stopped believing she was alive."

"Bullshit. He knew deep down, just like we all did. Maybe he didn't want to believe it, but he pissed away all their money and your future. You should be mad as hell."

"You don't understand." Haley turned back the dresser, yanking open the last drawer. "You were gone. It was different living here. Somehow finding Michelle alive seemed possible."

"I don't believe you. He may have hoped, you may have hoped, but after every year, he had to sense that she was never coming back. That she had died."

Haley shook her head, clinging to her denials.

"Come on. When you got the call, telling you they found her body, were you at all surprised she was dead? Or weren't you kind of expecting that?"

"Let's just finish this," Haley muttered, her fingers sliding between pairs of folded blue jeans. "It's been a long day and I'm tired."

"Fine, but when you get home, take the phone." Paige disappeared into the closet once more.

Haley turned and stuck her tongue out as she closed the drawer. She knelt next to the bed, lifting the frilled skirt. Nothing. Not a box, not a book, not even a stray sock.

Who didn't have something under their bed? Even now, Haley was certain if she checked under her bed, she would find a couple of battered paperbacks, maybe a shoe or two.

After dropping the bed skirt, she sat back on her heels and looked up. Her heart ceased to beat and her breath locked in her throat as she locked gazes with her mother.

"How could you?" Her mother's eyes narrowed to mere slits and her lips pulled back over her teeth in an ugly snarl. She curled her bony fingers until they looked like claws. She bent forward, poised as if ready to attack.

She looks like a vulture, Haley thought, just before her mother let out a high, keening wail and charged.

Chapter Twenty-Three

Haley jumped to her feet as her mother plowed into her side, knocking the breath from her lungs. Claire's small fists flailed ineffectively while a torrent of incoherent sobs and curses spilled from her mouth. As Haley struggled to grasp her mother's wrists, Paige rushed out from the closet.

She caught their mother in a bear hug from behind, trying to still her wildly waving arms. Paige almost had her when Claire caught Haley square in the mouth with the back of her hand.

Haley's head snapped back and her lips ground against her teeth. The metallic flavor of her own blood filled her mouth. She swore and turned away, pressing her fingers to her throbbing lips.

"How could you?" Claire screamed, shrill and furious. Paige had managed to subdue her. "How could you do this to her?"

Haley held one hand to her split lip while digging her fingernails into the palm of the other. Hot fury raged inside her, as she swallowed down the blood in her mouth and watched Paige continue to struggle with their mother.

"Get out," Claire screamed, shrilly. "Leave your sister's things alone. You are not to touch them. She likes her things neat and she doesn't like anyone going into her room."

"Mom, stop," Paige said, trying to calm her.

"I know. Nate told me who you've been carrying on with. I know why you're doing this." Claire continued as if Paige hadn't spoken at all. "It's because of him. You're doing this to protect him. How could you, you filthy tramp? After what he did to your sister!"

"It wasn't Dean," Paige said, while she tried to pull the older woman toward the door. "He didn't kill Michelle. There's proof."

"Don't tell me that. I knew what he was. I told your father, but he wouldn't listen and look what that bastard did. What he's still doing," Claire screeched.

Something snapped inside Haley's brain. She went to the dresser and her fingers curled around the cool porcelain of one of the knick-knacks near the mirror. A ceramic swan. She lifted the glass bird then winged it against the wall. It shattered in a tinkling explosion.

Claire let out a high, mewing howl, and sank to the floor. Paige sank with her, her arms still wrapped around her mother at the elbows.

With a methodical slowness, Haley yanked a drawer from the dresser, dumping the clothes inside into a pile on the floor. Urged on by her mother's uncontrollable sobs, she did the same to the next, and the next, until every article of clothing lay in a tumbled heap at her feet.

She hated this room. This Shrine stuck on permanent pause just like her life. Like a frustrated office worker, she swept her arm across the dresser's surface, sending a lamp and jewelry box sailing through the air. The lamp landed on the floor with a thud, the shade bent at an odd angle. Tiny silver earrings glittered like stars on the carpet.

Without hesitation, Haley turned to the bed, pulling off the covers in a single mighty heave and tossing them aside, then she kicked the bare mattress askew for good measure.

"She's dead!" she shouted, turning to her mother. "Do you understand that? She doesn't care what her room looks like or who's in it because she's dead!"

Grim delight filled her when her mother shrank back against Paige. She turned to the night table, knocking a second lamp the floor and yanking open the drawer. She dumped the ancient make-up with a clatter.

Enjoying herself now, she stepped onto the bed. The mattress teetered on the box spring as she walked across it to the other side. She pulled the drawer from the other nightstand, turning it upside down so magazines and scraps of paper fell onto the carpet.

She froze. Her gaze fixed on a greeting card, twirling to the floor. The fury drained from her as if someone had pulled a plug. She knelt and picked the card up.

Paige came to stand next to her. "What is it?"

Now free, their mother scurried to the middle of the room. She gathered Michelle's clothing to her bosom and sobbed inconsolably.

The whole thing barely registered with Haley. She stared down at the black and white photo of two young children dressed in grown-up clothing. A little boy gave the little girl flowers. When Haley opened the card, it was unsigned. Just as she knew it would be.

"This is just like the card I got the day of Michelle's funeral," she said. "The picture's different, but the same style. Black and white, little kids dressed as grownups. And unsigned."

"You think Michelle got this from the same person?"

"I do."

"You don't know that anyone gave the card to Michelle. She could have bought it for someone and never had the chance to send it."

"Maybe," Haley said, but she didn't really think so.

Her mother's soft cries pierced her like tiny pins. God, what had she done? Disgusted with herself she moved to kneel next to her mother, but Claire pulled away curling up tightly into herself.

"I'm sorry," Haley said. What had she been thinking? "I'll clean this up."

"Don't bother," Paige said, waving her hand. She grabbed Haley's elbow and pulled her to the door. "I'll worry about cleaning tomorrow."

"But Mom," Haley said, as Paige dragged her down the stairs.

"My God, don't worry about her. After a few drinks, she'll forget the whole thing."

Haley's stomach turned. "That's not funny."

"Yes, it is. Now go home and take a hot bath. And take

Dean's phone."

"For crying out loud."

"You know you want to."

"I suppose you're going to call him and let him know I'm leaving."

"Yes, I am. Now go straight home so we don't worry again."

For some reason, her sister's mothering didn't annoy her the way it had earlier. She slid on her jacket and grabbed her purse from the kitchen table.

"I'll come by tomorrow afternoon, okay?" Paige said.

Haley nodded, glad for the first time in years that Paige was her sister.

Haley's door was locked when she got home and her key didn't fit. Exhausted, and a little annoyed, she rang the bell. After a moment, the door swung open and Dean stood in the opening. Her annoyance faded a little as she took in the sight of him. His hair, messed and tousled, his black long sleeved shirt snug against his solid chest and arms. After the day she'd had, she wanted to press herself against that chest and feel his arms around her.

"Sorry," he said, stepping aside. "New locks. I have a key for you inside."

She moved into the hall and peeled off her jacket. "Thanks for installing them."

"No problem? Are you okay?"

"My mom caught us." The statement sounded ridiculous on her lips, as if they were teenagers pilfering a cigarette or sneaking out late at night.

Concern filled Dean's eyes and Haley had to look away. "What happened?"

"She freaked out, caused a scene. Same old, same old."

Before she could stop him she was in his arms, held tight against his beating heart. Hadn't she craved the feeling of security that she knew she would find there? And that craving terrified her more than anything else had today. She shivered a little and his grip tightened. His lips brushed the top of her head.

Stop being a baby. She had known form the start they were temporary. She went into this relationship with her eyes open, with no expectations, and she would keep it that way. *Just enjoy the time you have together and worry about what happens next after he's gone.*

"I'm starving," he murmured into her hair. "And you couldn't have eaten very much today."

No, she hadn't. Not since a muffin and coffee for breakfast. And that had wound up in the toilet at work. "I could eat. What do you feel like?"

"I found a Chinese food menu in your kitchen drawer when I was looking for a screwdriver. Why do you keep tools in the kitchen?"

She shrugged. "It's handier than going down to the basement."

"So Chinese?" he asked, hopefully.

"Okay." A faint smile touched her mouth. "I'm going upstairs to change."

"What do you want me to order?" He grabbed the menu from the counter and returned to the living room then lifted the phone from the side table.

"I'll eat pretty much anything, but order Szechwan beef for sure." Her stomach grumbled. She was hungry.

Dean nodded. "I'll check off what I was thinking about ordering and run it by you when you come back downstairs. Is there a pen around here?" He opened the drawer in the table next to the couch.

Heat flooded her cheeks. "No. Just leave that."

"What is all this?" He lifted the torn scraps of paper.

"Nothing. Garbage. Just forget it." Haley nudged him out of the way and tugged at the newspaper in his hands.

"They're want ads for accountants and bookkeepers."

"It's dumb. I need to throw them away. Here, give them to me." She tried to snatch the ads away, but he pivoted and held them out of her reach.

"Are you looking for job?"

"For crying out loud, give them to me. I'm not going to play keep-away with you."

"Answer me. Is that what you want to do?"

"I don't know, maybe. It's stupid, now give them to me so I can throw them out." Her face burned. She must look like a complete idiot.

"It's not stupid if that's what you want to do." He handed over the clippings.

"It is stupid. People dream of being artists and poets and astronauts, not accountants."

"If that's what you want to do, then you should do it."

She turned and started toward the garbage in the kitchen. "I have a job."

"You're unhappy running your father's store. You can't live your life doing what other people want you to do. At some point, you have to do what makes you happy."

Was he taking lessons from Paige all of sudden? "Sometimes grownups have to do things they don't want to."

"And sometimes children are manipulated by their parents." His words stung. She crumpled the papers in her hand into a tight ball, then tossed it into the trash.

"Everybody seems to know what's best for my life, but I'm the one who has to live it." She turned and started up the stairs. Dean grabbed her hand and stopped her.

"I don't want us to end."

A tiny thrill sparked inside her. A least she wasn't the only one dreading the inevitable. "I don't want that either."

"Then come back with me when I leave. I've got a place, the house is in mid-renovation, but it'll be nice when it's done."

"Just drop everything and go live with you?"

"You don't want to be in this house, working at the store. You could finally do what you've always wanted to."

The idea of trading a messy workbench for a desk and computer, or baggy coveralls for tidy little suits, appealed on an almost desperate level. He was right about one thing, she had always wanted that.

"I have responsibilities."

"They're not your responsibilities. Your mother has made her choice, you shouldn't let that cost you what you want in life."

"That's very easy to say, but I couldn't just sit back and let what happens happen. I'm not made that way."

"We could have a life together."

"I don't think so. I can't walk away from my mother, and while the store may not have been my first career choice, it's my father's legacy."

"Damn it, Haley," he said without any real heat.

She shrugged. "That's just the way it has to be."

Chapter Twenty-Four

Paige woke slowly and stretched on the soft bed. For a moment, she fooled herself into believing she was waking in her own bed, in her own apartment, until she rapped her knuckles off the window ledge with a painful thwack. No, not home. She sighed and opened her eyes.

Dull light flooded the room from the window. Exhausted, after finally calming her mother, she'd fallen into bed and had forgotten to lower the blinds. Squinting against the brightness, she rolled over to look at the clock. Ten-thirty.

Ten-thirty?

She jumped out of the bed. How had she been able to sleep until ten-thirty? Fear gripped her heart as she pulled on her jeans and sweater from the night before. Her mother should have been up by now. Could she have done something to herself after last night's fiasco?

As she scrambled across the room, still zipping the fly on her jeans, she flung open the door and froze. A rich, fragrant aroma filled the air in the kitchen. Coffee. Someone had made coffee? Haley must have come by to help clean the mess in Michelle's room.

The panic eased as she exhaled. With the urgency gone, she helped herself to a cup then started upstairs, but once she reached Michelle's bedroom, she halted. Cardboard boxes, some sealed, others half-full of Michelle's things sat in the center of the room.

Haley wouldn't just get rid of all Michelle's things, would she?

"You're surprised?" The voice behind her made her jump.

She turned and gaped at her mother. Dressed in blue jeans and a faded pale blue sweatshirt, both streaked with dirt in varying shades of gray and brown, she carried two empty cardboard boxes. Though her skin was pale and pasty, her eyes were unusually clear.

"What are you doing?" Paige asked. Had she woken up in The Twilight Zone?

"I'm putting some things away," her mother said. "I think it's time."

Claire moved past Paige into the room, setting the empty boxes down and kneeling next to them. Carefully, she began folding the clothes from the floor.

This woman was not the same person who just last night sat sobbing in almost the exact same place. She looked similar, but this woman was far more reminiscent of the mother Paige had known before Michelle disappeared. A tiny ember of hope lit deep inside her. Even though she knew better. Her mother's hands trembled as she folded and packed.

"Have you eaten?" Paige asked. A strange sense of uncertainty filled her.

"I can't eat yet," her mother said. She looked up at Paige, meeting her gaze. "I'm going to try. Really, I am this time."

"That's good." Paige swallowed and knelt next to her.

They worked together in silence for what seemed like hours. When her mother stood at last, her back made a strange popping sound.

"I'm tired now," she said. Dark circles smudged beneath her eyes, her face was ghostly white and her hands shook badly.

"Are you okay?" Apprehension twisted in Paige's stomach. She hated not knowing what to do.

Her mother shook her head "No. I need to lie down for a while."

After her mother slipped from the room, Paige finished packing the box she was midway through, filling it with outdated fashion magazines. As she stacked the periodicals, a flat, shriveled rose fell from between the pages of one. When she lifted the ancient flower, the petals fluttered to the floor like tissue paper.

He used to send me flowers.

Weren't those the words Haley had heard in her dream? The same words spoken by Sandra Gallagher's alleged phantom hitchhiker. Haley had received two bundles of roses in the past two weeks. Michelle had been getting them too, right before she'd disappeared.

Paige crumpled the rose in her fist. The petals and stem turned to dust and sprinkled to the floor when she opened her hand. There were only two flower shops in Hareton, one on Main Street and one in the mall. How many people bought a dozen roses in December? Not to mention, twice in a two-week span. Would the clerks at the flower shops remember? It couldn't hurt to look into it.

She showered and changed, and then gave Haley a quick call to let her know she had a couple of things to do before she went over to her house. She checked on her mother before leaving. Claire lay in the bed, dressed in her dirty clothes, her breathing deep and even.

Paige didn't like leaving her. This was the first time her mother had ever said aloud, at least to her, that she wanted to change. Paige pulled the bedroom door closed quietly. Hopefully, her mother would be okay.

Haley hung up the phone and twinge of guilt nagged at her. She and her sister had barely reestablished their relationship and Haley had just lied to her. Still, she couldn't help but think this morning's events were ruled by fate.

"Who called?" Dean asked as he joined her in the living room. The sight of him fresh from the shower, his dark hair still damp and his skin smooth from his recent shave, had her insides tightening.

"Telemarketer," she lied. Again that twinge of guilt.

"A wrong number and telemarketer within an hour. You should get an unlisted number." He set his laptop bag by the door.

"Are you kidding? That's the closest thing I have to a social life."

His eyes met hers, bright and turbulent. "I could stay here

with you."

"We talked about this already. Matthew said the problem was urgent and he needs you right away. Paige will be here shortly. She just has to finish with my mother and Michelle's room. I'll be fine on my own in the meantime."

"That's not what I meant," he said, taking a step toward her. "Instead of you coming to live with me, I could live here with you."

Her heart leapt at the thought. Yes, she wanted to scream. "Your business."

"I'm at job sites more than I'm in the office anyway. I'm working from here now."

"But your house. You never wanted to live in Hareton."

"I want to be with you. If that means living here or in a cardboard box under a bridge somewhere, then that's the way it is. I know what I feel for you, the rest is just logistics."

"Can I think about it?"

He frowned. "Yes. But I'm a little insulted that you need to."

"When you come back we'll talk. What you're suggesting is a big step and you should think about it a little more." Her heart all but exploded with the idea of him staying, but how could she ask him to give up his home and move back here just for her? What if it didn't work out?

"I will." He bent and kissed the tip of her nose. "But I don't need to. I really don't like the idea of leaving you alone."

"I won't be alone for long. Besides, you've put new locks on the doors, and I'll even carry around that cell phone you bought me."

His smile left her breathless. "Really?"

"Yes. I know I wasn't terribly grateful yesterday, but if the offer's still good, I'd like to keep the phone."

He yanked her against him and his lips met hers, hot and needy. Her entire body trembled beneath his touch. The urge to forget everything and drag him back upstairs nearly overwhelmed her, but opportunity had come knocking, or in this case calling, and she didn't know when she'd get a chance like this again.

"You should go," she told him, moving away. "Paige will be

here soon. If we time this right, she'll be leaving around the same time you get back and we can pick up where we left off."

"I like the sound of that." He kissed her again then slipped out the front door.

Haley stood in the window and watched him drive off. Once his car had turned from the street, she picked up the phone and dialed. Her heart thundered in her chest as the ringing at the other end filled her ear.

"Hello."

"Lara?" Haley asked.

"Yes, it's me."

"I'm coming now."

Lara lowered her voice until she spoke barely above a whisper. "Just you. Not Dean, right?"

"That's right."

"No one can know."

Apprehension shivered over her skin, but she squared her shoulders. She could handle Lara. "Fine. I'll be there in about fifteen. I can only give you about an hour, maybe two."

"I won't need that long."

The phone clicked in her ear before the dial tone sounded. Shaking her head, Haley hung up the phone and pulled on her coat. She figured she had maybe a two-hour window, if that, before Paige and Dean returned. With each believing she was with the other, they might not hurry.

When Lara had called and asked to meet Haley alone not ten minutes after Matthew had phoned asking for Dean's help with a client, Haley couldn't believe her luck. Then Paige called less than a half-hour after that and Haley was set.

Guilt nagged at her, but she clamped down on it. If Paige and Dean would act like reasonable people and stop hovering over her as if she was a child, she wouldn't need to lie to them. No, she wouldn't feel guilty. Especially, if Lara could bring her closer to the truth.

Tall fir trees marked the edge of the Williams' property line, blotting out the unsightly highway. Dark green and laden with snow, their tips stretched out into the charcoal-colored sky above. The radio announcer had called for five to ten inches of snow before tomorrow morning. By no means the worst snow storm Haley had seen, but a good dumping just the same. She hoped Dean and Paige made it back before the snow started.

As she turned from the highway onto the long, narrow lane winding through the trees on a gentle downward slope, the first flakes fluttered from the low hanging clouds. They swept over the hood of her car, big and fluffy, like white feathers.

Nerves gripped her as she parked in the circular drive before wide stone steps. Michelle had hoped to marry Jonathan, hoped to live in this house, but she was dead now and for all Haley knew her killer could be behind the heavy wood door even now.

She got out of the car. The wind, like an icy whip, stung her face and ears, seeping through her clothes, bringing goose bumps to her skin and chilling her bones. She climbed the steps and rang the bell.

A burly woman, Haley guessed to be in her late fifties, wearing a shapeless blue dress and white apron opened the door. She stared at Haley with pale eyes set in a ruddy square face. "What do you want?"

"I'm here to see Lara," Haley said, a little taken aback by the woman's abrupt demand.

"Thank you, Bonnie," Lara said, from behind the housekeeper. "I've been expecting Ms. Carling."

Bonnie glared a final time before slipping away.

"Come in." Lara moved aside so Haley could do just that.

"Is she the same housekeeper that worked here when Michelle disappeared?" Haley asked, taking in the marble entry, all soft shades of cream and gold. A huge Christmas tree stretched past the curving staircase, lit with tiny gold lights, and buried beneath gold and cream decorations. A perfect match to the foyer, and with all the personality of a department store Christmas tree. Though, she couldn't be too critical, at least they'd put up a tree, more than she'd done.

Lara nodded.

"I'd like to speak to her before I leave."

"You won't need to."

And why was that? Did Lara plan to confess? Maybe Haley shouldn't have come alone, after all. Or at the very least, she should have brought a tape recorder or something. If Lara did end up confessing, it would be her word against Haley's.

"I'm glad you came," Lara said, tucking a strand of straight, black hair behind her ear.

"Are you?" Lara didn't look glad. When she wasn't nervously picking invisible lint from her fitted black turtleneck and dove gray slacks, she was glancing over her shoulder. Lara looked afraid.

"I am. I have some things I need you to know. Come with me."

Lara led Haley down a wide hallway to a dark paneled study with furniture made up of smooth shiny wood and rich leathers. Jonathan's more traditional office?

"Sit down." Lara gestured to a high-backed chair before the desk.

Haley lowered herself slowly and the soft brown leather creaked under her weight. They stared at each other in silence for a moment, while Haley waited for Lara to begin.

"Could I get you a refreshment?" Lara asked.

Haley shook her head. "No, thank you."

Silence again. A last Haley asked, "Why did you ask me here?"

"I need to confess." A bitter smile touched Lara's mouth, making her look hard. From a small silver case on the desk, Lara removed a cigarette. After lighting the tip, she exhaled a thin blue line of smoke. "Jonathan hates me smoking. If he knew I was smoking in here, he'd be furious. My husband is a very meticulous man."

"I don't want to rush you," Haley said a little annoyed. "But I don't have a lot of time."

Lara flicked an ash on to the desk blotter. "None of us do. I would have spoken up sooner if I had realized that there was any real danger. I heard about Al. I'm sorry."

Haley nodded, her heart racing. What did Lara know? What would she confess to? Had she murdered her best friend for the affections of Jonathan Williams? But what did that have to do with Al?

For a moment, Haley thought of her life before Michelle's body had been discovered, the routine day-to-day that now seemed surreal and faded.

"I suppose you know I made up the story about Dean and Michelle still sleeping together."

Haley nodded again, and Lara inhaled deeply from the cigarette between her lips. "I wanted them to break up. The whole thing seems so childish now and yet back then it felt like life or death," Lara smiled bitterly. "I knew they were serious, but I wanted him. I didn't love him, but it had to be him."

"Why?" Haley asked. Would there be a point to any of this, or was Lara just looking to justify her adolescent foolishness?

"My father died when I was very young. My mother was ill-equipped to care for a toddler on her own, both financially and emotionally. Over the years, she lived with a series of men. All losers. I don't know if she had terrible taste in men, or maybe there are just a lot of awful people out there."

Where was this going? Haley didn't understand. Did she plan to fall back on the I've-had-a-bad-childhood-and-I'm-not-responsible-for-my-actions bit?

"Most of the men hit her or me or both of us. And they used her up, making her old long before she was. I knew I couldn't end up like that and Jonathan was just what I needed. If I married him, I would have the security and comfort my mother never did. I had nothing against Michelle, but she had opportunities I didn't. Your parents sent her to university, while I was stuck working at the diner during the week and Roy's Tavern on weekends. Hareton didn't offer a great selection of rich men. If not Jonathan, then who? How would I ever meet someone to give me the life I wanted?"

Lara inhaled deeply on her cigarette. The smoke from the glowing tip swirled and drifted in the air like a ghostly hand grasping at nothing. Haley suppressed the shiver running down her spine.

Could Lara be a borderline sociopath? No guilt, no regret. She'd lied and manipulated to get what she wanted and felt completely justified doing so.

"Why not admit what you did? My God, the people in this town practically ran Dean out and you sat there quietly, knowing none of it was true. What if he'd gone to jail?" Haley couldn't hide the disgust in her voice. Not that she wanted to.

"I was afraid," Lara said, her voice warbled some. "Because I knew."

"Knew what?"

Lara stood and moved around to the far side of the desk. She lifted the letter opener and worked it between the edge of the desk and the drawer. When the lock gave way with an audible click, she set the opener aside and slid open the drawer.

She removed a small black velvet box, popped the lid and held it open to Haley. The diamond ring glittered against the velvet inside.

"You see Michelle was pregnant and I think Jonathan had planned to ask her to marry him, but he'd heard by then. The night Michelle disappeared, she'd come here to try and convince Jonathan that only he could be the father, and that was the last anyone saw of her."

For a moment Haley's throat shrunk and her mouth dried up. She could barely form words, but she had to ask. "You think Jonathan killed her in a fit of jealousy, and then you kept quiet so you could marry him?"

"I kept quiet because he agreed to marry me. If he hadn't, I would have told the police and even his paid alibi couldn't have kept him from falling under suspicion."

"How did you know she was pregnant? That she came here to talk to Jonathan that night?"

"She was my best friend," Lara said, grinding her cigarette into the blotter. "She told me everything."

The words spoken so simply, so honestly, brought forth a fury she could hardly keep in check. "You're certifiable. I've never known anyone like you."

"We all do what we must to survive."

"No, we don't. We don't lie for killers so we can marry them, we don't let families suffer just so we can have what we want, and we don't let innocent men be accused of murder simply because it suits our needs."

Lara shrugged. "Needless to say, I will not admit to any of this if asked, but you might want to speak Erin."

"My sister-in law?"

"Yes. She helped spread the rumor, hated Michelle and she was adamant that I not speak up for Dean. I suspect she may have even contacted Jonathan. I'm not sure why one helped the other, but I think she knows more than she's admitting to. She might turn on Jonathan in an effort to protect herself."

"You really know what buttons to press."

A cold tight smile twisted Lara's lips. "Especially, when dealing with someone so like myself."

Haley stood and left the office without another word. A thin sheen a sweat covered her skin, and a sick feeling gripped her. Jonathan? Did she believe Lara? The woman was a survivor, she would tell Haley anything to protect herself. Even implicate her own husband—and Erin.

Still, Lara had to know Haley would ask Erin to confirm her story. Lara wouldn't have used her sister in-law, and told Haley just how to manipulate her if she didn't believe Erin would give credence to her tale.

Outside, the snow fell prettily to the ground. A soft blanket of loose snow had accumulated on the hood and windows of her car. She didn't bother to dig out the snowbrush from the backseat. Instead, she wiped it away with her coat sleeve, eager to get home.

After sliding behind the wheel, she managed to start the car on her third try. She didn't wait for the motor to warm up. She wanted to get out of here. Hopefully, by the time she reached town, and a traffic light, the engine would have warmed enough to keep from stalling.

She pressed her foot on the accelerator and sped along the winding drive to the road. How long had it taken Michelle to walk this distance all those years ago? Alone in the dark and cold. Or had she? Maybe she'd never left that house alive.

As the highway came into view, Haley slowed, but didn't stop. She pulled out onto the empty road and turned toward Hareton. Right away, the car at the side of the road caught her eye. A black Maxima, just like Dean's.

She swung onto the shoulder and stopped behind the

parked vehicle. That couldn't be Dean's car. Not so soon. She checked her watch. It was almost four. She'd been with Lara much longer than she'd planned.

Okay, maybe the Maxima could be Dean's, but why would he leave his car at the side of the road? Haley turned off the motor and opened the door. The wind, ferocious off the field to her right, nearly yanked the handle from her grip.

She stepped out into the deepening snow, already drifting onto the road and trudged toward the driver's side window. Cupping both hands at her temples, she peered inside. Dean's keys dangled from the ignition and his jacket lay in a heap on the passenger seat.

Her heart rate quickened. If he broke down, he wouldn't leave his keys and certainly not his coat. She edged along the side of the car. Snow had accumulated on the cold hood. The engine must have been off for awhile.

She went back to the driver side and opened the door. As she leaned inside and reached for his coat, her jacket brushed the keys dangling from the ignition. They jingled ominously in the quiet. His laptop sat on the floor behind the passenger seat.

Fear swept through her colder than the winter wind. She lifted his coat and his wallet tumbled from the folds. Something was definitely wrong. He didn't break down. He wouldn't have left his coat, wallet, keys and computer in an unlocked car. What had happened?

She dropped the coat back onto the seat and backed out of the car when the toe of her boot rocked on something buried in the snow. She knelt and dug into the ice and wet until her fingertips closed around the small phone. Dean's cell. She tried turning it on, but nothing happened. Maybe the wet had damaged it.

It didn't matter. She needed help—now. She rushed back to her car, getting in behind the wheel, her head filled with images of Al's battered corpse. Please, no. She couldn't think that, but what had happened and how long ago? She needed to call the police, or someone.

Damn it, damn it, damn it. The phone Dean bought her sat in the box on her kitchen counter at home. She turned the key and the car made its familiar, dry, high-pitched warble, but the engine didn't turn over.

"Start," she ordered aloud, and tried the key again. And again. And again. But the engine wouldn't start.

"Son of a bitch," she yelled. Panic swelled inside her like a balloon. Her eyes filled with tears, as she struggled to clamp down on the fear and frustration.

Calm. She needed to calm down. Closing her eyes, she inhaled deeply. On the exhale, she reached for the key and turned it once more. Nothing happened.

"Start, God damn it, start!" she screamed, stomping her foot on the gas and slamming the flats of her hands against the steering wheel. Still cursing, she reached for the key once more, but movement in the rearview mirror caught her attention. A car headed toward her.

She jumped out and waved frantically to flag down the driver. The battered pick-up truck rolled to a stop in front of Dean's car. The truck's door opened and Nate's long, thin legs unfolded, stepping out onto the snow-covered shoulder. He smiled as he approached, adjusting the red baseball cap on his head.

Relief nearly made her knees buckle. "Nate, I need you to drive me into town. I think something's happened to Dean." The words fell from her mouth in a panicked rush.

"Haley, calm down." Nate gripped her upper arms, his thumbs moving in slow circles over the puffy sleeves of her jacket. "What is it? Tell me what's wrong?"

Haley took a step back. "I think Dean's been hurt. Do you have a phone?"

"No, I don't."

"My car won't start, can you give me a ride into town?" Haley asked.

"Of course." Nate smiled. "Climb on in."

Haley frowned as she walked behind the truck. Did he not get what she was saying? The strange, almost indulgent smile made her wonder.

As she moved between the back of the truck and the front of Dean's car, movement in the truck's cab made her turn. For an instant, barely a flash, Michelle stared out at her through the dirty glass.

Haley stopped dead, frozen where she stood. Did she actually see that? And if she did, what did it mean? She didn't know, but the idea of climbing into that truck left her with a sick dread deep in the pit of her belly just like when she and Paige had been in her grandmother's basement.

"Haley?"

"Dean's phone," she said, turning toward his car. "I could call for help from his phone." She needed to get behind the wheel and get out of there. Damn, why hadn't she remembered his car before?

"It's been sitting in the snow, I doubt it works," Nate said, his tone easy, conversational.

And how would you know that, Nate? Paige had been right all along. She had to get to that car.

"Dean's computer," she blurted out. "And—and his wallet, they're still inside his car. I don't want anyone to steal them."

She turned and started toward the passenger door of the Maxima willing her legs to work. Her movements felt stiff and awkward. Don't let him notice.

Her heart thundered in her chest, echoing in her ears. Could he hear it? She reached the door. All she had to do was climb in and lock the door behind her. Closing her hand around the cold handle, she pulled it open. Almost there. Slowly she bent down—

"Don't do this, Haley."

He knew. She didn't look back, just dove into the car. Closer than she realized, or faster than she gave him credit for, his hand locked around her arm like a vise. He yanked her hard, dragging her halfway out. With a scream, she gripped the edge of the seat with her free hand, her knuckles going white.

She kicked out at him wildly, screaming all the while, until her foot struck something solid and Nate let out a gasp. He released her, and for a moment she was free. She scrambled back inside car, but his hand tangled in her hair. Stinging needles pierced her scalp. She cried out as he pulled her back outside.

When he released her hair, she made another dive for the door, but the back of his hand caught her across the cheekbone, and sent her sprawling back into the snow. While fierce pain burst in her face and rocketed to her eye, she didn't stop. She couldn't. If she did, she was dead.

Tears streamed down her cheeks, her breath came in hoarse sobs as she struggled to her feet. He struck her again, this time in the mouth, knocking her back into the snow. She could taste her own blood.

Nate straddled her, pinning her arms to her sides with his knees. She looked into his face and saw nothing. His features were void of expression. He could have just as easily been mowing the lawn, or grocery shopping as beating her down at the side of the highway and preparing to kill her.

She screamed, high and bloodcurdling, into the wind. The only fight she had left, but it didn't matter. There was no one to hear. No one to save her.

"Shut up," Nate snarled, fumbling with something in his pocket. A white rag loomed over her before he pressed it against her face, her mouth, her nose. She couldn't breathe, her lungs expanded until she thought they might explode.

Suffocating. Suffocating her. She choked on the sickly sweet stench, kicking and struggling until her world went black.

Chapter Twenty-Five

The wind howled and the snow fell heavily as Paige crept slowly along the highway. What a waste of an afternoon. After driving from one florist to another, in towns as far as an hour away, she'd returned empty-handed. But what had she expected? Did she honestly believe that someone would remember selling a dozen roses to the same person on two different occasions? Maybe not expected, but hoped.

Then, after a completely useless day, she'd wound up caught in the storm. She'd tried calling Haley twice so far and Dean's cell phone once. No one answered. They were probably warm and cozy in bed together while she was stuck out here in the elements.

With a sigh, she pressed a little heavier on the accelerator. Instantly, the car's back end swung out. Gritting her teeth, she let up on the gas, and brought the car under control. Christ, she wouldn't get back until tomorrow at this rate.

Paige popped a cigarette into her mouth and lit the tip, adding to the ever-present haze of smoke. Annie Lennox sang "Winter Wonderland" from the speakers. This had to be some kind of cosmic joke. She was in her own Winter Wonderland. Snow as far as the eye could see, but there was nothing wonderful about it.

The pine trees marking the Williams' property rose up on her left. Were she traveling at normal speed, she would be in Hareton in about twenty minutes, but unfortunately, traveling as she was, she probably wouldn't be home for another three hours.

Stifling a scream of frustration, she pressed on the

accelerator and again the back end skidded sideways. She let out a string of curses and swung the steering wheel into the skid. The car came around, but she over-corrected on the slick road, nearly sideswiping a car parked on the shoulder. She swore again and swung the steering wheel away from the car. Two cars, actually, parked end-to-end.

She stomped on the brake. Her car skidded slightly as she pulled in front. The first one, the one she'd nearly hit, was Haley's. She'd have recognized that rust heap anywhere. But what in hell was that hunk-of-junk doing here? And where was Haley?

A cold ball of fear formed in her belly as she emerged from her car into the bitter wind. Her feet slipped and skidded on the slick ground. She half-walked half-slid to Haley's car, her heart thundering against her chest, while something akin to raw panic seized her insides.

She passed a black car. Dean's car. What had happened? Once next to Haley's car, she opened the door and slid behind the wheel. She slammed the car door behind her, shutting out the wind and snow.

Haley's key was still in the ignition and her purse forgotten on the passenger seat. Something was wrong.

Paige jumped out of Haley's car and trotted to Dean's. She'd been so stupid to trust him. How could she have left her sister with him? How could he have fooled her?

The door of Dean's car was open also, and like Haley's car, Dean's keys were hanging in the ignition. His coat lay in a ball on the floor of the passenger side.

Where would he have taken her? And why would he leave his car? And his coat? Or could he be in trouble too?

She took a step back from the car. Hers were the only footprints in the rapidly accumulating snow. She moved to inspect the far side. Drifts from the wind off the field reached into the fenders. How long had the cars been here?

And what did she do now?

Trembling, as much from fear as cold, Paige hurried back to her car and got inside. She needed help. Her hands shook badly as she slipped a cigarette between her lips and lit the end. With the filter clenched between her teeth, she dialed Garret's number, smoke filling the car's small interior. When she opened the window a crack, the wind howled and whistled through the narrow gap like a ghost. She shivered.

"Hello."

The sound of Garret's voice turned her limbs weak with relief.

"Garret, it's me. Something's happened."

"What is it? What's wrong? Is it Mom?"

"No, worse." Paige told Garret about finding Haley and Dean's cars with their belongings still inside.

"Do you think he's got her?" Garret asked his voice hard.

"I don't think it's Dean," Paige said. "We've been doing our own little investigation, and I think someone just put a stop to it."

"What kind of investigation? Does this have something to do with what happened to Al?"

"I don't have time. Call the police and get them out looking for Haley and Dean. I'm going to stop in at Mom's, then I'll be over to see you."

Paige didn't wait for him to reply. She snapped her phone closed, tossed it onto the passenger seat and flicked her cigarette out the window. Then continued to crawl toward Hareton.

Dark silence greeted Paige when she finally returned to her mother's house. Her shoulders ached with tension and her knuckles cramped from gripping the steering wheel.

As she entered the kitchen, fear's icy claws dug deeper into her flesh. Not a light on, no TV, nothing. Just silence. She fumbled with the switch on the wall until at last the room filled with wondrous electric light.

Where was her mother?

"Oh, Christ," Paige whispered.

On legs made of rubber, she left the kitchen and started up the stairs. As she climbed, her heart hammered in her chest, reverberating through her body. Light seeped out from under

Michelle's closed door, but no sound, only chilling silence.

With a deep breath, Paige turned the knob and pushed the door open. She exhaled slowly and rolled her eyes. Her mother slept on the floor in a pile of Michelle's clothes. Clothes that Paige had packed into boxes that morning. A bottle of rye, two-thirds the way through, tilted onto the pile. Nothing wrong. Everything here was just as it usually was. The typical end to a typical day for Claire Carling.

Paige knelt next to her mother and slid an arm under her shoulders. Her mother stirred and her eyes fluttered open.

"Paige," she whispered, hoarse and dry. Her breath stunk of booze. Was it possible to get drunk from the fumes alone? If so, Paige could be in trouble.

"Come on, Mom, time for bed." She helped Claire to her feet.

"I tried, Paige," her mother said. Her voice cracked and tears filled her bloodshot eyes. "I'm so sorry. I tried, I really did."

"I know." She guided her mother down the hall.

"It's just so hard," Claire said as they entered her room. "To lose a child. Unless you have one you can't know."

Paige helped her mother into the unmade bed. She should make her eat something, but there wasn't time. Missing one meal wouldn't hurt. Besides, it certainly wouldn't be the first time.

Her mother continued to prattle on, slurred and barely coherent as Paige pulled the blankets over her withered frame. She'd unplug the phones before leaving. The last thing Paige needed was Mrs. Yolken or some other do-gooder, calling and telling her mother Haley was missing. By now, Garret would have called the police and once that was done word would spread. The storm would slow them some, but nothing Mother Nature had to offer could hold back the tide of good gossip in Hareton.

"It's like I told Nate when we looked at the pictures, until you have a child of your own, you can't know what it is to lose them."

As Paige yanked the phone cord from the wall, her mother's words registered and a chill rippled down her spine.

"When did you say that to Nate?" Paige asked.

"We both agreed there was never a little girl more beautiful than Michelle. She was like an angel."

"Mom, listen to me." Paige grabbed her mother's hands in hers, trying to penetrate the alcohol fog that encased her brain. "When did you look at pictures with Nate?"

"When he was here."

"I know," Paige ground out. "When was that? Was it before or after the memorial?"

"After," Claire mumbled, struggling to keep her eyes from closing. "The day you were away."

Nate here the same day she'd been away. Coincidence? The very next day her mother accused her of hiding her keys—and Haley's break-ins started.

Paige looked down at her mother asleep in the darkness. If she lost Haley too, she would fall over the edge she'd been teetering on for years. Paige had to find Haley. Alive.

Dean woke on a hard, dirt floor. He shifted slightly and pain soared through his body. What the hell had happened? He forced his eyes open, but his vision blurred and his stomach turned dangerously. With a curse, he squeezed his eyes shut and willed himself not to throw up.

The agony receded some, except for the back of his head. With that kind of pain, surely his skull had cracked, and even now a fragment of bone stabbed his brain.

Memory returned slowly. Confused images that he couldn't quite make sense of. He tried to focus, tried to piece it together, but the pain became too much. A thin layer of sweat dotted his forehead despite the cold seeping through his clothes. He slipped from consciousness back toward glorious pain-free oblivion, but somehow managed to stop himself. He couldn't sleep. Time was short. He didn't know how he knew that, he just did.

Where was he? How did he get here?

He forced his eyes open despite the bone-jarring pain in his head. Pale shafts of light seeped through gaps in the weathered plank wall facing him. He started to sit up, but his arms wouldn't cooperate.

Thick twine dug into the skin at his wrists. His arms were bound behind him. His jaw throbbed around a filthy piece of cloth fit into his mouth like a horse's bridle. Exhaling a deep breath, he relaxed and lowered his cheek to the gritty dirt floor.

He closed his eyes and concentrated on breathing through his pain. The stink of rotting hay and animal feces assailed his nostrils and tickled the back of his throat. When the pain eased a little, he opened his eyes again. In the bleak shadowy darkness, he could make out the outline of empty horse stalls.

A barn. He was in a barn! The sense of triumph left him abruptly. There were hundreds of barns outside the town limits of Hareton. He could be anywhere.

Again he closed his eyes and tried to remember how he'd wound up tied and gagged in a barn.

Snow. He'd been driving in the snow. The beginning of a storm. He was about twenty minutes away from town when he came upon Nate's pick-up at the side of the road.

Nate stood with the truck's hood open and Dean assumed he was having car trouble. While Nate was no fan of his, at one time the man had been his boss. Dean could at least offer him the use of his phone or a ride back to town.

Dean stopped and climbed out of the car. As he approached, Nate let the heavy metal hood slam shut.

"Looks like she's finally done for," he said, his smile warm and disarming.

The other man's reaction surprised and relieved Dean. "Can I help?"

"Do you have a phone?" Nate asked.

"Yeah, in the car."

Nate followed Dean and hung back as Dean opened the door and bent inside. He grabbed the phone from the console and started to turn when pain exploded across the back of his head. A dull clang rang in his ears, but he couldn't tell if it was real or just the reverberation from the blow. He staggered back, reaching for the oozing wound.

Nate had hit him.

The clang came again, then nothing until the hard barn

floor and the agony of varying degrees rocketing through his body.

Nate murdered Michelle, but why? How? He'd likely been responsible for Darren's missing first wife, too. But the question remained; why? Why kill Eleanor James? Why kill Michelle? And why club him over the head and dump him in a barn? Had Haley been right? Had he been the target all along?

From somewhere in the shadowy darkness, a heavy creak cut through the quiet followed by shuffling footsteps moving toward him. Dean closed his eyes once more and forced his body to relax. While feigning unconsciousness, he listened as the footsteps drew nearer then stopped.

Someone stood next to him, but didn't speak or move. Rough hands tugged the gag from his mouth while Dean struggled to keep his breathing even and ignore the muffled thundering of his heart.

"I know you're awake," Nate said at last. "Open your eyes."

Dean hesitated, keeping his eyes closed. Nate could be testing him. If he didn't move and Nate no longer perceived him as a threat, maybe he would do something stupid like untie him. Or at the very least keep him alive long enough to figure out how to escape.

Nate shifted. The soles of his boots scraped against the dirt floor. Maybe he was leaving.

Mind numbing agony, sharp and intense, pinnacled in his middle, where Nate's foot connected. The breath sucked up inside him, his eyes popped open and his vision grayed. He forced himself onto his shoulder, unable to keep his stomach contents at bay.

Still retching and choking, he edged away from the steaming puddle. Nate loomed over him, his usually mild mannered expression gone. His lips curled into a sneer and his eyes were wild and glazed.

Dean struggled to pull himself onto his knees. Whatever Nate had planned for him, Dean wouldn't lie there and wait for it to happen.

"I knew you were awake," Nate said. His voice was dull, almost robotic.

"Well," Dean panted, still struggling to catch his breath. "If

I wasn't, I am now."

"Shut up," Nate snarled. The sudden flip in his voice, from quietly menacing to boiling rage shocked Dean enough to do just that. "I almost missed her because of you."

"What?" A sinking feeling settled over him.

"I would've too if she hadn't stopped for your car, and hers wasn't such a piece of shit. I guess I should be thanking you." A smile touched his lips, chilling Dean.

"Where is she?"

"You shouldn't have come back, Lawson. You shouldn't have tried to interfere. She was meant to be mine. Did you really think you could keep her from me? I love her."

Hot and cold waves of panic washed over him. "Where is she?"

"That's not for you to worry about." He started to turn away.

"You're lying," Dean accused, desperate to keep Nate talking. He had to figure out where Haley was. "Why would you keep me alive? You're using me for bait."

Nate laughed a rich chuckle. "Oh, you're a dead man, Lawson, a living corpse. I'm just keeping you alive in case I need you. You were so helpful when Michelle died."

"Where is she?" Dean tried to yell, but his voice was too dry and hoarse.

Nate stopped, turned, and walked back to Dean. He bent to fit the gag in Dean's mouth. With his hands still tied behind his back, Dean fought the only way he could. With one sweeping motion he threw his head back then swung himself forward, bouncing his forehead off Nate's. A loud hollow clunk filled the quiet, and Dean's head nearly exploded. He fell back onto the barn floor, gritting his teeth and struggling to keep from crying out.

Groaning like an injured animal, Nate pressed his hands to his forehead and staggered back a few steps. He pulled his hands away revealing a large red welt. With eyes darkened by fury, Nate stomped back to Dean.

Had he pushed the man too far? Would Nate kill him now, whether he needed him or not? Nate bent down, tangled his fingers in Dean's hair then yanked his head back and stuffed the gag into his mouth.

Without so much as a backward glance, Nate walked away, leaving Dean on the floor almost the same way he'd found him.

Dean tried to yell from around the gag, but his words came out muffled. Where was Haley? And how would he ever get to her tied up the way he was?

Chapter Twenty-Six

"Erin?" Paige called, letting herself into her brother's house. Not that she thought Garret or Erin would be home. Both her van and his SUV weren't in the driveway when Paige arrived. Not that it mattered. Paige wanted Nate's current address, and preferably without a big discussion.

The more she thought about Nate, the more convinced she became. The way he used to watch them, stare at them when they were teenagers at the store. He'd always given Paige the creeps.

And hadn't she suggested Nate as a possible suspect just the other night? "Oh, no," Haley had said. "Not Nate. It couldn't possibly be Nate." When would people listen to her? If there was one thing she could do well, it was read people.

Paige marched into the kitchen and rooted through drawers and piles of envelopes on the counter, searching for anything that might have an address or even a phone number. Anything that would lead her to Nate. And Haley.

After tearing apart the first floor and coming up empty-handed, Paige bounded up the stairs, taking them two at a time. She went into her brother's office and started rifling through the papers on his desk, then in the drawers. Still nothing.

Did these people not own an address book? She darted across the hall to the master bedroom. Framed photos of her nieces sat next to a large crystal bowl filled with potpourri on the surface of the wide dresser. Paige opened drawers and dug through neatly folded clothes, leaving them neither neat nor folded.

While rummaging through Erin's underwear, her fumbling fingers fell on a small box, the kind jewelry stores placed the velvet box inside. As soon as she touched the thin cardboard, goose bumps raced up her arm and the hair on the back of her neck stood on end. The temperature in the room dropped and Paige shivered.

She lifted the small white box, a perfect square, unremarkable in every way, except her reaction to it. Carefully, she lifted the lid. Waves of sadness and loss washed over her and tears stung her eyes as she peered down at the contents. A ring, a necklace, earrings and a bracelet. All Michelle's.

Separately, only the earrings, plain gold hoops, may have given her trouble recognizing them as her sister's. The rest, though, were Michelle's. The necklace with the gold cursive M pendent that Jonathan had given her for Christmas, and the pearl ring her parents had given Michelle for her twenty-first birthday, and lastly, the bracelet. A dark pinkish gold bangle with intricate patterns engraved into the gold. Her grandmother's name and the year her grandfather had purchased it in India during the war engraved on the inside.

Michelle's jewelry, the jewelry she had been wearing the night she disappeared tucked away in her sister-in-law's underwear drawer. What did it mean? Had Erin murdered Michelle? Where did Nate fit in? Or did he? Did Erin take Haley? And Dean? Or was Dean an accomplice? Or was Haley's abandoned car just a coincidence?

"I didn't take them for myself."

The voice out of nowhere made Paige jump and she nearly dropped the box as she spun around. Erin stood in the doorway, looking tired and much older than her years. Snowflakes melted in her hair and on her clothing.

"Why do you have these?" Paige asked, her voice deceptively calm.

"I thought if she were found, it would keep them from identifying her." Erin smiled ruefully. "I was barely twenty, what the hell did I know about anything?"

"Why did you kill her?"

"I didn't," Erin said, sounding genuinely surprised. "I just helped bury her."

"You didn't bury her. You wrapped her in a blanket and stuck her in a hole in the floor."

"I didn't want to. I just didn't know what else to do."

"What the hell happened? Who killed her?"

Erin looked at Paige, long and measuring. Paige wanted to strangle the stupid bitch, but she waited. Here was the answer to Michelle, and the way to Haley. Erin sighed and flopped down on the edge of her bed. Her shoulders slumped in defeat.

"My father did it, he killed her," Erin said. "My mother was away at my aunt's, and when Garret dropped me off that night I found him standing over her. He looked so confused, I didn't realize what had happened. There was so much blood."

Dear God, Paige thought, what had he done to her? Paige didn't want to hear more, but she had to.

"I knew he was attracted to her. I even knew he was sending her the flowers and cards. I encouraged Lara to blame Dean so no one would suspect. I never thought he would hurt her."

"Why didn't you call the police?" Paige asked. She could hardly believe the calmness in her voice, so incongruent with the chaos in her mind. Like a tornado tearing through her brain.

"He was my father," Erin said. "And he was so sorry. He just wanted to talk to her, to explain how he felt about her, but it had gone so horribly wrong. He didn't mean to, it was an accident."

"If it was an accident, why hide it? Why bury her in my grandmother's house?"

"Perhaps accident is a poor choice in words," Erin said, coldly. "The point is, he didn't mean to do it. He didn't want to hurt her. It just happened. We didn't know what to do. I thought of going to the police, I really did. I saw what it was doing to your family. I was there, remember?"

"I remember."

"But he cried and begged me to help him. It had been three days by then, I was afraid that if I went to the police, they would think I was his accomplice."

"But you were," Paige said. "Whose idea was it to hide the

body in my grandmother's basement?"

"It was Dad's," Erin said. "She was staying with you by then and he had offered to pick up the mail and shovel the driveway. Your father gave him the key. We couldn't keep the body in the shed much longer. The police had released Dean by then and they were beginning the house-to-house searches. The ground was frozen, so he thought he could hide it there until he could think of something else. It was only supposed to be temporary until we saw the dirt floor in the basement."

Paige couldn't speak as she tried to equate Erin's confession with her memories of those first awful days. She remembered Erin's presence like a shadow next to her brother, her expression stricken when the police said they feared the worst. And Nate's anger that something like this could happen. His kind and supportive words to her father. She remembered her father giving Nate the key to her grandmother's and thanking the man for all his help when all along Michelle's battered body lay hidden in his shed.

Perhaps if her father had never given him the key, he would have been found out. Erin would never have married her brother. Her parents may have found some comfort in at least knowing what had happened to her sister. Dean wouldn't have been labeled a murderer, and most importantly, Haley wouldn't be missing now.

"Nate has Haley," Paige said.

"I know," Erin replied. Her eyes filled with tears. "You have to believe me when I say I never wanted this to happen."

"But it did, and you knew it would," Paige said, clenching her fists at her side. Fury boiled deep inside her the minute the first tear slid down Erin's cheek. That single tear enraged Paige more than anything Erin confessed.

"I didn't want it to," Erin said, on a choking sob. "I wanted to stop him, I thought I could this time. Dean was staying there—"

"Yes, he was, and did you not stand in my mother's kitchen three days ago and call him a killer?" Paige asked, cutting off her sister-in-law's tearful denials. "You knew it wasn't him. So why did you sic me on him?"

Erin looked at her with wide, glassy eyes. She opened her

mouth as if to speak, but snapped it shut again. Her face paled and Paige knew she'd caught Erin in a lie.

"You're lying to me," Paige said, taking a step toward her.

"No," Erin denied. "Everything I've told you is the truth."

"You wouldn't know the truth if it walked up and bit you on the ass." With her patience all but gone, and time ticking away, she clamped down on her temper and lowered her voice. "I'm going to ask you two questions, and I want the truth no matter how ugly it may be. If you tell me the truth, I won't tell Garret how you lied to him for the past twelve years."

Erin said nothing, but she nodded and Paige took that as a good sign.

"How did Dean fit in?"

"I didn't want my father to hurt Haley," Erin said, tearfully. "But if he did, I wanted you to know that Haley had been with Dean."

"So he would get the blame again," Paige said.

"I didn't know what else to do," Erin sobbed.

"Where is Haley now?" Paige asked.

"My father bought a place on Old Base Road. Number 12. He has a silver mail box."

"Give me the keys to your SUV," Paige demanded.

"What?"

"I need your keys. I'm taking your truck."

"Garret went out to meet the police at Haley's car. He has the SUV. I have the van."

Impatience exploded inside her head. "Fine, give me the keys to the van."

"Why?"

"Because it has to be better than my Mustang in the snow."

"I'll go with you."

"I don't think so," Paige said. "Just give me your keys."

Paige lunged for them, but Erin lifted her arm above her head, like a child playing keep-away. Paige was taller than Erin by an inch and a half, and had little trouble reaching her hand, but Erin clenched the car keys tightly in her fist. Paige tried to pry her fingers open. When that failed she gripped Erin's hair and gave it a hard yank. Erin cried out, the sound filling Paige with grim satisfaction.

Erin dropped the keys, reaching back to grab Paige's hand, and they jingled as they hit the carpet. Instantly Paige let go and swept the keys from the floor.

"What in the hell is going on here?" Garret demanded, standing in the doorway.

"Nate killed Michelle, and Erin knew the whole time," Paige said, Erin's confession spewing from her lips like a broken water main. "She helped hide the body and kept his secret. Now Nate has Haley and that's where I'm going."

"You said you wouldn't tell him." Erin gasped.

"I lied," Paige said. "That's a concept I thought you'd be very familiar with by now." Paige turned and dashed down the stairs, the keys digging painfully into her flesh.

Where was she? Haley sat up straight on the large bed, her gaze darting about the dark room she'd awakened in. Her head pounded, and her throat burned. She scrambled off the bed and went to the window, pulling back the greenish gold drape and peering out at the white flakes swirling against the black sky.

Her body ached like she had been hit by truck, and as she stepped away from the glass the sight of her reflection in the window stopped her. Her lips were swollen, a thin cut split the lower one. Dark purple bruises had formed around her mouth and on her cheekbone. Memories of Nate punching her at the side of the road rushed through her.

She had to get out of there. But where was she? She turned back to the window. Aside from the vague outline of a barn, she could make out little else through the falling snow.

Barns were found on rural properties. She was on a rural property, but where? She could be anywhere. Miles away from anyone who could help her.

She glanced at her stocking feet on the dark wood floor. What had Nate done with her boots and coat? She didn't see them. It didn't matter. She'd hike miles in the snow barefoot and naked to get help if she had to. Hopefully, it wouldn't come to that.

Determined to escape, she tugged at the window, but the glass wouldn't budge. She ran her fingers over the frame, searching for a lock. Nothing.

Could she break it? Haley looked for something to smash the glass. And again found nothing.

With fear and panic expanding inside her like a poison bubble, she went to the door. Weak light shone under the crack at the bottom. Pressing her ear against the smooth wood, she listened for any sign of life. Nothing.

She closed her hand on the cool metal of the knob and turned it. Unlocked. The door was actually unlocked.

She stuck her head into the hall. To her left, an open door led to a dark room, and another across from where she stood. To her right, the hall opened into the rest of the house.

As quietly as possible, Haley crept toward the opening. Her heart beat crazily, echoing inside her head as she reached the edge of a sunken living room and stopped. A fire burned in the stone hearth on the far wall. The flickering flames cast long shadows over the small open kitchen and dining areas facing her.

No sign of Nate. Perhaps he'd stepped out. Maybe he'd gone to kill Dean. The image made her head swim. No. She bit back on the overwhelming fear. She couldn't think like that. If she wanted to save Dean and herself, she needed get out of there now.

She started toward the front door, glancing over her shoulder, terrified that Nate would emerge suddenly from the shadows and put a stop to her escape. The orange glow from the fire lit a photograph on the table. With a frown, she moved closer. Bits of clipped and torn photographs littered the wood surface.

She lifted the scrap that had caught her eye. Paige, at about twelve, sat on a large rock surrounded by forest and tried not to smile. Haley remembered when that picture had been taken. Her entire family had been camping in Algonquin Park. The last vacation they had taken as a family. She remembered her father teasing a smile from Paige. She remembered the moment well because she'd once been in that photo. Someone had cut her image out.

A large soft-cover book lay in the center of the photograph scraps, the word "Scrapbook" typed across the front. With trembling fingers, she turned the first page and her stomach dropped. The thick paper was covered in pictures of her at various ages arranged in a collage.

She flipped to the second and third pages. More pictures of her a little older, right up until last week. Photos taken while she'd been locking the store, getting into her car. Pictures taken of her through her living room window while she read the paper. God, he was crazy.

"It's something, isn't it?" A voice from nowhere made her jump and step back. She turned in the direction of the kitchen, where the disembodied voice had come from.

"I put a lot of work into that." Nate stepped out from the shadows and Haley's breath clogged in her throat. "Worth every moment though. Many a night, while you were fucking Lawson, I was thinking about you."

"How did you get these?" Except for the most recent photos, the rest had been in a cardboard box at her mother's.

"I visited Claire the day your sister was away. She and I looked at the pictures together. When she went to lie down, I helped myself to my favorites. She won't mind. The others I took whenever I came back to see Erin. I've been watching you for a long time, Haley."

He took a step toward her. She took a step back, edging closer to the door. He smiled, clearly amused.

"Where will you go?" he asked. "You've no shoes, no coat. It looks cold out." He took another step forward.

Haley glanced at the door and then back at the man who inched closer to her by the second. Barefoot and naked, she thought, then turned and ran.

Chapter Twenty-Seven

Haley burst through the door into the black night. Her stocking feet sank into the wet, cold snow, but she ignored the slow numbing burn and ran. Without direction or thought, gripped with a nearly blinding panic, she fled past a decrepit barn, down the driveway, toward the road.

Her feet thudded against the fresh snow in time with her heart, the only sound reaching her over her own ragged breathing until the dry rev of a car engine ripped through the night. She didn't dare look back. Instead, she ran faster.

The engine grew louder, and the snow-covered ground around her glowed under the glare of the truck's headlights. Was he going to run her down? She'd never reach the road before he caught her.

She veered right, leaping over the high snow bank at the driveway's edge. Her foot caught on a jagged outcrop of snow-covered ice, sending her tumbling down and knocking the wind from her as effectively as a kick in the gut.

Gasping, she scrambled to her feet. Her legs sinking in the much-deeper snow. Blood pounded inside her head as she struggled forward, her movements slow and sluggish as though she were running under water.

A thud followed by a high pitched whine made her turn sharply. In his attempt to follow her, Nate had driven his truck onto snow bank and lodged it there. The tires spun uselessly as the truck rocked forward and back on its narrow perch. A small fragment of relief flickered inside her until the driver side door opened and Nate climbed out. His long legs moving through the snow much faster than her height would allow.

Haley turned and forced herself to pick up her pace. Her small lead wouldn't be enough to elude him. The field sloped gently downward, and through the falling snow she caught a glimpse of light. Warm, yellow and definitely electric. A house.

She could make it, she would escape. All she had to do was get there. Then she could call the police and Nate Johnson would spend the rest of his life rotting in prison.

Her breath left her lungs in a small yelp as something smashed into her and sent her sailing through the air. She landed hard, skidding over the snow like a human toboggan. Nate landed across her legs.

Gasping for air, Haley tried to wriggle out from under him, but he scrambled over her, using his body to press her deep into the snow. His fingers gripped her hair tightly, and her scalp came alive with a sharp tearing pain. He pulled her head back and pressed the cold barrel of a gun to the side of her head.

"Enough," Nate panted, his voice furious and harsh. "We're going back, and if you try anything like this again, I'll have no choice. Do you understand?"

She nodded.

Would she regret that decision later? Was it better to stand and fight while she still could? And wouldn't a quick death now be better than what waited for her inside?

No, don't think like that. Play it smart.

Nate pulled her roughly to her feet. With one hand he gripped her elbow and pulled her toward the driveway, keeping the gun leveled at her with the other.

She was shivering nearly uncontrollably by the time they reached the house, her clothes soaked and cold against her skin. She wrapped her arms around her middle and her teeth chattered.

"You should be afraid," Nate said. The anger had left his voice and he sounded like an annoyed parent. "What you did was very foolish. I'm disappointed in you."

I'm not too thrilled with you either. "Why are you doing this?" she asked.

"You need to understand," Nate said, shoving her inside. He turned the bolt in the door. "Don't try anything stupid."

He stepped around her, sat down on the sofa, facing the glowing fireplace and unlaced his boots. Haley didn't move. She stayed shivering and dripping on the hallway floor, searching for an escape.

"I love you, Haley," Nate said, pulling off one boot, then the other. His words made her stomach turn. Her gaze jumped around the room. There had to be a way out. "I didn't realize right away, but all along you were the one."

"You sent the flowers and the card?" Haley asked, though she already knew the answer.

"Did you like them?"

"Just like you sent flowers and cards to Michelle."

"Michelle was a mistake," Nate said. "I was wrong about her. It was you."

"Was my father's first wife a mistake also?" Haley couldn't keep the derision from her voice. Even beneath the layers of fear, anger throbbed hot and strong.

"No. She got what she deserved. She should never have tried to come between your father and me."

His words were spoken like a jealous lover rather than a close friend.

"Is that why you killed her?"

He was quiet for a moment his eyes hard and measuring. "I don't like your tone, Haley."

You've got to be kidding me. "Really? I don't like being attacked at the side of the road and dragged somewhere against my will. And I especially don't like having guns pointed at my head."

He stood and came toward her. Still shivering she backed up, but the wall behind her wouldn't let her go any farther. "I'm sorry. I didn't want to hurt you like that, but Lawson threw me off. He nearly ruined everything. I almost lost you."

A smile touched Nate's mouth, his eyes looked far away and frightening. He ran his fingertips down the side of her face and she tried not to shudder in revulsion. "No," she said.

He frowned.

Be careful, be very careful. "I don't understand what all of this is about."

241

He smiled warm and guileless. "You need to get out of those wet things."

Somehow she managed to keep from throwing up on the spot. "Not yet." She edged away from him. "I'll sit here by the fire." The orange light from the hearth flickered over the dark metal of the gun on the table as she sunk onto the ottoman next to the fireplace. If she could grab the weapon, she could get the upper hand. She tensed, ready to spring, but relaxed again as Nate sat on the sofa opposite her. She couldn't beat him to the gun. He was closer.

"Why did you kill my father's first wife and Michelle? Help me to understand." Her gaze flicked from his face, to the gun then back to his face.

He smiled at her like he would sometimes when she had said something that amused him. The way an uncle smiled at a favorite niece. Not the way a madman smiled at a potential victim. How could any of this be happening? How could Nate have murdered her sister?

"She tried to come between us." His expression darkened and the madman who hit her and dragged her here clouded his features.

"How?"

"Darren and I were like brothers. Maybe not by blood, but we were as close as people can be without sharing the same parents. Closer, maybe. We grew up together, did everything together. Then he met Eleanor and everything changed. He moved away and left me."

"You were jealous."

"Shut up," he snarled, suddenly furious. For a second, her heart ceased to beat. "I wasn't jealous. That's nonsense, but I knew what was best for Darren, and that wasn't Eleanor with all her plans."

She met his blazing stare. "You killed her?"

"She got what she deserved. She thought she was so much better than the rest of us. But she learned."

"No one found her."

"And no one will," he snapped.

She nodded and swallowed, a feat all on its own

considering her throat had shriveled to the size of a pin. He had been obsessed with her father. But why murder Michelle? And why had he suddenly fixated on her?

"So Dad came here?" Haley asked, cautiously.

"I told him that would be best. He was upset that Eleanor had left him. That her family had accused him of murder, but I knew he would get over it. I helped him to start again. I introduced him to Claire, she was a friend of Joan's. We opened the store together. In the end, I was right. He was happy, with his friends and family."

"Yes he was, until Michelle disappeared."

He looked at her sharply. "You didn't know your sister the way I did."

"And how did you know her?" Though she doubted very much she really wanted to hear.

"I thought she and I were meant to be together. Since she was about sixteen, and I would see her at the store. She shared your father's goodness. I knew she was for me. She needed someone to guide her, just as your father had. I thought she needed me, but I was wrong. She wasn't good at all."

"Is that why you killed her? She didn't meet your expectations?" She knew she sounded accusatory, but she couldn't help herself.

"First Lawson then Williams and then Lawson again behind Williams's back. She was a little slut."

"That was a rumor," Haley snapped. "And even if it had been true, who were you to judge, lusting after a sixteen-year-old girl."

In a flash Nate stood, the back of his hand connected with her already-bruised cheek. Pain exploded in her face, searing up the side of her head as she tumbled from the ottoman.

"Why do you make me do this?" Nate's voice had turned almost shrill. "I don't want to hurt you, Haley. I love you."

Trembling , Haley shrank away from the madman towering over her. Would he kill her now? Had she pushed too far? She needed to keep her mouth shut and her temper in check.

Nate turned away from her and started pacing, muttering to himself as he did. His mind was gone. How did he manage to go through life fooling people? Fooling her?

"She was pregnant." Nate stopped pacing and looked directly at her. "She told me. She actually believed that would make a difference."

"Is that why you killed her?"

"I loved her," Nate said. "I thought we were meant to be together."

Nate resumed his pacing as Haley shifted back onto the ottoman. She slid the seat closer to the table before sitting down, and prayed he wouldn't notice.

"She wouldn't have me, though." Nate stopped again, looked at her. "She was carrying a child and didn't know who the father was, but she wouldn't have me."

With her toes, Haley gripped the wood floor and slid the ottoman closer. The legs scraped against the wood and she tried not to cringe.

"I was so wrong," Nate took a step toward her. Haley froze. "It wasn't Michelle I was meant to be with. It was you. You are so like your father. I didn't see it before. You were young and not as outgoing as she was, but you're good like him. You need someone to keep you safe and protect you."

He moved between her and the coffee table—her and the gun—and bent down. Gripping both her shoulders, he pulled her to her feet. He smelled of perspiration.

"I've thought of you, of this, for so long." He lowered his head and pressed his mouth to hers, grinding her already-swollen lips against her teeth. She twisted her head away and those cold reptilian lips fell on her neck. Her stomach heaved, but she fought the nearly instinctual need to shove him away.

Michelle had rejected him, and he'd killed her for it. Despite the terror and loathing writhing inside her, she had to be smart. She had to stay calm.

When his fingers fumbled with the fly of her jeans all thoughts of smart and calm flew out the window. She pushed away from him hard. His furious eyes met hers.

With her heart thundering against her chest she wracked her brain for an excuse, something to stall him. To buy her time. To get her closer to the gun.

"Not yet," she said. Just saying the words made her cold. "Not like this. It's too fast. I need a little time to digest everything you've told me."

Nate released her almost instantly. Relief flooded through her system making her knees weak. She sank back down to the ottoman. For a moment or two, Nate stayed where he was, standing over her, searching her face with his narrow gaze.

"This is a surprise for you," Nate said at last. Then he smiled. "I've been in love with you for so long, I forget this is new for you."

"How long?" How long had she trusted him as friend while he'd been obsessively planning for this moment?

"Just before I left Hareton. I was getting ready to tell you, but Joan got sick. I may not have loved her, but she'd been a good wife to me and deserved to have me with her during her final years."

"You were gone for six years," she said stunned.

"I tried to visit, but Joan's illness made it difficult for me to get away. I might have ended her suffering sooner if that damn sister of hers hadn't always been hovering." Bitterness turned his voice hard, then he smiled brightly. "But I knew you would be here waiting for me. Someone had to take care of Claire."

Haley sat stunned. No wonder he'd been so cooperative when she'd bought out his half of the store. One more thing to keep her tied to Hareton, and available for him. But she hadn't been available the whole time. "I was engaged to Jason."

The smile vanished and Haley tensed waiting for him to hit her again, but he didn't. "He's lucky your sister helped him show his true colors, otherwise I would have had to deal with him."

For the first time, Haley thought so too. Jason might have been a fickle bastard, but she hated to think what Nate might have done to him.

"And I forgive you for him, Haley. Just like I've forgiven you for Lawson."

Her throat tightened. Had Nate dealt with Dean the same way he'd planned to deal with Jason? She glanced at the gun, but Nate took a step toward her.

"Wait." She held up her hand to stop him. "I still have

questions. I know this may be difficult to talk about, but Michelle was my sister."

"Of course, you want to know about Michelle." He sat down again on the couch. "I've always regretted having to keep what happened to Michelle a secret, but I know it was for the best. Your parents would have been devastated to learn what Michelle had become."

Haley forced herself to keep her tone even, to bite back on the furious words bubbling in her throat. God, she hated the man before her. She'd never known she was capable of such intense loathing.

What kind of person could justify murdering a pregnant twenty-one year old woman and believe that he had done the right thing? How could he convince himself that he had done her family a favor by keeping the truth from them for more than a decade? The sincerity in his voice, in his expression, his firm belief that Michelle had gotten exactly what she deserved was horrifying.

"You said you believed you were meant to be with her when she was about sixteen. Why did you wait to act on your feelings?"

He chuckled. "She was only sixteen. I'm not a monster."

Her cheek and mouth still ached from the pummeling he'd given at the side of the road. Not to mention when he'd knocked to the floor just now. Or tackled her in the snow like a football player.

No, you're not a monster. Now, please continue to explain how you came to murder my sister.

"I thought once she finished university, I would speak to her. I had my own family to think of. Garret and Erin would be married by then and I would no longer need to worry about my daughter, she'd be taken care of." His voice had turned conversational, as if he enjoyed having someone to tell at last. Someone he could voice his rationalizations to aloud.

"What about Joan, your wife?"

"Joan would understand, once I explained things to her."

And if she didn't, the poor woman probably would have found herself buried in someone's basement too.

"Michelle hadn't finished school when you started sending

the flowers and cards," Haley said.

"I had to move forward sooner than I'd planned. She and Williams were getting serious, and I'd heard he might propose. That couldn't happen. She was meant for me."

His words sent a shiver down her spine. He must have assumed from the minute he told Michelle how he felt they would live happily ever after. He never considered that Michelle would reject him. Her feelings had never been a factor. For Nate, she wasn't even a real person, just a player in a drama where he was the star. Now Haley filled Michelle's role.

"When she told you she was pregnant, did you realize she wasn't meant to be yours after all?"

Nate frowned. Damn, that had sounded entirely too flip. She had to watch her temper.

"I knew about her and Lawson," Nate said. The vehemence with which he spoke Dean's name alarmed her. Was Dean already dead? She struggled to push away the image of his cold empty car. If she could get to the gun, she could make Nate tell her what happened to Dean. "I knew he was trash. I told your father not to hire him, but your father wouldn't listen, and look where it got him. Everyone knew Michelle was going behind Williams's back and messing with Lawson. She denied it, of course, once she had found herself knocked up. Couldn't have her golden boy knowing that she was sleeping around."

"How do you know this?" Haley asked trying to seem curious rather than disgusted. His smile had gone and his voice had turned furious. A dark malignancy glowed in his eyes.

"She told me when I picked her up," Nate said. "I had been following her for some time, waiting for the right moment for us to talk. I needed to tell her how I felt. When I saw her walking away from the Williams's place, I knew the time had come."

Talk about history repeating itself.

"So you stopped," Haley said, almost to herself. "And of course, she wouldn't have hesitated accepting a ride from you. You were our father's friend. She would have been relieved to see you."

"Haley," Nate said. "Don't do this to yourself. Michelle was not the person you thought she was. She told me right there in the truck about the mess she was in. How Williams wouldn't have her because he knew about her carrying on with Lawson."

"She would have been afraid, and confiding in you as a friend."

"Don't try and turn this around on me," Nate shouted. "I would have taken her still, loved her, but she wouldn't have me. Williams and Lawson had both abandoned her, and she wouldn't have me. A slut like that and she wouldn't have me."

"Nothing happened with her and Dean after they broke up," Haley snapped, anger and fear swirling in her brain and pushing her toward the edge. "It was a rumor spread by Lara Kramer and your own daughter."

"Is that what he told you?" Nate jumped off the couch. His body, taut and trembling with fury, towered over her. Bright red blotches spread out over his face and his eyes nearly bulged from their sockets. "Is that what he told you, to worm his way into your bed? Well, not to worry, he'll get his."

Get, not got. A thin shaft of hope speared her heart. Could Dean still be alive?

"Dean's innocent. He had nothing to do with Michelle." She swallowed back the bile rising in her throat. "You should let him go. I didn't know how you felt before, but I do now. We can be together, but you need to let Dean go. Where is he?"

"We can be together?" His eyes narrowed.

She nodded. "But let Dean go. Is he here in the house? In one of the rooms back there?"

"I love you, Haley." Then in a single almost graceful move, Nate turned and swept the gun from the table, leveling the barrel at her face. "Why don't I take you to Dean."

Haley's heart ceased to be beat. She closed her eyes tightly and waited to die.

Chapter Twenty-Eight

Garret stood frozen in place unable to move, speak or even think. Around him the world continued on. Erin gasped in shock and Paige smiled triumphantly before racing down the stairs with Erin's keys. Both women seemed unaware that the air had been sucked out of the space around him. That he now stood paralyzed in a lifeless, soundless vacuum, watching them from a void.

The front door slammed shut with a resounding whack and suddenly he was back. Sound, thought and movement rushed over him and through him, like a wave crashing against the shore, so powerful he nearly had to take a step back to steady himself.

"Garret," Erin said. She wanted something from him. What, he wasn't sure. He felt drunk. The room spun and only he and Erin remained still.

"You knew," he said. At least he thought it was him. The voice, dry and hoarse, as if unused for years, sounded unfamiliar.

"Please, Garret." Erin choked back a sob.

"How could you do it? All these years. You were there. You saw what it did to my family, to my mother and all along you knew."

"So many times I wanted to tell you," Erin said. "I love you. It hurt me to see you go through that. I never wanted to lie to you."

"Then why did you?" The hardness in his voice made her take a step back, a dark thrill raced through him. The haze muddling his mind was lifting, and only black fury remained.

"I couldn't, he was my father."

"He murdered my sister," Garret exploded.

Big glassy tears ran down her cheeks, and he wanted to hit her. "It was an accident. He didn't mean to kill her."

"He has Haley now?"

She nodded.

"Accident my ass," he muttered pushing past his wife. Blindly, she reached for him. Her hands, like claws, grasped the front of his shirt, twisting the material in her tightly gripped fists. Garret looked into her red, swollen eyes and something inside him snapped.

He hated her. This woman he once loved and cherished, with whom he shared children and a home. In an instant, she had killed his love and tore apart all they shared. Everything he depended on, gone in a single moment. Oddly, he hated her for that more than the secret she'd kept all this time.

He raised his hands from his sides slowly. The temptation to wrap them around her neck and squeeze was almost unbearable, but instead, he gripped her wrists and pulled her clutching fingers from him. He turned on his heel and started downstairs.

"Garret," she sobbed, but wisely didn't follow.

Once outside, both Paige and his SUV were gone. He would try the van, but he had no idea how far he would get in the weather. He went back inside and called the police from the phone in the kitchen, ignoring their instructions to stay where he was.

Was there still time for Haley? He couldn't go through losing another sister, and lose his wife at the same time.

Paige gripped the steering wheel until her hands ached. Garret's truck allowed for more control on the slick road and greater speed, but when she braked, the SUV stopped just like any other car. So she tried to stop as little as possible. Fortunately, the storm was keeping most people at home and off the roads. Particularly the back roads. Only she was crazy enough to be using them on a night like this. Crazy or desperate. Both really.

She should have called the police before she left, but the all-consuming sense that time was ticking and every second counted kept her from making decisions based on common sense. If she hadn't left her cell phone in her car, this wouldn't be an issue. She missed her tiny technological wonder the same way she would an appendage had someone come along and lopped it off.

The road north of Hareton was winding and hilly, treacherous even in Garret's SUV. The falling snow turned her visibility to slightly better than nothing. She had missed Old Base Road twice. A thick layer of snow clung to the green sign, hiding the road's name.

The truck's headlights fell on a silver mailbox, poking through a mound of loose snow. Excitement leapt inside her. This could be it. She squinted to read the number. This was it.

She swung the wheel and the SUV fishtailed slightly as she started up the drive. She straightened out with little effort. The trees closed in around the truck, their branches scraping the sides like grasping fingers, scraping her nerves raw.

Within seconds, the woods fell away to a flat open expanse of field covered in a blanket of pristine snow. The outline of something huge loomed in the darkness before her. A large hulking mass, rising out of the road. Then her headlights hit, illuminating faded red paint and the dents caused by years of use. Nate Johnson's truck teetered on a snow bank.

Paige stopped a few feet from the truck and climbed out. The snow fell in a thick curtain, but the wind had died down some, taking the bite from the air. Deep impressions in the snow led away from the truck into the field.

Cursing, she plowed her way into the deep snow, following the half-buried footprints. They ended abruptly nearly thirty feet from the driveway. Here the snow was smooth and untouched except for a much larger imprint, as big as a body.

Paige lifted her gaze to the darkened field around her. Just ahead, the ground sloped toward a line of trees. A pale light glowed from between their branches. A house. Maybe Haley had gotten away. She considered the body size imprint in the snow and shivered. Maybe not.

Her heart pounded a wild rhythm against her chest. She turned and started toward her car, then stopped mid-stride. She could call the police from the house. This could be her last chance to do so. But the feeling that she needed to hurry, that time was slipping away, kept her moving toward the driveway.

A fresh wave of fear washed over her, cold and numbing. Her pace quickened with every step until she was running. Every second seemed to matter, and she couldn't ignore the feeling that there were precious few left.

She jumped the snow bank, clearing the hump easily, but slipped on the snowy drive and landed hard on her backside. Her teeth clicked together with her tongue in between.

The warm metallic flavor of her own blood filled her mouth. She spat a red wad into the snow. Fabulous. Ignoring her throbbing tongue, she scrambled to her feet and ran toward the truck. As her hand closed around the cold metal handle, a shot rang out, echoing in the quiet stillness like a thunder crack.

Paige's knees buckled and she sank down into the snow. Time was up.

How long Nate held the gun pointed at her, Haley didn't know. She might have stood frozen, her extremities cold and paralyzed, for years. Nate dropped his arm, but before she could take a breath he was next to her, grabbing her arm and yanking her outside. His fingers dug painfully into her flesh.

"You disappointed me," he muttered. That same blank expression he wore when he knocked her out next to the highway slid over his features.

He was going to kill her. If not by gun, then perhaps something more personal. He'd slit Michelle's throat, maybe he needed a knife. She swallowed back her rising panic.

With the gun pushed hard against her kidney, he shoved her toward the barn, releasing her only long enough to open the door. She could run now, this might be her last chance.

As if reading her mind, Nate growled, "Don't move or I'll kill you right here, and Lawson too."

Dean was alive, but for how long? How long did either of them have? Was Nate taking her to him? Would he kill them together? There had to be a way to get the gun from him. Maybe charge him, catch him by surprise.

Nate thrust her into the darkened barn, pitch black except for the small pool of light at the door. She stumbled over the uneven floor. A match scraped and sparked from behind her. She turned as Nate ignited a thin propane lamp.

"Move." Nate shoved her again, sending her stumbling into the side of a stall. The rakes and shovel leaning there clattered to the ground. She caught her balance just before she joined them.

Something moved at the corner of her eye. She turned to see Dean, tied and gagged, struggling to pull himself to his knees.

"Oh God," she gasped. Blood streaked his ashen face, stemming from the back of his head where his hair was thick and matted. More blood smeared his hands and forearms, from where he'd been fighting the rope binding his wrists.

Instinctively, she took a step toward him, but Nate grabbed her arm and yanked her back. Dean's eyes filled with fury and fear, he muttered something unintelligible from around the gag. As he struggled against the ropes, a thin stream of blood dripped from his fingers.

"Don't!" she shouted. He lifted his gaze and met hers. "I'm okay." Though tears pricked her eyes for the first time since she woke to find herself in Nate's house. He'd kill them both and no one would see either of them again.

"Let him go," Haley said, turning to Nate. He ignored her, staring blindly at the man in front of him. "Please let him go. He has nothing do with this. I told you, we can be together." And still he didn't respond.

Haley glanced around the barn desperate for a way out. Nate's lantern only illuminated a small circle around them. The rest of the barn remained in shadow.

Her gaze lit on the shovel she'd fallen into. Maybe she could knock him out with the shovel.

Nate turned on her suddenly and she took an involuntary step back nearly tumbling over the shovel and rakes again.

"Do you love him, Haley?" Nate asked. Haley's breathing turned rapid and shallow. A trick question. No matter how she answered he would kill Dean. She had to stall for time. If she could just bend and grab the shovel. She needed to distract him.

"Answer me," he shouted.

"Let him go. I'll do whatever you want, just let him go."

"You're the same as her. You're nothing like Darren." Nate said, his voice choked with emotion. "I thought you were good. I loved you."

"Please let him go," she whispered.

Without another word, he turned and fired the gun. Dean had pulled himself to his knees, and was edging closer. The bullet caught him in the side and knocked him backward to the floor. His shirt stained red almost instantly.

"No!" The scream, primal and ferocious, ripped from her lips. She bent and gripped the shovel's wood handle, swinging wide, with all her fear and hate. The flat side of the spade struck his face and his nose exploded in a mass of bloody flesh. He stumbled back, turning a little, and she swung again, catching the side of his head. He fell to the ground, and the gun spun uselessly into the shadows.

He didn't get up again.

She dropped the shovel from her trembling fingers, the metal spade clanged in the quiet when it hit the ground. Shaking all over, tears filling her eyes, she went to Dean.

He lay where he fell, his breath coming in quick ragged gasps. Blood soaked shirtfront, but he was still alive. How long could she keep him that way?

Gently, she worked the gag free from his mouth. She had no car, no way out of this hellhole. She needed to call 911, but how long until someone finally showed up?

"You're okay."

Haley jumped at the sound of Paige's voice. Her sister rushed over and fell to her knees, throwing her arms around her, squeezing the breath from Haley's lungs. "I thought—oh my, God, I thought—"

"He's shot," Haley said, on a sob. She'd never been so grateful to see anyone in her life. "Nate shot him. We have to get him to a hospital."

"Oh, Christ." Paige shrugged out of her coat and handed it to Haley. "Put this over the wound. Hopefully, it will stem some of the bleeding while I get him untied."

Haley pressed her sister's jacket over Dean's stomach while Paige struggled to loosen the stiff ropes from his ankles.

"I've got to lift him to get at his hands," Paige said. Haley nodded. She pressed the coat to Dean with one hand while she helped Paige lift with the other.

"He's bleeding back here too," Paige said. "The bullet must have passed through him."

"Is that good or bad?"

"Am I a doctor?" Paige snapped. "Sorry, I'm freaked."

Haley nodded. "Can you hold him by yourself?"

"Yeah."

Haley sat back and pulled off her still damp sweater, leaving her in a thin white T-shirt. She handed the sweater to Paige. "Put this under him."

"You'll freeze," Paige said. Haley shrugged and pressed down once more on the coat while Paige lowered Dean back to the ground. His eyes fluttered open and fixed on Haley.

"You were shot," she told him. "But you're going to be all right. Paige is here, and we're going to get you to a hospital."

"Nate?" he asked.

Haley glanced over her shoulder at the man lying perfectly still where he had fallen. The side of his head was swollen where she'd hit him, and a round blue-black bruise had formed. Blood trickled from his ear and nose.

With huge eyes, Paige crawled over to him and pressed her finger to his neck, then his wrist. She pulled her hair away from her ear and tilted her head so her ear was inches away from his mangled and bloody nose.

"I think he's dead."

Haley's insides clenched. "Good."

"Can you stand if we help you?" Paige asked, crawling toward them. "I've got Garret's truck outside."

Dean nodded and both Paige and Haley helped him to his feet. He leaned heavily on them, each shouldering his weight.

As they left the barn, the high-pitched whine of distant sirens rose up from the night, growing steadily louder.

"Garret must have called the police. Hopefully, paramedics too," Paige said.

Haley nodded, relief crashing into her and leaving her shaking. It was over. After twelve years it was finally over.

Chapter Twenty-Nine

Erin stood in the silent den. Behind her, the multi-colored lights from the Christmas tree she'd decorated with her husband and children less than a week ago glowed in the dark room. Christmas Eve and she was alone. But Garret was coming. He'd called this morning and told her he wanted to see her.

A hope she didn't dare acknowledge grew inside her as she paced the small room. Everything was as she wanted it. From the quilted Christmas stockings she'd made herself, hanging from the mantel over the fireplace, to the book Garret had been reading, carefully placed on the coffee table to appear carelessly laid. She'd cleaned the house until every corner of every room was spotless, all to achieve her ultimate goal—tidy, warm and homey.

Surely Garret wouldn't throw away their life together. Not after so many years. She drew in a shuddering breath and expelled the air slowly.

She'd feared the worst when he came home from the hospital in the early morning after her confession. He told her Haley was okay, Dean would live, and her father was dead. Then he took the girls and left. She hadn't spoken to any of them since. Five days. The darkest, longest days of her life.

Still, he hadn't told the police what she'd done, and he hadn't let his bitch sisters tell either. From that, the first kernel of hope had bloomed.

At the sound of the front door opening, she froze and her heart fluttered. She stopped pacing and wrung her hands.

"Erin?" Garret called.

She took a deep steadying breath. "In here."

His footfalls echoed on the ceramic tiles, purposeful and headed her way. She wiped her damp palms on her thighs. He stopped at the threshold of the den as if hitting an invisible barrier.

He glanced around the room and when his eyes lit on her, they blazed like smoldering onyx. For the first time in her life she saw a resemblance to Paige. His hard gaze swept up and down the length of her then his lips curled back in a sneer.

"I don't have a lot of time, Paige is watching Lilly and Tess."

"I miss them," she said. "How are they?"

He shook his head. "Confused. We all are."

"Where are you staying?"

"My mother's."

"Garret, I don't like the girls around her. The way she drinks, she's unpredictable."

"Funny, you had no problem leaving them alone with your psychotic, murdering father."

The words hit her like a slap and she dropped her gaze to the floor. "How is Haley?"

"She's okay. Her face still looks like she was hit by a truck, but she seems better."

"And Dean?"

"He comes home from the hospital today."

"Good, I'm glad."

Garret snorted and shook his head. "Are you?"

"Of course I am. I can't believe you can ask that."

"Neither can I. How could you have kept this from me?" His voice was terse and filled with fury. She wanted to touch him, but his body practically hummed with pent-up violence, and she was afraid.

"I wanted to tell you, so many times." She choked on a sob. "I just didn't know how."

Garret stared down at his wife's bent head. No this woman wasn't his wife. This lying bitch was a virtual stranger to him. "You could have started with, 'Garret, my father murdered your sister, and you'll find her body buried in your grandmother's basement'."

The urge to hit her, to punch her right in her manipulative, lying mouth, the same way her father had hit his sister was overwhelming. He turned his back to her, the sight of Erin dressed in the clothes he gave her on her last birthday, wearing the perfume he liked, looking soft and hurt only enraged him further. Everything from her to this house felt staged.

"I wanted to. I did." Her hand closed over his forearm.

He jerked away and snarled, "I guess you couldn't tell me though, you were an accessory to murder after all."

"No, it wasn't like that," she denied again.

"Then what was it like? What was it like covering up a murder with your father while playing the mourner with me?"

"He was my father, what else could I do? I had to protect him and my mother. What if it had been your family?"

His hand closed into a tight fist. "It was my family. We were just on the other end. The falling apart and losing our minds end. For God's sake, he murdered your friend. How could you have protected him? Helped him? Let alone stand back while he did it again. Innocent women, and you let him get away with murder."

"Innocent women?" she asked, narrowing her eyes. The big glassy tears dried. "They lured him, Garret. He was a good man, a family man, but Michelle flirted with him just to hurt me. And Haley was no better."

The hate glowing in her gaze made him take a step back, and strengthened his resolve. He was doing the right thing. "You're as delusional as he was."

"Don't say that." She turned weepy again. "Please forgive me. I'll do anything to get back what we had."

"What we had is dead," he said. His heart felt like a stone in his chest. Heavy and cold. "If it existed at all."

"Think of the girls."

"They're all I've been thinking of. They're the only reason the police haven't carted you off—yet."

"What do you mean?" Her voice was soft and wary.

"This is a document signing over all of your parental rights for the girls to me. I've started the paperwork for a separation."

"No," she gasped.

"You can't honestly be surprised."

"We can get through this. I will spend every day of my life making it up to you."

"You can't make this up to me. You were a part of Michelle's murder, and you very nearly let Haley end up the same way."

"There has to be hope for us."

"There is no us. Now, sign the papers and give me the girls."

"You can't take away my babies."

"You would rather have them see you go to prison?"

"I don't understand."

"We're getting a divorce. You can have the house and everything in it, I don't care, but you're going to give me the girls. I'm going to take them and start over somewhere else. If you don't, I'll go to the police, and you'll be arrested for your part in what happened to Michelle."

"Do you hate me that much?"

"Yes."

She cried, but she signed the papers. Her sobs filled his ears as he left.

Once he climbed into the truck, he closed his eyes and rested his forehead against the cold plastic steering wheel. Again doubt filled him. Memories of Lilly crying for her mama and Tess staring at him with reproachful eyes gripped his heart and squeezed.

Nate had done this. It wasn't enough to murder Michelle and destroy his parents. It hadn't been enough to ruin Dean. Or torment Haley. Now Garret's own children, innocent in every way, were suffering.

His stomach twisted. Was it wrong to take their mother from their lives? How could Erin have lied to him all that time? Let her father try and kill Haley, then to blame Michelle and Haley for what happened? There had to be something fundamentally wrong with her. What choice did he have?

He backed out of the drive and headed to the mall. He had Christmas presents to buy, and Santa would be overcompensating this year. Then, when he returned to his mom's, he'd find the old artificial Christmas tree that had been his family's when he was a kid along with the old ornaments.

For the first time in more than a decade there would be Christmas in his mother's house.

"Here, you can lean on me," Haley said, helping Dean from the passenger seat of her car.

"I think I can manage." She ignored his indignant tone and gently took his arm. He rolled his eyes. "The bullet barely grazed me. It was nothing."

"Then why did the doctors make you stay in the hospital for five days for nothing?"

"They were more concerned about my head than the gunshot wound."

"Stop your whining and come inside," Haley told him, leading him up the walk to her front door. "It's cold out here."

"And me in my delicate condition."

She unlocked the front door and they stepped inside. Over the past five days, she'd returned home only a few times to shower and change. Now, the air smelled stale. Empty.

She clutched her keys, the cool metal pressing against her flesh. Why did she feel so awkward and nervous? She knew why. She might want to pretend everything was the same between her and Dean, but it wasn't.

There was no reason for him to stay now. They had the answers they'd been searching for. Nate had killed Michelle, and she had killed Nate. Something quivered inside her and she forced the images of those terrifying moments in the barn to the back of her mind.

More than once she'd tried to bring up the subject of what happened next, but every time she worked up the courage one of the nurses, or a doctor, or Paige, or Garret would interrupt. They were alone now, though. Finally, they could talk.

"Sit down," she instructed, helping him to the couch.

"I'm fine." Gingerly, he lowered himself to the cushion.

She knelt in front of him. "I'll get your boots."

"I can take off my own boots," he said, exasperated. He leaned forward and winced.

"Stop being stubborn. You're going to rip your stitches."

She unlaced his boots and pulled them from his feet. He scowled all the while.

"I'll get you a blanket from upstairs."

"Haley, I don't have pneumonia, I was shot."

"I know." The image of him falling, hitting the barn floor, his blood spreading out over his shirt played again in her mind, turning her stomach and leaving her cold.

His hand cupped her cheek and gently forced her to meet his gaze. "I'm fine," he told her, gently tracing her bruised cheek bone with his thumb. The swelling had gone and the ugly purple had faded to an uglier yellow-brown. "I hate that he hurt you."

She smirked. "I wasn't so wild about it myself."

He drew her closer and covered her mouth with his. She melted into the kiss, sinking into his warmth, momentarily finding the reassurance she sought.

Her arms wrapped around his neck, as if of their own volition. His teeth tugged at her lip and heat pooled between her legs. The need to touch him, to feel him against her, warm and living rushed through her, driving away the uncertainty. She shifted closer, running her hands over his chest. His sharp hiss made her scramble back.

"Oh God, are you okay?" What the hell was she thinking, making out with an injured man?

"I just need to lean back." He shifted on the sofa. "Now, come here, I've missed this."

"No, you'll hurt yourself."

"I'm fine, damn it," he whined.

"You're not that fine."

A sharp knock at the front door ended the discussion. Before Haley could answer, Paige let herself in. "Am I interrupting?"

Yes! Haley wanted to scream. At this rate, she'd never get a chance to talk to Dean.

"You seem to be settling in," Paige said to Dean, shrugging out of her coat and flopping into the armchair. "Your color looks better."

He looked at Haley. "That's because I'm fine."

"Mom wants to see you," Paige said. "I told her Dean had just gotten out of the hospital, but she's a little high-strung today and wants to see you now. I think she's afraid that you've died and Garret and I are just hiding the fact from her. Oddly, had you died, that's probably what we would have done. For a drunk, she's quite astute."

"How much does she know?" Haley asked, standing.

"Everything, except Erin helping Nate hide the body."

"Has Garret decided what he's going to do?"

"He's leaving her and wants her to give him custody of the girls. He won't tell the police or anyone else about what she did as long as she never tries to contact any of them again. Personally, I think he should have hung her out to dry, but I guess he's worried about the effect on their kids."

"Nate was crazy. There's no telling how he manipulated Erin as she grew up," Haley said.

Paige shrugged. "You're much more forgiving than I would be."

"Don't misunderstand, I don't want to be her best friend or anything, I just think she's as much his victim as any of us. More so, maybe."

"Well, you better get over to Mom's. Don't worry, I'll invalid-sit for you."

Dean scowled. "I'm sitting right here."

"Thanks." Haley dug out an orange plastic pill bottle from her purse. "Here's his painkillers." She glanced at her watch. "He can have another one in two hours."

"Thank God you're both here. Getting shot in the side did make me illiterate and caused me to forget how to tell time."

Both women ignored him. "I'll try not to be long."

"No rush," Paige shrugged.

"Speak for yourself," Dean muttered. "Whatever happened to my car?"

Surprise and hurt speared her heart and she did her best to squash the unpleasant sensation. She would do what she had to do. She had hoped Dean would be a part of that, but if he wasn't she would manage on her own. She always had before.

"The police impound," Haley told him. "I'll take you tomorrow to get it."

"You can't." Paige leaned forward and snatched the remote off the trunk, flicking on the TV. "Tomorrow's Christmas."

"Right. I'll have to take you after the holidays."

Dean shrugged. "No big deal."

"Okay, I'll see you both in a bit."

As soon as the door closed, Dean hauled himself off the couch, went to the window and waited for Haley to back out of the driveway. His side throbbed dully. Maybe Haley was right. Maybe he was trying to do too much.

Once her car had left the street, he turned to Paige who eyed him suspiciously. "I need you drive me somewhere."

"Haley will kill me if I let you out."

"Come on, Paige, help me. It's Christmas Eve." He met her gaze.

After a long measuring stare, Paige snapped off the TV and stood. "Of all the disgustingly romantic clichés."

Doubt flickered inside him. "You don't think she'll like it?"

"She's a big sap. She'll love it."

He hoped so.

When Haley got to her mother's, Garret and her nieces were in the living room setting up a misshaped Christmas tree. While Garret bent the wire branches covered in dark green plastic needles in a sad attempt to hide the gaping holes, Lilly chattered and played with the dusty ornaments. Tess sat on the sofa, arms folded over her chest, glaring at her father.

"Is that from before?" Haley asked.

Garret looked up and smiled. "Yeah, how does the tree look?"

264

"Good," she lied.

"What happened to your face, Aunt Haley?" Lilly asked, studying her with pale eyes. Her long, light hair was a mass of wild curls. She looked like her mother.

"I was in an accident."

"That tree looks like it was in accident," Tess muttered. Dark haired, dark eyed and sullen, she was a Carling, all right. "Our tree at home is better. I don't understand why we can't just go home."

"We've never spent Christmas with your grandmother. Think about how nice this will be for her."

"She's always sleeping. She wouldn't notice if we were here or not."

"I miss Mommy. Why can't Mommy come to Grandma's for Christmas?" Lilly asked.

Garret rubbed his mouth with the back of his hand. Haley's heart went out to him. How would he tell them? Or should he?

"Mommy can't, she has some problems she needs to take care of."

Tess rolled her eyes and stood. "I'm going to watch TV."

"Okay." Garret nodded.

"Oh dear, Garret," Claire said, from the top of the stairs. "Your tree is tilting left." As she came down farther, her eyes fell on Haley. Without a word, she walked straight over and hugged her, holding Haley tight with her skinny twig arms.

"I was so afraid," her mother said, taking a step back. "The things I said the last time I saw you. I'm so sorry."

"I shouldn't have done that to The Shr—Michelle's room. I had no right."

Claire shook her head, more coherent than Haley had seen her in ages, but her breath still smelled faintly of alcohol. "I wouldn't say that. Let's go somewhere and talk."

Her mother led her back upstairs, to Haley's old bedroom. They both sat on the edge of the bed. Nerves made Haley's stomach tight, and finding her mother rational had ruined the script she'd mentally prepared.

"How is Dean? I understand the hospital released him."

"He's doing better. I left him to Paige's tender mercies."

A faint smile touched Claire's lips. "I was under the impression you liked this man."

"You look good, Mom."

"Do I?" She laughed shakily and her fingers brushed her smooth hair. "I'm not good, but I'm trying. I don't want the girls to see me bad. They seem to be going through enough. I don't know what's happened between Garret and Erin. I can't see Garret turning away from her because of what her father did. Do you know?"

Haley nodded. "You'll have to find out from Garret, though."

"I can still hardly believe that it was Nate. That he could do something like that and still play the part of our friend."

"Believe it."

"Why did he do it? I don't understand." A rasp tinged her voice. "Did he have a perverse obsession with her?"

"Yes." How much should she reveal? Her mother's grasp on the world was shaky at best, and Haley didn't want to say anything to send her on another bender. Though, once Haley explained how things were going to change, she very well could.

"You can tell me everything. I won't break, and I think knowing will help."

So Haley did. She told her mother about Nate's strange obsession with her father that shifted to Michelle and then to her. She explained about her father's first wife. When she finished, her mother's cheeks were wet with tears.

"Had he been looking for a female version of your father?"

Haley sighed. "I don't know. Find a team of psychologists and maybe they'll be able to explain it. I think for Nate it was all about control. I bet if we knew more about his relationship with Joan and Erin, you would find he controlled every aspect of their lives. That's what he'd been trying to do with Dad."

"Why did he fixate on Michelle?"

"I have no idea. Maybe just another way to manipulate Dad."

"He took so much from us—all of us." Her mother's hand shook badly as she tucked a strand of Haley's hair behind her ear. "And he would have taken more still."

Haley looked away. The naked pain and love in her mother's eyes was strange, making her uncomfortable, and what she had to do even harder. Still, it had to be done.

"Mom, there's something I need to tell you."

"I think I can guess, but go ahead."

"I'm going to leave here." Saying the words out loud bolstered her resolve. She was leaving at last. "This town, the store, I don't want it anymore."

Her mother nodded, her eyes glassy with unshed tears. "Will you leave with Dean?"

God, she hoped so. "He's not a factor," she said carefully.

"What will you do with the store?"

"Sell it. Close it. Whatever's fastest. I won't be here to take care of you anymore. Paige will be going back to work and Garret will have his hands full, but Paige and I have found a clinic that could help you. We want to help you, but we're not going to take care of you. You're going to have to make a choice."

"Sink or swim?" She chuckled again, brittle and a little lonely.

Haley nodded. This had been so much easier when she'd rehearsed the scenario in her head. Of course, in her head her mother had barely been conscious.

"I understand. I wonder if maybe you and your sister could do something for me before you get on with your lives. Two things, really."

Haley narrowed her eyes. Here it comes, she thought. "What's that?"

"Your brother is determined to have Christmas dinner tomorrow. Maybe you and Paige, and Dean if you like, will come for dinner and help me. Then the following day you could take me to this clinic."

Haley smiled. "I'd be happy to." And strangely, she meant it.

As Haley climbed out of her car, Paige came outside, a wide, goofy grin across her face.

"How'd it go?" she asked, meeting Haley in the driveway.

"Good." Haley nodded. "She's agreed to go to the clinic."

"All we can do is keep our fingers crossed. She's actually on her best behavior because of Garret's kids. I know she's drinking, but I think she's hiding in her room when she does."

"She wants us there for dinner tomorrow."

Paige screwed up her face. "Nothing says the holidays like family dysfunction."

"Dean inside?"

"Yeah, he's asleep. Those painkillers really knock him out. I left him on the couch."

"Thanks, Paige, for everything." She didn't just mean for keeping an eye on Dean, or smuggling fast food into the hospital for them so they wouldn't have to eat the meals the hospital provided, or even coming after her when Nate had her. It was all of that and so much more. She was glad to have her sister again.

"Think nothing of it." Paige gave her a quick hug. "Go inside, it's cold out here. I'll see you tomorrow."

Haley nodded and went in, but stopped short in the hall. A small, foot-tall, artificial Christmas tree turned on a plastic base in the center of the steam trunk. Thin white fiber optic needles and plastic snowflakes glowed brightly, while an electronic rendition of "Santa Claus Is Coming to Town" played on a loop from the speaker in the base. It was the tackiest thing she had ever seen. She smiled, strangely delighted.

Dean whistled along tunelessly from the kitchen as he opened and dug through drawers, stopping to curse when he couldn't find whatever it was he was looking for. She watched him from the living room with admiration and exasperation combined.

"You're supposed to be taking it easy," she said at last.

"I am," he turned and grinned, holding out a glass of red wine.

She came toward him and accepted the glass. "What are you looking for?"

"The Chinese food menu from the other night. I know, not very Christmasy, but I'm sick of pizza. Not that I'm not grateful to Paige for feeding us while we were in the hospital, but Hareton really needs to expand their takeout selection."

"On the fridge." She plucked the folded paper from the magnetic clip holding it in place. "How is Pizza Christmasy?"

"I always had pizza on Christmas Eve."

"I'm surprised you managed to convince my sister to take you out and get the tree." She lifted the glass to her lips and sipped the dry smooth wine.

"It wasn't all that hard, actually. Now finding the tree, that was a mission. Any idea how hard it was to get a tree so late on Christmas Eve?"

She remembered Garret struggling to put together her family's twenty-year-old artificial tree. "Some."

"I actually had to buy that one from a shop keeper's display window. He probably charged me twice what he paid for it."

She grinned despite herself. "It's a very nice tree."

"No, it's not, but it's festive, and I thought we could both do with a little festive." He leaned down and brushed his mouth over hers. She tasted wine on his lips.

She pulled back and turned to the counter, where his glass stood half-empty.

"You can't drink anything when you're taking painkillers."

"I haven't taken a painkiller since yesterday," he said on a sigh.

"I gave you one this morning."

"And." He dug in his front jean pocket, producing a long fat pill. "Here it is."

"You're palming your pain medication?"

"If I really hurt, I'd take it. Now, I've kind of planned a romantic night for us. We have an ugly tree, we'll order Chinese food, and then we'll sit back and watch *It's A Wonderful Life* or something."

She sighed and nodded. Maybe she was being a mood killer. "Okay. Should I just get the same thing as last time?" she asked and held out the menu.

He nodded.

As she ordered the food, he prowled the small living room as if suddenly restless. When she hung up the phone, he sat next to her, his expression inscrutable.

"We need to talk," he said and her stomach dropped. "I've wanted to for a while, but I feel like we haven't had a second alone."

"Me too," she croaked, her mouth suddenly dry.

He said nothing for a moment, a long, aching moment. Her throat grew tight. Here it comes.

"Everyone at the hospital thought we were engaged," he said slowly as if choosing his words carefully.

Her face heated. "That was Paige's idea. They wouldn't tell us anything about you at the hospital because we weren't family. So she lied and said I was your fiancée." She shrugged. "It worked."

He reached over her suddenly, opening the side table drawer and pulled a small package wrapped in silver paper. "Merry Christmas."

"What is this?" She asked as he thrust the tiny gift into her lap.

"A present. Open it."

As she tore the pretty foil paper he stood and paced. Inside, she came to a dark blue velvet box. Her breath caught as she opened it and lay eyes on the glittering diamond inside.

"It's a ring."

Dean stopped and ran his hand through his hair. His insides quivered as he met her bewildered stare. "It's an engagement ring."

She glanced down at the ring then at him, clearly baffled. This wasn't going as he'd planned. What had he been thinking? Look how she had reacted when he gave her a cell phone for God's sake.

"Are you asking me to marry you?"

Crap, he'd forgotten that part. He sat next to her on the couch and forced himself to pull it together. He reached for her hand, her skin was cold against his. Then he met her eyes, dark hot amber. "Will you?"

She smiled. "Yes."

"Yes?"

"Yes."

Laughing like kids, he slid the ring on her finger then wrapped his arms around her. She tilted her head back and he kissed her, sealing the deal.

"I hesitate to bring this up, but I think we'll need a bigger place once I'm recovered, which, despite your best efforts to convince me otherwise, shouldn't be very long. We should look for a house in January."

She frowned. "You want to move?"

"This place is great, but if I'm going to be working from Hareton, I'm going to need a home office and something I can use for a workshop."

"No."

Damn, too much too fast. He shouldn't have pushed. "Did you want to ask your landlord about adding to this place?"

"No. I don't want to stay in Hareton. I'm going to close the store, or sell it if any will actually buy it. My mother's agreed to rehab. I'll be taking her to a clinic right after Christmas. Then I'll, well I don't know what exactly I'll do, but it'll be for me. And maybe you."

Her face almost glowed with excitement, and she was beautiful. He kissed her again, but when she moved to pull away he held her in place, tracing her tongue with his. She moaned a little and leaned into him. He had her.

He slid his hand under her sweater and trailed his fingers over the swell of her breast a long the edge of her bra. He wanted her, hungered for her in a way he never knew possible.

The doorbell shattered the moment.

"If that is any member of your family..." His voice sounded ragged and hoarse even to his own ears.

She giggled. "It's the food."

With a curse he stood, willing his body into a slightly less embarrassing state before opening the door. "We're picking up where we left off."

"I don't want to hurt you."

"Then you'll have to be gentle with me."

She tilted her head and grinned, cocking a single brow. "Maybe just this once."

About the Author

To learn more about Dawn Brown, please visit www.dawnbrown.org or send an email to Dawn Brown at dawn@dawnbrown.org.

A terrorist plot puts their lives—and hearts—on the line.

Under Fire
© 2008 Beth Cornelison

When Jackson McKay and his daughter are kidnapped, their captors demand his research files on a devastating chemical weapon—or they'll kill his little girl. Jackson searches desperately for a way to save his daughter and also protect his country from the terrorists. No risk is too great. His daring escape sets in motion a deadly game of cat and mouse.

Arriving at the scene of a wildfire, smokejumper Lauren Michaels and her crew are caught in the crosshairs of Jackson's nightmare. Lauren is the only one who can lead Jackson off the burning mountain and to the police. In order to prevent a national crisis and save a child's life, they embark on a treacherous journey—one step ahead of a sniper!

But more than their lives are at risk, because an unexpected heat flares between them that may cost them their hearts...

Warning: This title contains sex, strong language, some violence, smart men, courageous women, and heart-pounding action. Possible side effects of reading include racing pulse, missed sleep, and nail biting.

Available now in ebook and print from Samhain Publishing.

Enjoy the following excerpt from Under Fire...

Jackson gaped. "You're a woman!"

Her *no-shit-Sherlock* glare rebuked him for wasting time with the obvious, but the pop of gunfire interrupted any verbal reply. Bark splintered from the tree beside him.

Jackson dove for the ground. He landed next to the woman, pain streaking through his shoulder. The smokejumper gasped and crab-walked through the leaves, scuttling away from him. Another crack echoed through the trees.

"Stay down!" He scrambled through leaves and thorny debris to tackle her, cover her with his body. Protect her.

She grunted and squirmed. Despite the sharp ache wringing his shoulder, he held on tight. No way would he let a woman get hurt in this nightmare if he could help it.

Damn it, a woman! The last thing he needed was another life to safeguard, another innocent snared in this macabre scenario.

With surprising strength, the woman used a wrestler's move to flip him to the ground and pin him under her.

Lightning-hot pain slashed down his arm and up his neck. An agonized cry tore from him, and spots flashed before his eyes.

The smokejumper gazed down at him, winded, her breath hitting his face in gentle puffs. Under other circumstances, the position would be a turn-on. The woman wasn't bad looking, even with dirt smudges on her cheeks and leaves in her hair.

Jackson squeezed the sleeves of her yellow fire shirt and snarled, "In case you haven't noticed, there's a maniac shooting at us!"

"I'm well aware of that!" she growled back. "I'm trying to save your sorry ass!"

Jackson blinked. Scowled. "You're saving *my*—"

Another bullet pocked the earth by his head.

"Shit!" With a hard tug on her arm, he twisted toward a cluster of barbed bushes.

The woman moved with him, and together they rolled into the briars. From their hiding place, she stretched her arm out and groped in the blanket of fallen leaves and pine needles. After a moment, she dug out the revolver she'd dropped and dragged it into the brush with them.

"Can you shoot?" he asked.

She cut her eyes to his, hesitated. "I can shoot. What I hit is another matter."

"Then I suggest you save your rounds until your target's at closer range."

She gave him another how-stupid-do-I-look look. Shifting to lie on her belly, she gazed out across the clearing again. "And just who is my target? Why is he shooting at us?"

Jackson rubbed his throbbing shoulder. Sighed. Where did he begin? "Suffice to say, he's merciless and will stop at nothing to protect his interests."

"What interests? C'mon, pal, you're not making a lot of sense!"

"Mike!" a thundering voice shouted from across the open field.

The woman's breath caught as another smokejumper staggered out of the woods across from them, dragging his right leg and clutching tree trunks for support.

She snatched the radio from her hip and jabbed the button.

"Boomer, get down! I'm all right. Oh God! Just stay outta sight. I'm on my way," she said in a low rushed voice and started scrunching forward, out from under their cover.

Jackson grabbed for her wrist, a thorn gouging his arm in the process. "Hey, whoa!"

She tried to shake loose of his grasp, but he clung to her hand. "You can't go out there. There's no cover. Rick'll pick you off like a fish in a barrel."

"Rick? You *know* the guy that's shooting at us?" She glanced back to her friend, and they watched Boomer slide to the ground and roll into cover behind a large pine.

"Not the way you mean." Jackson struggled for a breath through the searing ache in his shoulder. "Look, he's got a rifle with a scope. And a hell of a lot of other weapons in the van. He freaked when he saw you and your buddies jump from the plane. He doesn't want anyone seeing him or reporting a van or—"

"The plane!" She raised her small handheld radio again. "Jump 49, this is Michaels. Do you read me?" When she got no response, she repeated her call to the aircraft. "We have a man down! Do you read me?"

Static crackled in the cramped space under the brambles. No one answered her call.

"Damn it," she growled. "The repeater must still be out. They can't hear me."

The woman, Michaels she'd called herself on the radio, heaved a deep sigh and dropped her forehead to the walkie-talkie in her hand. "Please, God. *Please.*"

Jackson tried to shift, wanting a better view of the terrain. The movement shot pain through his arm again. He rubbed his shoulder, grimacing. "Geez-zus!"

The woman scooted toward him. "You're hurt. Were you shot?"

He drew a ragged breath through clenched teeth. "No. It's an old football injury from college. I aggravated it a couple days ago when Rick and his henchmen slammed me on the floor one time too many."

Her dirt-smudged brow furrowed. "Come again? Slammed you on the floor?"

"Mike!" the same deep voice called across the clearing.

She jerked her attention back to the injured man across the clearing, concern creasing her face.

"Hang on, Boom. I'm coming. Where are Birdman and Riley? Who's that in the clearing?" she said into her radio. Eyes closed, she waited for a response.

Jackson studied her. She seemed young, yet in control of her situation, her emotions. Even without makeup she had a fragile femininity about her, an appearance incongruous with the tough, take-charge smokejumper he'd witnessed so far. She glanced at him. "What's your story? Why are you up here?"

Jackson tried to steady his breathing then summarized the past two days as succinctly as he could.

Her eyes widened, and she shook her head then frowned skeptically. "How do I know I can trust you?"

"You don't. All you have is my word."

She turned away, lifted the walkie-talkie again. "Boomer, it's Mike. Do you copy?"

Nothing.

"Damn." She huffed. "Listen..." Grabbing the front of Jackson's Yale T-shirt, she shoved her face inches from his. Her green eyes blazed. "My partner is hurt," she said, through gritted teeth. "Another man's down over there, not moving." Her voice broke, and the first flash of grief or fear flashed over her face.

She sucked in a deep breath, her nostrils flaring as if in defiance of the emotions. Once again composed, she grated, "I have to get over to them. Now!"

He knew the fire and determination that lit her eyes well. Intimately. Janine had had the same passion, the same grit.

"Ah, hell," he muttered, holding her gaze. The energy and conviction in her eyes pulled him in, sucked him deep into their magnetic lure. *Never again.*

She averted her eyes and shoved him away. As she inched out from their hiding place, Jackson bit out a curse and followed.

"Wait! Go the long way around." He pulled himself along the ground with one arm. "Stay in the cover of the trees and skirt the edge of the clearing. Keep out of sight."

She glowered at him. "Anything else, Your Highness?"

He ignored her sarcasm. "Yeah. Lose the yellow shirt. You're too visible."

Still frowning at him, she climbed to her feet, staying in a squat, and looked down at her bright clothing. "Damn it, you're right. Help me get this thing off."

He crawled out and rose to his knees as she peeled the fire shirt down her arms. The T-shirt she wore under it was soaked in sweat and stuck to her like second skin.

Jackson's breath lodged in his throat as he scanned her shapely body. Her arms had definition and tone that spoke of a rigorous fitness routine. Admiration tugged at him when he considered the rigors of her job and the effort involved, just staying in condition for those demands.

Jackson dragged himself to his feet, holding his left arm close to his body to minimize jostling his shoulder. "All right. Stay low or behind trees as much as you can. Let's go."

"*You're* coming?"

"There a reason why I shouldn't?"

"Well...you'd probably be safer under there." She tipped her head toward the bush they'd just vacated. "Outta sight."

"Probably. But I can't hide forever. I want to help with your friend if I can."

Her eyes brightened. "You're a doctor?"

Jackson winced. "Not the kind you need." When she frowned her confusion, he waved his hand, dismissing the comment. "Forget it. Ready?"

She glanced again across the field of wildflowers then at Jackson. "Okay. And...thanks."

"Don't thank me yet. We still gotta lose Rick and his trigger finger." Without thinking about what he was doing, he reached out to tuck a copper wisp of her hair behind her ear. The strands curled intimately around his finger in a silky caress that shocked him back to his senses. He snatched his hand away and cleared his throat. "Then you're gonna help me find my daughter and get her off this mountain."

GREAT CHEAP FUN

Discover eBooks!

THE FASTEST WAY TO GET THE HOTTEST NAMES

Get your favorite authors on your favorite reader, long before they're out in print! Ebooks from Samhain go wherever you go, and work with whatever you carry—Palm, PDF, Mobi, and more.

Samhain
publishing ltd